Walter Wager, a graduate [...] former Fulbright Fellow [...] diplomatic adviser to Isra[...] editor at the United Natio[...] and editor of *Playbill* and *Show*. A prolific writer, he has contributed articles to sixteen magazines, authored eleven cloak-and-dagger novels under a pseudonym, and written television documentaries for three networks and films for the United States Information Agency. He is currently director of public relations for a music licensing society in the USA.

Also by Walter Wager:

TELEFON

Walter Wager

Twilight's Last Gleaming

Futura Publications Limited
A Futura Book

A Futura Book

First published in Great Britain 1977
by Futura Publications Limited

This book is dedicated to the memory
of my remarkable brother, Julie

ISBN 0 8600 7468 4

Printed in Great Britain by
Cox & Wyman Ltd,
London, Reading and Fakenham

Futura Publications Limited
110 Warner Road, Camberwell
London SE5

Everything in this book is imaginary and fictional – names, places, people, political entities, military organizations, events, spelling and punctuation. I hereby disclaim all intent to injure anyone's reputation, public image, credit rating or sexual magnetism. To be entirely frank, a rather decent colonel in the U.S. Air Force has suggested that it is quite unlikely that the events described in this work of fiction could actually transpire. I should *certainly* hope so.

It would be nice to be sure.

W. W.

CHAPTER ONE

Martin McKenzie was precisely on time, precisely as usual.

A number of people said that you could set your watch by McKenzie's morning appearances, but they never said it to his face.

They thought that he wouldn't have liked it, and they had no wish to offend a man of such immense power – the new power that isn't measured in votes or fame or money but in megatons and fire storms and other modern forms of apocalyptic annihilation. They were, of course, wrong. Martin McKenzie felt that his line of work made it his duty to be on time – precisely and invariably – and he wouldn't have been the least bit offended by such comments. He certainly wasn't pompous or stuffy – business-like and impatient with small talk but far from either pompous or stuffy. As a matter of fact, his still pretty fifty-one-year-old wife or any of his seven children – six now that Eddie had been killed in Vietnam – could truthfully tell you that Martin McKenzie was a decent, considerate fellow with a better than average sense of humor and no false pride.

They could tell you that quite easily if you got past the armed men who guarded Martin McKenzie's pleasant medium-priced house, a four-bedroom split-level residence that McKenzie's employer rented to him rather reasonably. McKenzie – a vigorous, fit person with a square face and only a few gray hairs to hint that he was fifty-six – saw nothing unusual about the armed men who guarded his home. They were exactly like the armed men who guarded his office.

As mentioned earlier, this morning – this cool, clear Sunday morning – he arrived on time. At 7:25 A.M. Central Standard Time, the blue staff car pulled up to the front entrance of a three-story building approximately twenty miles from the swinging center of Omaha, Nebraska. The exact distance is of very little consequence, although there are at least 168 officers attached to the GRU – the Glavnoye Razvedyvatelnoye Upravlenie, or Chief Intelligence Directorate of the Red Army General Staff – who could tell it to you quite accurately. On the other hand, they probably don't know that Nebraska's state flower is the goldenrod and its state bird the Western meadowlark – a sad commentary on the Soviet educational system and the failure of the Moscow Birdwatchers Society.

Of course, the structure itself is hardly a cultural landmark. It is a large rectangular office building decorated with numerous radio antennae, a functional building in the architectural style that is sometimes summarized as Federal Frugal. No frills, no beauty and no particular taste – but not quite tasteless either. Atop a low grassy knoll at Offutt Air Force Base, this ecumenical edifice is the global headquarters of the Strategic Air Command. You remember the Strategic Air Command, the US Air Force's Sunday punch? Peace Is Our Profession? Long-range bombers and intercontinental missiles? Right, *that* Strategic Air Command.

When the staff car stopped at the main entrance and a crewcut, whippetlike major bounded out of the vehicle to open its rear door, the armed men flanking the portico prepared to salute Martin McKenzie. As soon as he stepped out of the car, four of these sentries – keen-looking young chaps in Air Force uniforms, berets, boots, and pearl-handled pistols – hurled their Number One salutes with a synchronized dash that would have delighted any Radio City Music Hall Rockette. Martin McKenzie always got everybody's Number One salute, for he was entitled – being the CINCSAC. As commander in chief of the Strategic Air Command (CINCSAC), he got salutes, respect, a corner office with a rug, a good deal on the rented house and a salary just a bit higher than a union plumber. Higher than a union plumber's *salary*, for no one is suggesting that union plumbers tipple – not with double overtime being what it is. General Martin P. McKenzie – he didn't get those four stars on each shoulder from crackerjack boxes – snapped back *his* Number One salute with a sharpshooter's accuracy, drilling it exactly between the two pair of sentries. As he did so, he automatically scanned the four guards from head to foot to make

8

sure that every inch of each man and his attire was exactly as crisp and clean as it should be. He did this without breaking his stride, reaching the door just as Major Winters jerked it open with the efficient deference one might expect of the CINCSAC's aide.

The lobby area was large, with a barrier across it and a desk near the center of that barrier. McKenzie headed directly for the narrow entrance beside the desk, walking briskly as if he meant to go through without any unnecessary delay.

'Sir?' said the sergeant seated at the desk.

The general almost smiled, pleased that the security NCO was alert and competent.

'Your badge, sir?'

The CINCSAC stopped to permit the sergeant to check his face against the photo on the badge McKenzie wore clipped to the left breast of his beribboned tunic. Some thirteen months earlier, another security NCO at this desk had recognized the senior SAC general and waved him through respectfully – with disastrous results. That stupid ass-kissing bastard was now at a remote Arctic outpost, a living, suffering example of the CINC-SAC's total passion for total security. This sergeant studied the badge, nodded.

'Thank you, sir,' he acknowledged briskly.

The guards flanking the entry snapped to attention as General McKenzie strode through, and for one moment Major Douglas Winters wondered which it would be – the office or the bunker? The SAC command post was buried in a large blast-proof bunker some forty feet beneath this building, and the morning intelligence briefing always took place in this subterranean redoubt, but senior generals could watch it in their own offices over closed-circuit color television – one of the perquisites of rank. The office on the second floor was nearer and more comfortable, and since this was a Sunday – a day of rest to almost everyone except SAC officers, professional football players and Christian clergymen – it seemed likely that McKenzie would head for his office. For just that reason, the aide silently guessed that the CINCSAC would choose the bunker.

'The Hole,' announced the general curtly.

That was what most people at Offutt called the bunker. Its

9

code name was Touchdown, but almost everyone at SAC headquarters referred to it as either the CP or the Hole. Pleased that he'd guessed right for a change, Winters followed McKenzie through the swinging doors, down the stairs, and along the low-ceilinged zigzag corridors leading into the earth. The zigzag design was to cut off blast effect, the TV cameras on the walls were to scan who was coming down, and the armed men checking badges and identification were there in the tunnels for the same reasons that the other armed men were stationed upstairs – to keep out the wrong people. When McKenzie and Winters passed the first checkpoint, the guard on duty punched a button on his wall phone and passed the alarm.

'*He's* on his way down,' he warned the Command Post.

'Fine. The coffee's ready.'

It was. It always was at 7:28 A.M. when the CINCSAC wasn't away – hot, black with one sugar. At 7:28:30, McKenzie and Winters walked into the large subterranean room – 140 feet long, 39 feet wide and 31 feet high – and they headed directly for the second level, where Battle Staff desks, chairs and phones overlooked the Situation Display System. This SDS – much more factual than the tempestuous teen version that grabbed all those 1968-1969 headlines – consisted of twenty-foot-high and eight-feet-wide panels mounted on trolley rails. Normally pulled aside to expose a large world map, the panels were covered with global weather maps, 'force deployment charts' and displays showing the operational status of US missile and bomber units. Above were electric clocks exhibiting the local time in Peking, Moscow, London, Washington – and Omaha, Nebraska. Thick rubber-clad cables snaked from two TV cameras on dollies that squatted near the center of the floor, while behind them and to the left the Duty Controller – always a cool sensible colonel with plenty of experience and practically no nerves – sat at a console dominated by several telephones and many switches. There was a black telephone and a red telephone and a gold telephone – each for a different purpose – and there was a carton of coffee and an oval ashtray inscibed with Chinese calligraphy that some humorist had picked up in Hong Kong.

It was the only light touch in the Command Post. The atmosphere wasn't grim but it was earnest, and the thirty-odd Air Force personnel on the main floor – a diverse group that ranged from a blonde female communications sergeant to a bald lieutenant colonel who knew a great deal about radar jamming – were relaxed but purposeful. At 7:29 – just as McKenzie sat down and his mug of coffee was simultaneously placed on his desk – a thin young Air Intelligence captain walked up to the front of the big map and glanced at the sheaf of papers on his clipboard. Thirty seconds later, the red lights on the TV cameras glowed and a black airman handed the captain the special flashlight that would project an arrow image. Thirty seconds after that – exactly as the sweep second hand hit 7:30 – the A-2 officer spoke.

'Good morning, gentlemen,' he said to no one in particular, because he knew that it might be bad manners to acknowledge the presence of the CINCSAC. 'Let's begin the briefing. To start with, it's DEFCON Five.'

Defense Condition Five – the lowest alert status and the normal one for the US armed forces when there was no significant threat or crisis. During the Cuban missile confrontation, the Joint Chiefs had gradually escalated the 'readiness' to DEFCON Two – one level short of war – but now it was only DEFCON Five. McKenzie sipped at his second cup of coffee of the morning, waited.

'Battle readiness,' continued the captain, 'is ninety-four percent for manned bomber squadrons.'

'The Old Man will be pleased,' Winters told himself, for that was a two-percentage-point rise over Saturday's figure.

'Shit,' General Martin McKenzie brooded. It was probably those slobs down at Homestead, soaking up the Florida sun instead of making love to their B-52s. A number of vulgar expressions and obscene thoughts passed swiftly through the general's transistor-quick and computer-cruel mind, words that he rarely used aloud because they were unbecoming to the dignity of the CINCSAC. Some of his hard-boiled predecessors – gutsy, colorful cigar chewers such as able Curt LeMay – talked like that quite freely, but it wasn't Martin McKenzie's style. As a matter of fact, McKenzie was not only smoother and cooler than previous CINCSACS but he was also giving up smoking – as an example to his men.

'Shit,' the CINCSAC thought as he considered that 94 per cent figure and wished he had a cigar. He'd be checking that 94 percent as soon as the briefing ended.

'Snakepit status report,' the briefing officer continued. 'Snakepit' was the code word for the US intercontinental ballistic missiles buried in underground silos in the middle and northwestern states. Each strategic missile wing had as its own code name that of some species of poisonous snake such as cobra or rattler, and the condition of all the ICBMs was collectively summarized each morning in the status report. 'Ready to fly, ninety-three percent,' said the captain in his flat Ohio voice.

Now *that* wasn't too bad. Idiots – a catch-all term that included journalists, congressmen and at least one Assistant Secretary of Defense – always expected that every single plane and rocket would be ready at a moment's notice, but that was because they didn't know anything about maintenance and didn't care either.

'TAC operational readiness, eighty-nine point nine percent.'

That made McKenzie smile. It always pleased him to hear that he was doing better than the fighter-bomber boys of the Tactical Air Command, a difference that was a product of superior maintenance – of course. Top maintenance was the key, and a ruthless intolerant CINCSAC didn't hurt either.

Then the briefing proceeded to flying weather over various parts of the globe, the numbers and most recent movements of Soviet trawler squadrons in the Atlantic and Pacific, the location of Russian submarines in the Sea of Japan, the Mediterranean, Caribbean and North Sea, the start of Warsaw Pact nations' autumn military maneuvers in southern Poland, the locations of top political and defense leaders in China and Russia and a CIA report on the next Chinese H-bomb test, scheduled for the coming week.

No major troop movements toward any frontier.

No significant air movements or signs of prestrike dispersal.

No unusual naval activity.

No signs that Soviet or Chinese leaders were leaving their

capitals, which would be obvious targets for US retaliation if either Red nation attacked. As a matter of fact, the Russian Prime Minister was due in New York on Friday to address the General Assembly of the United Nations.

Not bad, McKenzie reflected.

Aside from that goddam 94 percent, not bad at all.

The briefing ended at 8:02, and at 8:03 Martin McKenzie was on the scrambler telephone to the head of the heavy-bomber forces at Homestead Air Force Base south of Miami. Then he spoke to the generals who commanded other SAC B-52 forces in the ZI – the Zone of the Interior, the United States – and overseas, bluntly but without losing his temper. It was understood that the CINCSAC – no CINCSAC – would ever be satisfied, but it was also unseemly for him to blow up except in cases of serious dereliction or crisis.

At half past eight, McKenzie stood and headed for the ramp up to the surface. On the way up, he passed two guards flanking a metal door marked STB – NO ADMITTANCE but he kept walking. The Strategic Targets Board was an ultra-hush-hush inter-service intelligence outfit that was a world of its own, a subtenant in the SAC bunker and one that dealt directly with the Joint Chief of Staff in the Pentagon. A tight mouthed and tight-assed group, the CINCSAC reflected as he walked steadily up the zigzag tunnel that finally brought him up into the lobby again.

The sun was breaking through when McKenzie and Winters left the building, and a fresh breeze was blowing in across the Nebraska plains. The general paused – and the aide paused – to sniff and experience, but almost immediately the CINCSAC's restless mind moved on to the test exercise designated True Blue that was scheduled for that night and the budget meeting planned for lunch the next day. McKenzie was to go before the Senate committee on Friday, and he meant to be fully prepared to justify the two wings of the new bomber he needed so badly.

'You'll have those figures on the Ninety-One,' he told Winters.

'They'll be ready this afternoon,' the aide promised.

The four-star general nodded. With no way of guessing that there would be no budget meeting the next day, McKenzie stepped into his car and glanced at his wrist watch. It was 8:42. His wife and children were to meet him at the church at 8:58 for the regular Sunday services, and Martin McKenzie didn't want to be late.

CHAPTER TWO

The dark-blue station wagon rolled inexorably through the chill October drizzle, drilling its private tunnel into the clotted morning mists that all but obliterated the highway. There was never much traffic on the few roads across these bare Montana plains, and at 7:58 A.M. – it was 8:58 in Omaha – on such a wet, dreary Sunday there was almost none. The endless, curve-less ribbon of concrete and the rhythmic nagging of the vehicle's windshield wipers combined in a soothing hypnotic quality that was somehow greater than the sum of its parts, but despite this the three men in the front seat of the station wagon were totally alert.

They were also completely focussed, wholly committed.

The road and the weather didn't affect them at all.

Like the vehicle itself, the driver was dressed in blue and wore the insignia of the United States Air Force. He was a powerfully built young black in a sergeant's uniform, cool-eyed and obviously competent in the way he handled the wheel. Beside him sat a beefy, balding captain who seemed at least ten pounds too fat for his crisp white coveralls, the costume that identified him as one of America's new breed of rocket tech-nicians. On the far right – staring out the window for familiar landmarks – was a lean thoughtful first lieutenant of such rugged good looks that he resembled some idealized figure from a recruiting poster. His sunken gray eyes were oddly old for a junior officer, but this minor flaw did little to detract from his almost theatrical handsomeness. There was also a hardness in that impassive, arresting Warner Brothers face, a toughness that was both mental and physical.

Strong. This strong man had an air of unmistakable author-ity and intelligence that precisely suited his missile-specialist's coveralls, and the dashing gold scarf at his throat only completed the picture. The multi-colored Strategic Air Command patch on his left shoulder was almost superfluous, for this man was obviously born to serve SAC or some equally dramatic and high-powered organization. A little too cool, a little too taut, a little too ruthless to be the All-American Boy, he radiated a command quality that promised he wouldn't remain a lieutenant very long.

'Keep it down to thirty,' he said to the driver in a voice that was used to giving orders.

The road was wet.

The launch site was near.

It would be stupid to take any unnecessary chances of an accident now.

All this was implicit in his voice. The husky Negro behind the wheel nodded, clearly as accustomed to taking orders as the officer was to giving them. Both trained veterans, they understood each other well. For the next dozen seconds, the only sound was the hum of the motor and the annoyingly relentless squish-squish-squish of the mindless wipers. Then the perfect-featured lieutenant spoke again.

'Mind if I turn on the radio, sir?' he asked crisply.

The chunky sweating man in the captain's uniform didn't bother to reply. He merely reached forward to the dashboard, flicked a switch and settled back with a sigh. He was not a talkative person, and the perspiration generated by the tight coveralls and the station wagon's heater and the humidity made him even less conversational than usual. He was not happy. The look on his pudgy face and his heavy complaining breathing confirmed that he was not happy.

The small speaker in the dashboard suddenly came alive.

'For the whitest wash of all!' the announcer's voice promised in the synthetically intimate cadences of every well-read commercial. Next there sounded three chimes, followed immediately by the staccato clatter of teletype machines.

'Eight A.M. and here is the news – the *big* news from the *big* station, KMOX – the Great Voice of Great Falls,' the broadcaster recited briskly. 'With the election only twelve days away, the Harris Poll reports that President Stevens now holds only a two point lead over Senator Baylor Caldwell in the race for the

16

White House. Some fifty-one percent of the voters currently support the Chief Executive for re-election and forty-nine percent favor the colorful senior Senator from California, whose blistering attacks on the Administration's defense policies and social-welfare programs have made this one of the bitterest campaigns in recent US history. Caldwell has gained six points in the past month, and political experts now give him a fifty-fifty chance to win on November fourth. Both candidates were on the campaign trail yesterday, President Stevens speaking in Los Angeles, San Francisco and Seattle and Senator Caldwell wooing voters in Miami, Atlanta and New Orleans. The rivals will meet in Washington on Wednesday night for the third and final broadcast in their series of nationally televised debates. ... Closer to home, State police are expanding the manhunt for the five convicts who escaped from Helena penitentiary late last night. The fugitives – all condemned murderers – broke out of the Death House shortly after midnight, seized Assistant Warden Patrick Claiborne as hostage and used him as a human shield to force the tower guards to open the main gate. Taking advantage of the heavy fog, they drove out in Claiborne's black 1967 Chrysler sedan and have apparently by-passed or slipped through the first set of police roadblocks.'

Blank-faced, the damp beefy captain stared ahead into the mist as if he hadn't heard a single word of the sensational account crackling from the radio two feet away.

'The fugitives are now heavily armed. While they had only two revolvers when they escaped, the are now equipped with submachine guns, bulletproof vests, tear-gas grenades and respirators,' warned the announcer in tones that communicated both awe and a certain professional excitement – if not glee. This was the biggest local news in two years, perhaps three. 'Less than an hour ago, Governor Wilcox announced that the killers had seized this material in a three-A.M. raid on the police station in the town of Millegan – some one hundred thirty-eight miles north of the penitentiary. The governor has advised that these five desperate criminals – wife killer Lawrence Dell, underworld assassin Jimmy 'Stud' Falco, sex slayer Harvey Schonbacher, religious fanatic Marvin 'Deacon' Hoxey and barroom brawler Willieboy Powell – are extremely dangerous.'

The station-wagon driver suppressed a yawn that was bred of fatigue, not boredom. Desperate criminals? Escaped murderers? Of course, he was interested.

'Citizens with any information as to the fugitives' whereabouts should immediately notify local police and should not – repeat, *not* – attempt to stop them alone,' warned the Great Voice of Great Falls. 'Falco alone is believed responsible for sixteen deaths, paid underworld executions, spread across seven states. Bad weather has hampered the manhunt thus far, but when skies clear this afternoon helicopters and state-police cars are expected to—'

The porky captain clicked off the radio irritably, lit a cigarette to console himself. The lieutenant simply shook his movie-star head twice.

'Those cons sound like a real mean crowd,' he said.

'I certainly wouldn't try to stop that bunch,' agreed the sergeant.

'That's not *our* job. It's up to the police to—'

'How far is it?' the chunky man in the middle interrupted impatiently.

'Less than a mile, sir. I've been out here so many times that I could find Viper Three in my sleep,' the junior officer assured him cheerfully.

Directly ahead there was a break in the fog.

'The fence,' the driver announced.

Running parallel to the left side of the highway was a five-strand barrier of barbed wire, nine feet high and connected to the central alarm system that protects each such US intercontinental ballistic missile launch site. Somewhere within that fence and some sixty feet underground was the massive blast-proof, radiation-proof, bacteria-and-gas-proof steel and concrete 'command capsule' that housed the controls of the launch site designated Viper Three. The two US Air Force missile specialists – there were always two down in 'the Hole' – who sat at Viper Three's complex consoles controlled ten Minuteman rockets, each weapon with a range of 6,500 miles and a nuclear warhead that could incinerate a city of 1,000,000 people. There were eight identical Viper launch sites spread out over – no, under – many square miles of these Montana prairies, scientifically dispersed to assure the survival of the 168th Strategic Missile Wing's eighty Minutemen. The responsibility of and pressure on the men in each 'hole' in Viper Three and the others – was tremendous, and standard Strategic Air Command procedures called for the Missile Combat Crew of each subterranean capsule to be changed every twenty-four hours.

The armed Air Police who protected the launch site entrance and the cooks who manned Viper Three's kitchen in the surface guardhouse were not quite so lucky. Their work was less demanding, their shifts three times as long. Their responsibility was also substantial – as they were often reminded – but somehow less glamorous and urgent, and the routines for protecting the entrance to 'The Hole' had inevitably become boring after nineteen months. Even the surprise 'no warning' security drills and occasional mock attacks no longer helped much in the struggle against tedium atop the rocket base code-named Viper Three, so the earnest, well-trained guards fingered their carbines and drank their coffee patiently but without any traces of either passion or enthusiasm. They had been waiting a long time for a crisis – a moment of glory – that they knew would probably never come, so this foggy morning when they heard the familiar and expected toot-toot of the station-wagon horn at the gate the Air Police at Viper Three responded quickly but unemotionally.

In the sparely furnished but inexorably overheated guard room, a lanky Memphis-bred sergeant put down his cup and glanced at the round electric clock on the wall.

'Oh-eight-oh-six, eight minutes late. Not *too* bad for a dirty Sunday morning,' he said philosophically as he reached for his waterproof poncho. The gung-ho efficiency-expert types at Wing wouldn't like this, of course, for they expected absolute on-time perfection. The sergeant rechecked the names on the list on his clipboard again. He'd studied the replacement schedule a dozen times during the previous hour, but SAC training had programmed him to take no chances. There was an inflexible, approved, safe routine for handling these shifts in Missile Combat Crews, and examining the names and credentials of the replacement duo was Step One in the official security regulations.

'Kincaid, Roger F., Captain. ... Witkin, Harry O., First Lieutenant. Right, Sarge?' a swarthy young corporal joked from across the drab room.

'Nobody likes a smart-ass, Mendez. Just do your job and remember that,' the Southern senior NCO reproved mechanically. The names quoted aloud had matched those on the list, but SAC Minuteman security procedures were certainly no subject for humor.

A third Air Policeman – as husky and practical as the son of a West Virginia miner should be – watched as the other two donned their rain gear, checked the safeties on their carbines and slogged out into the foggy drizzle. They trudged the forty yards to the gate in silence, each completely familiar with what he had to do. This low-visibility weather complicated matters a bit, for the sergeant usually required the newly arrived replacement crew to line up outside the electrified fence so he could study their identification badges and photos before he unlocked the gate. In this fog, the senior NCO would have to go outside to check them off in the station wagon. Corporal Mendez would remain about a dozen yards back, covering the replacements warily with his finger on the trigger and the carbine set on 'automatic.'

It was all specified in the manual.

The procedures had been developed and approved by both SAC headquarters outside Omaha and the meticulous security experts of the Defense Atomic Support Agency in Washington, the Pentagon's little-known custodians of US atomic and hydrogen warheads.

As the long-jawed sergeant reached to unlock the gate, he heard a door of the nearby vehicle open and he knew exactly what to do. He barked an immediate order into the blinding mist.

'Stay in the wagon – sir,' he snapped impatiently.

He said 'sir' because he knew that both members of the replacement crew were commissioned officers. Sergeant Russell didn't know where Viper Three's ten intercontinental ballistic missiles would land if fired, but he knew that only carefully screened, well-trained, emotionally stable officers were assigned to SAC Missile Combat Crews.

Sergeant Bruce V. Russell flicked the switch, swung the barrier open and strode forward through the puddles and fog until he could peer into the wagon's rolled-down window beside the driver. He looked in, saw the familiar white coveralls with the gold scarves and blinked in automatic approval of the hexagonal green badge that each missileman wore clipped over his heart. Then he thrust his flashlight and head inside to study the identification photos on the security badges, paused for a moment to test the replacements with the day's coded 'challenge.'

'Daniel?' he queried.

'Webster,' the pudgy captain replied correctly.

No sweat, no problem – as usual. The lanky AP leaned in to complete the final check of faces against badge pictures, ignoring the black driver to get a better look at the officers who would actually enter Viper Three.

'Now,' the handsome lieutenant whispered.

The two big hands resting on the wheel suddenly leaped and closed like some radio-controlled vise around the Air Policeman's throat, choking off his cry before a single sound emerged. The numbing shock of the attack caused the carbine to slip from Russell's fingers, and the flashlight was jerked from his other hand by the beefy man wearing captain's insignia. It was all happening very swiftly and crazily, unlike anything in any SAC manual. The driver squeezed harder and harder, ignoring the agonized terror in the sergeant's astonished eyes. After a while, it was clear that the guard was unconscious and the husky chauffeur relaxed his grip.

'Kill him! Finish him off!' urged the sweaty man in the middle.

'What for?' the driver challenged scornfully. 'What the hell are we, Apaches collecting scalps?'

Willieboy had a gift for language, the lieutenant thought, but he didn't say so. Nobody in the station wagon bothered to answer the chauffeur's bitter question, for there was still a great deal to be done – and very little time.

CHAPTER THREE

Some sixteen yards away, Corporal Rafael Mendez was peering earnestly – and uncomfortably – into the wall of fog and wondering what was delaying the sergeant. Mendez detested these cold Montana mists, so different from the sensible man-warming weather of his native Arizona. Shivering and grumbling and cursing softly in savage sibilant Spanish, he didn't hear the two barefoot men who had slipped out of the back of the blue wagon. He had no way of guessing that they were circling him in the gray cotton-candy mist. Mendez heard a sound of metal striking something – it was the carbine – and wondered. Finally the uneasy young corporal walked toward the station wagon, advancing slowly until he could make out the sergeant leaning into the open window to talk to the driver. But there was no sound of voices, no movement.

Nothing seemed to be happening, and after several seconds the corporal began to wonder why. He took one step forward. At that instant, he was struck a stunning blow on the back of the neck. He was dazed as he crumpled to his knees; he could barely see the two pairs of oddly naked feet move nearer. Then gun butts smashed at his head from either side – twice – and Rafael Mendez sprawled on the concrete like one of those ruined rabbits whose corpses litter the sides of busy highways.

The purposeful men who had fractured his skull did not loiter. One rolled the corporal's body into a drainage ditch while the other picked up the dying man's carbine. Next they edged toward the station wagon cautiously, taut and wary until they saw that the sergeant's body hung limp – according to Dell's plan. The taller of the two barefoot men tapped on the door frame with the muzzle of his submachine gun. Then the driver released his hold, and the unconscious Air Police sergeant collapsed beside the vehicle as if someone had let the air out of him.

'Deacon and I cooled the other one,' the olive-skinned man with the machine gun reported to his confederates inside the station wagon. 'Stud' Falco spoke quickly but calmly, as was befitting a man of his profession who had a good deal of experience with violence. There were few people in the United States – aside from a number of television producers and script writers for 'Western' films – who had more experience with violence than this veteran assassin.

'Good,' approved the handsome raider in the lieutenant's coveralls as if he were running down a check list – which he was. 'Tie him up, and let's get on to Phase Two,' Dell continued in that voice so used to giving orders.

It was Lawrence Dell – the one whom the Great Voice of Great Falls had so glibly summarized as wife-killer – who'd planned the operation with military precision. It was Dell who'd conceived the prison break, who'd passed the word to each of them furtively during a month of brief whispered talks in the exercise yard, who'd made them wait for this weather, who'd briefed them again on the details after they'd seized the station wagon. It was Dell who commanded this strange 'strike force', whose knowledge, boldness and cunning were their only hope. Aware of this reality, Falco moved swiftly and it took him only a minute to truss up the unconscious sergeant with the NCO's own belt.

'Finished, Larry. Lead on, Major Dell,' said the underworld executioner.

'It is the Lord's will,' the thin, pale maniac standing beside Falco in the mist chimed in piously.

Dell couldn't see his face clearly in the fog, but he knew the look that Marvin Hoxey was wearing. Marvin 'Deacon' Hoxey – who'd helped Falco assault the young corporal a minute earlier – was a lunatic. He was clearly insane to almost anyone, anyone but a jury of angry Montana farmers and ranchers. Lawrence Dell realized that Hoxey was a grotesque religious fanatic, but the Plan – *his* plan – would need every man and gun if this extraordinary gamble were to succeed. This pious psychopath was a remarkably accurate shot, as he'd proved in

23

slaying three of the deputies who'd come to arrest him for the church burnings, and he could be useful. Of course, it would take considerable luck and plenty of careful handling to keep this volatile madman in line – focussed and obedient to orders and the requirements of the Plan.

'You're right, it is the Lord's will,' Dell reassured the gaunt lunatic smoothly. 'You're right, Deacon. We're going in now, so would you please cover the back door?'

Moving carefully and quietly, the five fugitives fanned out through the dense, dim drizzle as Dell had rehearsed them. Some forty seconds later, the third Air Policeman of Viper Three's security team heard someone at the crew door of the prefabricated guardhouse. The rangy AP swiveled in his chair, his hands coming to rest – lightly – on the carbine on the desk before him. The crew door swung open, letting in a gust of rain and one of the replacements. The new combat crewman – a tall lieutenant in the familiar white coveralls – backed in still talking over his shoulder.

'Hope you've got some hot coffee ready, Sergeant,' he said to someone behind him in the mist.

It was so completely normal and routine that the AP relaxed for a second.

That was all it took.

The man in the coveralls turned around – and there was a .38-caliber Police Special revolver in his right fist. It pointed directly at the seated guard. For a moment, the blinking Air Policeman wondered whether this was some new test or perhaps a jest. Then he recognized the face of the invader in the lieutenant's coveralls.

'Major Dell,' identified the startled sentry.

'Who'll shoot you dead if your sweaty fingers move one half inch closer to that alarm buzzer,' answered the former Deputy Intelligence Officer of the 168th.

The Air Policeman froze.

'I'll splash your brains all over the walls,' Dell promised.

The patriotic guard was willing to die to protect Viper Three from enemy saboteurs, but Dell – and the others whose escape the radio had reported – were common criminals and not Red raiders. They didn't – couldn't – threaten either 'the

Hole' or the United States. Still Dell was alone and the AP was beginning to calculate the odds when two more armed men entered. There was a beefy captain with a gunnysack in one hand and a regulation Air Force revolver in the other, and behind him a husky black sergeant who cradled a submachine gun in a manner that reflected considerable experience.

'Cover him! It's Dell!' the AP called out exultantly to the missile crew.

The Negro swung his machine gun, aimed it at the guard's stomach.

The guard gaped.

'Meet Sergeant Willieboy Powell,' Dell invited. 'Willieboy knows all about automatic weapons. I hear he was a fine Marine, decorated in Vietnam.'

'A damn fine Marine,' Powell remembered aloud.

It was difficult to tell whether the man with the machine gun was being proud or simply truthful. His voice was flat, controlled.

One thing was clear, however. Dell was in command, and there was no glimmer of indecision in his large gray eyes. When the ex-SAC intelligence officer waved his ·38, the muzzle moved only an inch – but the guard got the message. *Move.* The helpless Air Policeman stood up slowly, raised his hands and began to step away from the desk.

Then he suddenly got his chance.

Across the overheated room, the door to the adjacent kitchen opened to admit a cook carrying a metal pitcher of steaming coffee. The glances of the three convicts turned slightly with their weapons, and the alert, conscientious Air Policeman made a frantic grab for the carbine on the desk. He succeeded, just the way they do in the movies. He seized the gun, spun to fire – and then something went wrong with the script. He died.

The window behind him disappeared as Falco's machine gun erupted in one short terrible burst. The big .45-caliber slugs threw the corpse across the floor with the impact of a high-pressure steam hose. So awfully real and final that it was almost unreal, it was very ugly and very frightening. The cook with the aluminum pitcher stood rigid, his throat knotted and his eyes wide as he tried to cope with the coppery taste of terror in his mouth and the incredible shock. It wasn't supposed to happen like this. The training had made it clear that the attack would come in a salvo of ICBMs over the Arctic, and the multibillion-dollar Ballistic Missile Early Warning System would detect these rockets by excellent long-range radar and flash a warning to the SAC command post buried in that bunker near Omaha. Then the command post would alert Viper Three and all the other launch sites – at least twelve, perhaps fourteen minutes before the enemy assault hit the United States.

It wasn't supposed to happen *like this*.

The cook stood there with the coffee vapors rising before his eyes, wholly uncertain of what was happening or what to do. He was only a twenty-year-old cook. This stunning savagery was beyond both his training and his experience, so he clutched the pitcher as if it were a cross or some other magic talisman and he hoped that he wouldn't be killed too. He was still hoping a few seconds later when the other cook ran into the guard room, took in the situation in one look and raised his hands immediately.

He was a born survivor.

'Don't shoot, don't shoot, Major!' he blurted.

Dell considered, nodded, smiled.

'See that? I'm still an officer to my old buddies in the 168th,' he mocked in oddly muted tones. 'Still *Major* Dell – despite my domestic and legal problems.'

The black man in the sergeant's coveralls shrugged.

'Do we really have time for that kind of creative dialogue?' Powell asked.

Practical and intelligent as well as brave and tough, he had been a damn fine Marine all right.

Dell smiled again, shook that perfect profile.

'No, we don't. You're right, Willieboy,' he admitted calmly. 'I'd rather hoped that a little wife-killing conviction wouldn't affect the 168th's loyalty to me,' he continued sardonically, 'but we can go into that after we've completed Phase Three.'

Phase One had been to penetrate the compound.

Phase Two had been to capture the surface guardhouse.

Phase Three of the Plan called for the seizure of the sub-terranean command capsule, 'the Hole' and its instruments which lay behind a door that was four feet thick. There were elaborate alarm devices and an armed SAC Missile Combat Crew within Viper Three's command capsule, and these wary, disciplined men operated under complex security procedures that had been developed and perfected during more than a decade of Cold War.

Phase Three was, of course, impossible.

CHAPTER FOUR

First things first.

First, Harvey Schonbacher opened his sack, took out three sets of handcuffs stolen from the police station, turned the two cooks back to back and manacled their wrists together. He chained the right wrist of one to the left of the other, then reversed the process. After that, he removed their belts and lashed their ankles together in accord with Dell's instructions. As the fat man was completing this, Hoxey and Falco entered the guardhouse — drenched, barefoot, beaming.

'Beautiful, just beautiful,' the assassin said while he mopped his wet face with his left hand. His right still held the machine gun.

Hoxey said nothing, nothing clearly audible. His lips were moving animatedly, however, and Dell was reasonably confident that he was intoning a prayer for the dead Air Policeman's soul. For a moment, the former Deputy Intelligence Officer of the 168th was tempted to add a solemn 'amen' to the lunatic's litany but then decided that Hoxey was too unpredictable to risk it.

'Nice shooting, Stud,' he said to Falco instead.

The underworld professional flashed his broad Mediterranean grin, lots of good teeth, male pride and earthy peasant charm.

'I sure saved your ass,' he agreed as he noticed the box of Kleenex on the desk. 'That kid had plenty of guts and the way he dived for the carbine — well, he was going for the long ball. He'd have taken at least one of you with him,' Falco estimated.

He pulled out a fistful of the paper tissues — ten or twelve — and dried off most of his face. 'Yeah, I saved your ass — your asses — all right,' he repeated in tones edged with good-humored complacency.

'Done,' Schonbacher announced from across the room.

He was breathing hard from the relatively modest exertion that had been required to bind two unarmed and unresisting cooks, Powell noticed. The pudgy rapist was in poor condition physically, Powell judged, and when he glanced across at Dell he saw that the ex-SAC officer had reached the same conclusion.

'Not quite done, Harvey,' Dell responded, 'but almost. We've got to gag them and put them out of sight – that closet over there would do – just in case someone might come by. A very remote possibility, I admit, but let's not risk it. Let's do a clean job.'

'Cleanliness is next to Godliness, my Uncle Tom used to say,' announced the black man.

Falco smiled, Dell nodded affably and 'Deacon' Hoxey looked up in puzzled surprise. Hoxey didn't have a very high opinion of black people, and this apparent show of piety on the part of Willieboy Powell came as an unexpected delight to the religious fanatic.

Harvey Schonbacher was less impressed. 'Your uncle was a preacher?' he challenged irritably.

'No, a street cleaner.'

Dell and Falco both chuckled, but Hoxey still wore that earnest, puzzled face. Harvey Schonbacher gagged the two prisoners with strips of cloth ripped from white kitchen aprons, opened the closet door and glared at Powell. The former Marine understood, helped bundle the cooks into the broom closet.

'Good,' Dell rated their effort. 'Now, Willieboy, would you please drive the wagon inside the fence? It could attract attention out there.'

'Lock the gate too?'

The man with the film star's face – the man whom Montana newspapers and broadcasters had been describing as 'the handsomest murderer ever imprisoned in the State Penitentiary Death House' – nodded. Powell thought ahead regularly and neatly, neatly and coolly and purposefully. He and Falco were the best – by far – Lawrence Dell computed, and he was counting on them.

'Switch built into the gatepost – left gatepost – locks it electrically,' Dell explained.

There was nothing remarkable about the fact that he knew such details, that he knew it all. As Deputy Intelligence Officer, he'd been in charge of launch-site security for the 168th and it had been his job to know it all. It was easy for him to learn, for he was a good student with an exceptional memory and a passion to know it all – all that counted anyway. Dell had all the poise and the brains and the nerve – the cool, the courage and the cunning – to win a general's star eventually, the black man reflected as he walked out into the fog. A handsome, careful, clever WASP like Major Lawrence Dell could have gone all the way, Powell thought with only a trace of bitterness. Then the ex-Marine slid into the stolen wagon, drove the dark-blue Ford inside the electrified fence, closed the gate switch and re-entered the guardhouse with a pair of shoes in each hand.

'You fellows might need these,' he said curtly.

Falco and Hoxey thanked him for his consideration, but Dell merely smiled. Dell was the only one who realized that Willieboy Powell had spoken the literal truth. He hadn't meant to be considerate or helpful at all – simply practical. He ran nobody's errands, for he was nobody's servant. Powell had thought – rationally – that these two men who were now and temporarily his allies might need their shoes, might do their share of the work better if shod. If they did their best, his life and his future might be saved and that was all he cared about – all he had cared about for a long time.

Dell could have told the others this, but that wouldn't have been wise, for it might anger Powell. Instead, he said something else that was much safer.

'Let's eat,' he advised.

A few minutes later, the five fugitives from the Death House sat munching thick ham-and-rye-bread sandwiches and drinking coffee. Hoxey was chewing abstractedly, faintly humming some almost tuneless hymn and nodding to the rhythm that sounded only in the private labyrinth of his mind. It was a psalm to God who had sent him into this strange place with these strange companions. Powell consumed his sandwich slowly and systematically, his eyes wandering to the windows every twenty seconds on 'routine patrol'. Dell's attention was focussed on his allies, for he knew how remote was the chance of anyone else visiting Viper Three on a morning such as this, and he found himself studying the gross way that fat Harvey Schonbacher was gorging himself. It seemed appropriate that the sex murderer should eat like some large swinish animal, for the homicidal pharmacist was a vicious hypocrite and sly sadist who represented most of what Dell detested. Back in the Death House, Dell had described his project – this project – as 'the greatest crime in history', and now it seemed unfortunate that anyone as gross, shifty and contemptible as Schonbacher should participate.

Well, flabby Harvey Schonbacher didn't matter that much.

It was the mission that counted, Dell reminded himself. They had trained him to think that way, and now all those years of training were going to pay off in the next sixty minutes. This was going to be bigger than the Brink payroll theft or the British mail-train robbery or anything. Within the next hour, the five fugitives were going to do something that would make then internationally famous.

Or dead.

'Now pay attention,' Dell announced in that crisp clear voice he'd used at so many briefings, 'because this is the last time I'm going over it. We've talked this operation backwards and forwards a hundred times, but now it's for real. If you do exactly what I've told you – *exactly* – we can make it. On paper, this is a suicide mission. I say it isn't – not for us. I say we can make it.'

Falco nodded. He'd been on tricky jobs before, like that 'hit' in Vegas or the time he'd gunned the government witness right on the steps of the U.S. Court House in Manhattan's Foley Square. Willieboy Powell's eyes narrowed, but he kept on eating.

'Maybe nobody else in the world could make it,' Dell admitted. 'Maybe the best Red Chinese commando team or the toughest Russian paratroop company couldn't, but *we* can make it – and alive. Okay, take a look at this squawk box on the guard's desk. First, Deacon will talk to the missile crew down in the capsule on this squawk box and he'll tell them the new

31

shift is here. He'll give the names and the ranks they expect. Second, I'll step up to the box and recite the code phrases we squeezed out of the replacement crew when we ambushed their station wagon.'

'Why should *Deacon* talk to the capsule?' challenged Schonbacher.

'Because he's the only one of us who speaks with a Southern accent like that sergeant I choked outside,' Powell explained coolly.

Falco nodded again. It made sense.

'Willie's right,' confirmed the former intelligence officer, 'so let's give it another run-through.'

They rehearsed the routine four times before Dell was satisfied that Hoxey was letter perfect. The fact that the religious fanatic was a lunatic didn't appear to interfere with his 'country boy' cunning; in fact, he appeared to enjoy the role and was an impressively quick study. He had it all right the second time, didn't waver when he was asked to repeat the lines twice more. Even Falco, who regarded Hoxey as a 'Hick creep', was impressed.

'Good. Okay, here we go,' ordered Dell.

Hoxey sat at the chair behind the dead guard's desk, took the clipboard and watched Dell press down the switch on the intercom.

'Attention, the Hole; attention, the Hole,' Marvin Hoxey repeated as he'd been drilled. 'This is the guardroom. Security detail now processing replacement Missile Combat Crew 962-B reporting for duty. Names and ranks: Kincaid, Roger F., Captain and Crew Commander, and Witkin, Harry O., First Lieutenant.'

The reply was almost instantaneous.

'Affirmative, affirmative. Names and ranks check properly with those on our list. Please put Captain Kincaid on the box for the challenge,' the metallic voice of the capsule commander directed.

As Lawrence Dell leaned forward, he wondered – for one moment – whether the genuine SAC crew had supplied the correct passwords when the convicts had hurt them so badly. Some dedicated men might be tricky despite the pain, but other very brave men might crack under the brutal beating and shock. Dell had to say the right things – all the right things and in the correct sequence – or the massive door to the capsule would remain closed and the commander of the Missile Combat Crew inside would sound the alarm. Red Indian. Red Indian was the SAC code phrase for an attempt to sabotage or seize a nuclear-weapons base, and that was what the commander would shout into the microphone as he punched the alarm button.

Red Indian.

That would do it all right.

That would kill them all.

At this moment – at every moment – there were two 'alert platoons' of Air Police standing by in a 'ready room' at Malm-strom Air Force Base. Malmstrom was the headquarters for the 168th, and it was precisely nineteen point seven miles from Viper Three. That was the distance from outer fence to outer fence. It was actually a bit more than twenty-two miles from the helicopter pad near the 'ready room' to the front door of the guardhouse at Viper Three. They would come by helicopter, eager young men with automatic weapons and enormous mo-tivation. Motivation – that was the armed forces' synonym for a willingness to die so long as it was done purposefully and stylishly. The three twin-rotor helicopters that were always on the pad could be loaded and airborne in no more than four minutes, and in another thirteen the keen APs – all qualified as sharpshooters on the range each month – would be ringing the launch site and firing.

Dell didn't think about any of this.

He didn't have to.

He knew it.

He also knew that he couldn't hesitate any longer now, and he couldn't turn back either. This plan and this hole added up to their only chance.

'Captain Kincaid here, requesting permission to come down,' he lied evenly.

He didn't smile meaningfully. A lot of vulgar people might have done that in this situation, but Dell, a worldly connoisseur of Marcello Mastroianni and Steve McQueen films, didn't. He was much too tense.

'Captain Kincaid, would you please present the security password?' the squawk box rumbled.

'Bunker Hill.'

'And?'

'Yorktown,' Dell added.

'Now the third part, please.'

Fear.

Terror.

Harvey Schonbacher was so frightened that he might vomit. Lawrence Dell could see it in his face, and he didn't have to ask why. The missile crew they'd captured and beaten so brutally – no, tortured was a less mealymouthed description – hadn't yielded up three parts to the security password. They'd given only two, Bunker Hill and Yorktown, and there was no way that anyone – not even a man as intelligent and cunning as Dell – could possibly guess the third.

Powell and Falco exchanged glances, saying nothing to avoid distracting the man who'd masterminded the prison break and brought them this far. It was up to him, completely up to him. Their strength and weapons couldn't help him now. They watched, saw his eyes swing to the United Air Lines calendar on the wall.

'There is no third part,' the ex-major said firmly.

'I'm sorry,' responded the crew commander in the capsule, 'but I must insist on the third part.'

Now Dell grinned.

'There is no third part. I challenge you,' he said into the squawk box.

There was a moment of silence.

'All correct. You are correct,' announced the man some twenty yards below their feet. 'We'll be ready to switch the keys at oh-eight-twenty. Okay, Kincaid, you can come on down.'

CHAPTER FIVE

'Balls of brass,' Falco complimented a second after Dell had flicked the intercom switch.

'Nice work, Major,' agreed the black Vietnam veteran.

His voice was much calmer and less enthusiastic than Falco's, for he was merely expressing one professional's opinion of another. Willieboy Powell wasn't giving compliments or anything else away.

Schonbacher's uneasy eyes swung back and forth, flashing out the fear still within him like some electric sign. There was an utterly different look on Hoxey's face, tranquil beatitude.

'Lord's will,' he sighed.

Dell nodded.

'I'm sure it was,' he replied, 'but that calendar on the wall helped too.'

'You weren't just guessing?' probed Falco.

'Not after I saw that calendar. Once I checked the calendar and made sure this was the start of the third week of the month, I knew I had him cold. SAC sometimes uses three-part passwords, but only in the first half of any month. Don't ask me why; some security genius made the rule a few years ago.'

Then he held up his right hand, showing four fingers.

'Four minutes!' he said in the confident, driving tones of a football coach giving a half-time pep talk to a team that was already twenty points ahead. 'Four minutes – two hundred and forty seconds, and we're home. Once we're inside and I've fixed the wiring, it's the whole damn ball game!'

The generals – all those cold, busy men with the stars and the power who spoke so authoritatively to Senate committees and television cameras – would never believe it. Of course a hydrogen bomb could be lost off Spain and nerve gas could

35

accidentally kill 6,000 sheep in Utah, but nobody could *ever* seize a Minuteman capsule.

'We'll be safe inside,' Dell promised.

The others looked at him hopefully, wondered.

'What's it *really* like inside?' Schonbacher tested.

'Marvellous. No air pollution, no crowds, no noise problem, no annoying door-to-door salesmen, no junk mail, no screaming demonstrators and no burglars or muggers. It's even germ-free. Law and order, USA., and clean as Doris Day's undies – the American dream come true.'

'But no broads,' Falco observed.

'When they make the picture, they'll put in a few broads,' Powell assured him.

It was an attractive prospect.

'I want Dean Martin to play me,' Falco stipulated.

'You've got a deal,' pledged the black man.

'Look at it this way, Stud,' reasoned the ex-SAC officer wryly. 'No broads – but no police and no roadblocks and no helicopters hunting you down like an animal. It's a perfect hideout, but even if it wasn't we've got no place else to hole up out here in these goddam prairies anyway.'

Powell sighed.

'It should be quiet and restful anyway,' he judged, 'and that'll be good because I'm tired – tired of sweating and tired of running.'

'I give you my word as an ex-officer and a former gentleman,' Dell vowed, 'that once we bolt that eight-ton door behind us the running is over. And the sweating too. As soon as I disconnect those cutoffs and make that phone call, *they'll* do the sweating. The fat men at the top, the men so high up they never heard of us and wouldn't care if they did!'

He spoke with the special bitterness of a man who'd been on the way to the top himself, who'd been part of the Establishment and had been expelled-betrayed-abandoned by it. Hoxey was speaking too, or at least his thin lips were moving in what was probably some righteous prayer. There was something ironically incongruous in this, Dell reflected, for the madman was in almost continuous communication with *his* God but the same people – the respectable sensible jurors who'd voted to

36

end his life – were content to relate to *their* deity only one day a week. Sunday – this was Sunday, when they put on clean clothes and prayed for lower taxes and an end to student riots. The 'impossible' assault on Pearl Harbor had also been on a Sunday, Dell recalled.

No more time.

'Let's go,' he ordered.

They followed him past the open door of the closet in which the bound cooks lay watching, with Falco winking at the captives and Deacon Hoxey making an awkward sign of the cross with his carbine. Powell didn't do anything so colorful; he simply closed the closet door. The convicts followed Dell through another door that led from the guardroom into a corridor, down that passage and around the corner where they faced the accordion gate of a typical freight elevator. It was smaller than most, and the five invaders found themselves crowded uncomfortably when Dell closed the metal grid behind them.

Down.

Slowly.

As the elevator began to descend, the former Air Force intelligence officer automatically glanced at his watch again to check the time, as SAC had trained him to. This part of the holy ritual – like the others – presumably contained some special magic of its own, and – like the elaborate security system for the launch sites – was designed to produce perfect results for imperfect men.

Flawed men – such as these in this elevator, he reflected.

Perhaps not quite that flawed, but men who could take orders or lives or flight as the situation required.

0818.

Two minutes to go.

When the elevator stopped at the bottom of the shaft, Dell guided the raiders out into a well-lit room lined with green metal lockers, a door and a large cork bulletin board that was almost completely covered with mimeographed copies of recent 'standing orders' from Wing headquarters. There was also a SAC poster reminding and re-emphasizing and repeating the need to maintain the tightest security at missile bases, to keep

the secrets of America's ICBM weapons and installations from
... It didn't say from whom, but you couldn't put that on a
poster anyway because the nation's – any nation's – enemies
changed from year to year. Now the Germans and the Japanese
were our friends and the Russians and the Chinese were our
foes, and the Apaches were no longer the villains in film and
fiction and young people from the best families shouted obscenities at policemen instead of playing tennis. None of the
convicts said any of these things, of course, or anything else.
They simply looked around curiously and silently, waiting for
Lawrence Dell to do what he had to do next.

He pointed to the gray telephone on the wall, walked to it
and raised the receiver.

'Kincaid and Witkin ready to enter Launch Control Center,'
he told the men inside the capsule. 'One hundred and twenty
seconds? Roger. We're standing by at the hatch.'

As he hung up the phone, the convicts all turned to face the
door at the far end of the room. It looked like a ship's hatch, but
the rectangular metal plate was actually an eight-ton slab of
torch-proof steel. It was made of the same material used in the
exterior walls of bank vaults, a choice based on the fact that
something much more valuable than Xerox shares or diamonds
or tax-free municipal bonds was stored here. Something so
precious and potent as to be priceless rested inside, ten small
red switches and two unique keys worth more than all the gold
in Fort Knox or the rerun rights to every TV situation-comedy
series ever made. They were invaluable, but nevertheless no
one could steal them or sell them, for they were valueless outside of this subterranean redoubt.

0819.

Sixty seconds.

'Our one chance,' Dell warned. 'Harvey and I will go in first
– in the coveralls. Stud, you and Willieboy will stand by with
the tear gas. Deacon, cover the elevator behind us – and say
another prayer.'

They heard the clicking sounds of the heavy bolts being re-
tracted, and the big metal door swung out smoothly on well-
oiled hinges. Framed in the opening stood First Lieutenant
Philip Canellis, a thin, twenty-eight-year-old Bostonian in the

standard white coveralls with the standard .38-caliber pistol on his right hip. With no reason to expect trouble, he'd left the gun in its leather sling when he'd unlocked and opened the four-foot-thick door. He saw 'Captain' Harvey Schonbacher, blinked at the unfamiliar face. If he'd seen Dell, the face wouldn't have been unfamiliar and he wouldn't have blinked. He'd have grabbed for his side arm and shouted 'Red Indian!'

But he didn't see Dell.

Dell was hiding, just out of sight on the left side of the opening.

He was hiding and waiting, with one of the stolen police revolvers in his right hand.

As soon as Canellis blinked, Schonbacher nodded in the pre-arranged signal and the former major stepped forward. He swung the gun at the same time. The lieutenant recognized *him* instantly, reached for his own weapon and opened his mouth to scream 'Red Indian!' At that moment, Lawrence Dell hit him. First he struck Canellis in the mouth with the revolver, and some one and a half seconds later hit him in the throat with some sort of judo blow. The attack was brutal, barbarous, un-provoked, deplorable and successful. The missile officer fell to his knees, and when Dell struck him twice more on the back of the head he sprawled on the floor – full length, face down, unconscious.

Phase Three was going well.

Not a shot, not a shout to sound the alarm.

Some thirty feet down the tunnel in the Control Center itself, a tall blond captain seated in a swivel chair faced a large console covered with dials, switches and gauges. There was also a red alarm button, isolated on the panel so that it wouldn't be pressed by accident. Dell couldn't see the button at this dis-tance, but he knew exactly where it was and what would happen if the commander of this Missile Combat Crew pushed it.

Everything, and the Plan would fail.

They would have the hole but not the birds, and without the birds Viper Three would be a trap instead of a weapon. The birds – the ten ICBM's – were crucial.

Dell pointed to Falco's submachine gun, and the underworld

assassin handed him the weapon unquestioningly. Then Dell pointed to Schonbacher, gesturing a command to precede him up the passage. The sweaty-faced rapist winced, hesitated and finally swallowed nervously. None of those things would have mattered if he'd moved up the tunnel, for Dell wanted someone else – someone whose face wouldn't trigger the crew commander into hitting that red button – to be point man. But Schonbacher didn't move. Son of a bitch, Dell thought angrily. Son of a bitch, the son of a bitch was a coward as well as a sex murderer.

Schonbacher had to go first – and now.

Right now, or the captain at the console would wonder.

Schonbacher had to go first because he was the only other raider in white coveralls.

Dell had to decide instantly between the carrot and the stick, the reassuring words or the machine gun in the belly. He guessed that force or even the threat of force might panic Schonbacher, so he smiled confidently and leaned close.

'We've got it made, Harve,' the former major lied in a confidential whisper. 'Just amble up the shaft – it's only fifteen or twenty steps – and screen me until I can cover the man at the console.'

Schonbacher swallowed again, took a deep breath and started walking slowly. Dell followed, holding the machine gun behind Schonbacher so the crew commander wouldn't see it. This weapon wasn't standard equipment for missilemen, and everything had to look routine and standard – for another fifteen seconds. They were that close to success. As Schonbacher approached, the yellow-haired crew commander – Captain Sanford Towne – smiled and spoke.

'You guys are late. Fog again, huh?' he said as he rose from the swivel chair.

Schonbacher wondered what to answer, a dilemma that ended swiftly.

Dell pushed him aside.

'Don't move, Sandy,' he ordered. 'One step and you're dead.'

One step. Towne was one step from the instrument panel and its red button. He looked at the machine gun, the man who aimed it and the distance to the red button. One step.

'You'd never make it,' Dell warned, reading his thoughts. 'You'd be dog meat before you got halfway.'

Towne took a deep breath, tensing as if to move.

'Don't try it, Sandy. This gun throws six hundred slugs a minute, and they go a lot faster than you do. I'll put ten holes in you before you can blink.'

The crew commander's eyes flickered, shifted toward the tunnel.

'No, he isn't coming. We took him at the door,' Dell replied to the unspoken hope.

Now Powell and Falco – the latter still in prison uniform – appeared in the doorway, each carrying a gun and each pointing it at Captain Sanford Towne. Dell couldn't see them, but the look on the crew commander's face told him that they were there.

'Willie? Stud?' the ex-major tested.

'We're here.'

The odds were hopeless.

Towne sighed, raised his hands slowly in surrender.

'Good, very good. Very intelligent,' Dell complimented. 'Now take three steps away from the console – three very careful steps, Sandy, or you'll be dead.'

'Larry,' the crew commander began.

'No, no talk. Move.'

Towne obeyed.

'Take his gun, Stud.'

The professional assassin advanced, disarmed the missileman and glanced at the pistol in his hand. He nodded – as if remembering something – and abruptly hit Towne on the back of the head with the gun. The crew commander dropped to the gray linoleum floor.

'Sometimes guys get second thoughts,' Falco explained calmly, 'and we don't have time to screw around with heroes.'

Falco was right. Towne might have made another try. Neither Dean Martin nor John Wayne would have slugged an unarmed man like this, but they had their images to consider. One of the rare Americans who didn't care about being popular, Falco was thinking solely of his own survival. He did this with the knowledge that no one else was.

41

'Okay, chain him up,' Dell said after one long glance at the man on the floor. 'Stud, would you help Harvey?'

'Sure.'

'Good. Willieboy, come with me.'

Powell followed him back down the short tunnel toward the door, stopped to look down at the young lieutenant whose bruised cut mouth was now bleeding.

'He's still out,' the ex-Marine reported.

Dell nodded, called to Hoxey to enter. The madman walked inside and was studying the dimly lit shaft as Dell and Powell put down their machine guns. He watched as they leaned against the massive portal, saw it move slowly and close with a jarring crash of metal against metal. Then the handsome hard man who'd once been Major Lawrence Dell slammed shut the two-inch steel bolts and spun the wheel that locked out the rest of the world.

0824.

Phase Three completed.

They had achieved the impossible.

Now only the unbelievable lay between them and a fantastic victory.

CHAPTER SIX

Cunning, check.

Violence, check.

The cunning and violence were finished, but – from a technical point of view – the most difficult part of the operation still lay ahead.

Directly ahead, to be precise, and Dell knew that he had to be perfectly precise. It was now a question of seconds and millimeters, he thought as he noticed Hoxey staring dreamily up the tunnel toward the brightly lit Launch Control Center. The sharp-featured Arkansan had never seen anything like this, of course, and he was studying it with the curiosity of a sly, hostile child. He was wholly absorbed, indifferent to the mounting menace of time.

'Wake up, Deacon,' Dell ordered in tones of barely controlled irritation. 'Deacon, we're in a critical bind – a time bind. Somebody might find the real missile crew on the surface at any moment, so there's no time for sightseeing now. There's too much to be done.'

'Can I help, Larry?' the madman asked politely.

Dell nodded.

'Help Willie move this fellow off the floor and get him up to the Control Center – up there. Harvey and Stud will tie him up,' the former major promised.

Dell glanced at his wristwatch as Hoxey and Powell lifted the unconscious lieutenant. Numbers, it was all numbers now just as it had been in the Air Force. Viper *Three* controlled *ten* Minutemen, but *four* other Viper launch sites within *sixty* miles also had some control – a negative control – over these same missiles. If any *one* of the *eight* alert men in the other *four* capsules saw an alarm light blinking to signal that Viper Three was preparing to fire its rockets, he could flick an 'inhibitor' switch that would make any such launching impossible. There was a cable linking each other Viper capsule to the main instrument control console here in Three, and these wires permitted SAC teams outside Viper Three to cancel Three's effectiveness as a weapon. Dell had to find and remove these cutoff devices without setting off any of the sensitive and tricky anti-sabotage alarms or booby traps. Some worked by pressure plate, others by trigger, still others by tension or electric circuit. A number were cleverly disguised.

Dell had to disconnect or neutralize all of them.

Then he'd make the phone call, the one he'd been planning so bitterly during the long weeks in the Death House. He'd worked out every word, for this would be an important – perhaps historic – conversation. He had no doubt about what he'd say, and the only question was whether he still remembered the complete wiring diagrams he'd last seen in the TOP SECRET 'security maintenance manual' nearly a year earlier.

He started up the shaft after Powell and Hoxey, stopped halfway to the Control Center to open a four-foot-high gray metal locker standing against the tunnel wall. He pulled out a toolbox stenciled USAF EMERGENCY MAINTENANCE, hefted it and walked quickly to the command capsule itself. Falco, Hoxey and Schonbacher were finishing the binding of the two unconscious Air Force officers, but Willieboy Powell stood aside cradling his machine gun and watching.

'Hurry up, dammit,' Dell commanded. 'Aren't you finished yet?'

Schonbacher turned, sniffed defensively.

'Almost,' Falco answered pleasantly. 'Just about ... yeah, that's it.'

He stepped back, inspected and approved.

'Finished, Larry,' he said.

'Dump them both in the bunks – over there – and clear out. Back into the tunnel – all of you,' Dell instructed curtly. 'This is going to be damned delicate, and I don't want anybody breathing down my neck.'

The major's feeling the pressure too, Powell thought.

The prisoners were manhandled into the bunks in the adjacent compartment and the four convicts withdrew to the

44

shaft, from which they watched Dell begin. As the condemned wife-killer started by unscrewing a panel on the left side of the commander's console near the red telephone, Powell let his eyes wander to study this strange place of which he'd heard so much. Using the only frame of reference he had, he'd half expected this instrument-crammed capsule to look like something out of a low-budget science-fiction movie or perhaps one of those Japanese flying-saucer-epics. It was a bit disappointing to see that this was simply a crowded rectangular chamber with two high-backed red swivel chairs – bomber-pilot seats mounted on metal rails – facing complex control panels. There were lots of dials and buttons and switches, and that helped some – but still it wasn't nearly as bizarre as it might have been. The Air Force engineers and designers were practical, untheatrical hardware men who were probably adequate for SAC, but they'd never make it with MGM or even BBC television.

Dell had told him a great deal about this room. Some twenty feet long, sixteen feet wide and nine feet high, it was the nerve center of the thick-walled capsule that squatted on massive hydraulic shock absorbers built to absorb the blast effect of an enemy's atomic weapon. Viper Three could survive a near miss; it would require a direct hit with a fair-sized warhead to knock it out of the psychotic global game – the thermonuclear trick-or-treat that great nations played so calmly 365 days a year. The exact target would be this room, Powell remembered, and now the words returned as if they'd been tape recorded.

Self-willed, Powell's eyes followed the silent sound track being played within his skull.

'The inner walls are metal, and almost every inch of wall space is used. The floor is linoleum, skidproof and easy to clean. The room is well lit with fluorescent tubes, perhaps a little too well lit because after a few hours on duty the crew often find there's a bit too much illumination for comfort. This may be deliberate, a calculated decision. The Launch Control Center probably isn't supposed to be too comfortable, because the crews might relax and SAC doesn't want anything less than full alertness. There are no shadows and no privacy in this place. The men are part of the weapons system. This place and this weapons system are not meant for living, although the capsule can provide adequate life support for two people for about fifteen days in an emergency. That means food, water, air, toilet and sleeping facilities – the minimum necessities for bare survival.'

Powell had thought that he would find it impressive and he did – but he didn't like it. It was unnatural, two men in a hole with chemical toilets and buttons that could kill great numbers of invisible, anonymous people thousands of miles away. He looked at the switches – the ten firing switches – and he wondered *which* people in *what* place. Women and children or fanatical enemy soldiers – he'd seen them all burned and broken and lifeless in the jungles and the rice paddies. He had slain people who'd been trying to slay him and others who might have been trying – there had been no time to talk – but this way of war seemed worse. It had been dirty, sweaty and real in Vietnam, real heat and real fear and real people, and this cool, scientific way of killing distant strangers from a temperature-controlled hole in the Montana plains seemed unreal. It was too cool and clean here. It was too quiet.

You didn't even know whom you were fighting, Dell had told him, for the missile crews were never informed what the targets of their rockets might be. The prudent security-conscious generals had rationally concluded that the men at the firing switches didn't really need to know, and SAC operated on a sensible 'need to know' basis. That made the whole thing even more unreal, the ex-Marine decided, and he wondered what sort of men could comfortably spend their days as part of a weapons system. Very ordinary men, if his memories of that other cruder war in Asia were correct, and that didn't make too much sense either.

The crew commander whom Falco had hammered groaned, and Willieboy Powell looked toward the sound. He couldn't quite see the bound captain in the bunk, but he had no doubt that this man was a superior person of above average intelligence, education, sobriety and integrity. Yes, the Minutemen launch teams were hand-picked and thoroughly trained and emotionally stable – as close to perfect as the rest of this weapons system – but somehow five much less stable and much less perfect jailbirds had conquered both. They could never have

46

done it without Dell, the ex-Marine reflected, for Dell was not only just as intelligent and well trained and perfect but he was also *angry*. That was his edge, his advantage over the emotionally stable types who designed and manned this underground redoubt. This was no startling discovery; Powell knew there were many situations in which only the bold, irrational or desperate could survive or succeed. He'd seen it in bloody battle in the Demilitarized Zone up north, in the Ashau Valley and in the Mekong Delta jungles a dozen times – the wild ones daring and defying and somehow doing. Sometimes they died in the process, and their proud, dazed, tight-lipped families in oddly named towns in Oklahoma and South Carolina received medals in ceremonies reported only in local newspapers. Of course, there would be no medals – posthumous or otherwise – for the five men who'd seized Viper Three, for they were committing an unspeakable act. They were defying not only the government and armed forces of the United States, but also the efficiency and magic of American industry and technology. If Dell's scheme failed, they could expect no mercy for this sacrilege.

Dell grunted, and Powell saw him put down the panel on the floor. After a moment, the former major reached for a pair of pliers in the toolbox and Powell turned away again to scan the rest of this control room that he heard Dell describe.

'Off the main room with the controls is a compartment with a toilet, two bunks and an electric oven. There's also a refrigerated box packed with enough frozen meals for two weeks, the emergency food to be used when the capsule is sealed in a war or brink-of-war situation. The entire capsule is constantly cooled by an air-conditioning system set for exactly sixty-eight degrees, and if the temperature varies a warning light flashes on the Missile Crew Commander's console.'

Powell wondered which of the bulbs on the panel would signal this; it was impossible to guess, for there were several. For a moment he wanted to ask Dell, but he could see that this was no time to ask 'tourist' questions. The former SAC major was totally and grimly involved in his race to disconnect the 'inhibitors' – peering into the opening with the total calculating concentration of a surgeon getting his first look at an abdominal cancer he'd just exposed. He hesitated, took a deep breath and reached forward with the pliers. Quite deliberately, Willieboy Justice Powell – that was the name he'd been christened in Baltimore some three decades earlier – turned his attention away from this critical business and back to the capsule.

There – up *that* passageway – was a Minuteman.

He couldn't see it from the doorway, but Dell had said that one of Viper Three's ten rockets was accessible from the Launch Control Center and if a man stood in the middle of the Center and the passage door was open he could see the bottom of one missile. It would be interesting to look at, to touch such a remarkable piece of hardware – if Dell said it was all right. They could do nothing here without his permission, for he knew about this place and they didn't. Cool and clean instead of steamy and filthy, metal and plastic instead of mud and jungle, this place had its own dangers that were just as frightening and fatal as the choking green rain forest he'd left nineteen months before.

Powell looked at the red switches on the console, remembered and stared.

'On the Deputy's control board, which is screwed to the floor about five yards to the right of the Commander's, are ten switches – up near the top of the console on the right side. Each switch is safety-sealed so that it cannot be tripped by accident, an extra precaution that's easily understandable if you know that each one of these switches arms or activates the electronic circuits in the nuclear warhead of one Minuteman. Under standing orders, the switches are to be thrown only if both missilemen agree that the TOP SECRET predetermined code phrase to launch – the specific signal that means World War III – has just come over the speaker from SAC headquarters and been verified by Wing.'

Powell looked at the twin speakers. He was a skilled auto and truck mechanic who didn't know much about communications equipment, but these small square loudspeakers – one above each of the control panels – seemed quite ordinary. They didn't look at all like the end of the world – just gray metal boxes with grilles. Now Dell swore, and Powell turned to see the former major tug at the zipper of his stolen coveralls. Dell was hot, tense, damp with concentration despite the steady sixty-eight-degree temperature here in Viper Three, and his breathing was growing more urgent and more visible by the moment. He put down the pliers, picked up a rubber-handled screwdriver and did something with it inside the open console.

'Booby trap, antipersonnel grenade on the cable,' he reported without turning around.

He didn't wait for a reply either, but simply continued his work. There really wasn't much that Powell could have said anyway, other than that he hated booby traps with the bitterness of the combat foot soldier who has seen comrades maimed and killed by such devices. Dell didn't know anything about *that* kind of war, the ex-Marine reflected with an odd, angry pride of possession, and if they were in *that* sort of battle now it would be Willieboy Powell who'd know and lead. Comforted by this, the Marine veteran watched Dell set aside the screwdriver to retrieve the pliers. It was disturbing not to be able to see what Dell was facing and doing inside the console, for if the SAC technicians were half as sly as the Vietcong had been the booby trap would be almost impossible to disarm. What the hell would a chairborne major know about booby traps anyway?

'Number One,' Dell announced as he severed the first 'inhibitor' cable.

It was only then that Powell realized how heavily he was breathing himself.

Nine miles away, a stocky red-faced farmer named Simon Liffey was breathing almost as hard as he peered into the drizzle. The poor visibility was only one reason for Liffey's sullen discomfort, a mere supplement to the endless nagging of his shrill voiced wife beside him in the front seat of the Dodge pick-up. It was always unpleasant driving with garrulous, critical Emma Liffey, who compulsively volunteered advice – usually wrong – on everything, but today she was in an especially critical temper because the Chrysler wouldn't start and she *deeply* resented the indignity of going to church in a truck. It was *deeply* embarrassing, she grumbled for the thirtieth time, and she blamed it all on her husband's carelessness.

'*Deeply* humiliating,' she persisted righteously.

Liffey said nothing, for there was nothing that you could say to this irrational forty-nine-year-old woman when she ignited in one of her emotional tirades. She was stupid, as stupid as the ridiculous hat she wore to church and other special occasions because she'd seen one like it in one of those stupid magazines.

'And now we're going to be late,' she complained as if Simon Liffey had planned the car breakdown, the rotten weather, the whole mess. She might go on like this all day, he realized, bitching and whining right through the afternoon. She could talk for hours, perhaps even into the football telecast that he'd been looking forward to all week. She'd done it before. Not this time, he resolved grimly as he fought down his impulse to reply. Not today, with the Jets playing Oakland. Any answer or comment would merely supply additional fuel for her fire, he told himself as he concentrated on the wet road ahead.

'What's that?' she said abruptly.

'Look out, Simon,' she added before he could answer.

This was another of her infuriating habits, wholly unconscious but extremely irritating. He saw nothing ahead at first, but then noticed a white figure on the left side of the highway. The woman's eyes were as sharp as her tongue, Liffey brooded as he tried to make out who or what the form might be.

'It's a man,' the farmer identified as he automatically slowed down the vehicle. 'A man in . . . in his underwear.'

'Probably drunk,' snapped Emma Liffey. 'See the way he's staggering. Drunk or crazy. Speed up, Simon.'

She might be right, although that was highly unlikely since she was almost always wrong. The man was probably sick or in some sort of trouble, Liffey reckoned, but he pushed down the gas pedal. She had a thing about picking up strangers on the road, and Simon Liffey wasn't going to risk his afternoon – his game – by stopping for this weaving half-dressed figure in the rain. The man waved futilely as the truck picked up speed and disappeared into the chill mist.

The man reeled, fell and somehow managed to get up to a crouching position. Now there was mud in addition to the blood stains on his face and undershirt, and his puffed, bruised face hurt as he shook his head to fight off the dizzying sheets of pain.

He could easily have fainted again, but he wouldn't permit himself that human weakness. Kincaid, Roger F., Captain, 168th Strategic Missile Wing, USAF, was much too highly motivated for that.

CHAPTER SEVEN

Dell wiped his sweaty hands on the sides of his coveralls, yawned and moved on with the screwdriver to open another panel down near the linoleum floor. He'd forced himself to sleep for two hours the previous afternoon, but now his body was beginning to feel the fatigue and pressure and it was only the tension-adrenalin and the defiant anger that kept him alert. The fear helped too, he realized, but that didn't bother him a bit. Weary but still tautly awake, he put the panel down and examined the complex of green, red, blue and yellow pipes and wiring. The Pop Art effect was purely coincidental, for the diverse shades of the wires and pipes reflected SAC's calculated color coding to assist maintenance crews rather than any youthful passion for psychedelic splendor.

The former Deputy Intelligence Officer of the 168th closed his eyes, waited until the appropriate page of the appropriate manual jumped into mental focus.

Yes, he could see the wiring diagram quite clearly now.

There would be little difficulty, if the bastards hadn't changed something during the past eleven months. Those systems experts in Omaha and Washington were always developing improvements – probably to justify their jobs and their budgets, Dell thought, and you never could predict what those clever engineers might come up with next. He took a flashlight from the toolbox, sat on the floor and shined the beam into the console.

There it was.

'Son of a bitch,' he complained in a whisper as if afraid that someone might hear him.

The second 'inhibitor' cable was booby-trapped with *two* devices, one a trip wire that would release deadly nerve gas and the other an electronic relay that would send a microwave signal to the other Viper launch sites alerting them that the cut-off wire was being removed. Both of these protective units were camouflaged as step-up transformers, but Dell remembered and recognized them. He found the wire cutters in the toolbox, took them in his right hand and aimed the flashlight beam with his left.

Then he stopped.

'Alarms on alarms,' he grumbled as he spotted the pressure plate concealed beneath the electronic signaler.

This was something new, but not really too surprising. It was the sort of little extra that you might expect if you were familiar with the other gadgets and techniques of SAC's security engineers, a logical extension of their previous thinking and hardware. Dell squinted, considered, reached in warily and finally closed the sharp jaws of the wire cutter with almost tender deliberation. He extracted the device like some poisoned tooth, instantly looked up to the Deputy Commander's console.

No flashing light.

No clanging alarm.

No booming klaxon.

Not yet anyway, but the job wasn't finished.

He took another look at the gas cylinder, shook his head.

'I don't know,' he said.

'Something wrong?' Falco asked from the doorway.

'Yes, but I'll handle it.'

'What are you going to do, Larry?'

Dell shrugged, sighed.

'I don't know,' he admitted. 'I haven't figured it out yet.'

His eyes moved to the clock.

It was 8:46.

'Eight forty-six and all's well with Big Ben Bell,' chortled the car radio. 'Here's an oldie and goldie, a disk that sold more than a million platters for delicious Dionne Warwick not so many years ago – "Alfie"!'

All these disk jockeys sound alike, the long-haired boy in the red Thunderbird noticed without malice. He couldn't afford to feel any hostility toward these glib radio 'personalities' even if he wanted to, of course, for he was – as the $900 guitar on the back seat indicated – a singer. He was more than that – a rock singer and one with great ambitions. If he was going to make it big – make it with the open-faced, teen-aged girls and the New York booking agents and the TV producers and the record companies – he'd have to make it with the DJ's, the powerful peddlers such as Big Ben Bell, who could put a record on the charts or in the trash.

'What's it all about, Alfie?' the silky, soaring voice demanded.

'Bread,' Terry Swift answered without hesitation as his eyes flicked to the Thunderbird's gas gauge. Bread such as Dylan and Donovan and Jim Morrison collected, a lot more bread than Terry Swift received for playing college concerts in South Dakota and Montana and Oregon. Of course, the bread wasn't all there was to it. Terry Swift had things to say about Love and Death and the Middle Class – nothing too original but quite sincere – and he had a rather good voice.

> And if only fools are kind, Alfie,
> Then I guess it is wise to be cruel.*

She was slick all right.

Now the driver began looking for the crossroad where 163 cut into Route 87, for that was his turn. He had another concert that afternoon at Carroll College in Helena, and he still had at least 110 miles to drive. Maybe more, he brooded, for signs were few and it was difficult to tell exactly where he was in this drizzle.

'I believe in love, Alfie,' she vowed as she slid into the final verse – and then Terry Swift hit the brakes. He was much too intelligent to do such a thing in a car moving fifty miles an hour on wet roads, but he did it to avoid killing the man. At that speed, the Thunderbird would surely have killed the man who'd staggered out into the highway, and Swift, twenty-three-year-old baritone advocate of Life and Love, couldn't risk that.

*'Alfie' – music by Burt Bacharach and lyrics by Hal David. Quoted with permission of copyright owner. Copyright © 1966 by Famous Music Corporation.

The brakes screeched and the car skidded in a short, frightening zigzag and Dionne Warwick kept singing – and finally the Thunderbird shook to a halt. It stopped about four feet from the man, close enough to leave Terry Swift tight-throated with panic and more than a little furious. He lowered the window beside him, leaned out to shout at the idiot in white. At that moment, the man fell down in the middle of the highway.

You couldn't be angry anymore.

You couldn't leave him there either.

Swift pulled his car to the side of the road, turned off the engine and got out to help the man. The man was bruised and bloody, clad only in socks and underwear and moaning constantly. As Terry Swift picked him up to carry him back to the car, the long-haired singer noticed two things about the semi-conscious stranger. He wasn't drunk – not a smell of alcohol – and he kept repeating the same odd phrase again and again.

'Red Indian at Viper Three. Red Indian at Viper Three.'

The words didn't mean anything to Terry Swift, but perhaps they could figure it out at the hospital in Great Falls. Concert or not, the young singer would have to deliver this man to a hospital in that nearby city, for that was the decent thing, the human thing, the only thing to do.

He moved the guitar to the front, gently placed the battered stranger on the back seat and pointed the car toward Great Falls. Big Ben Bell was babbling something about a 'groovy new platter by Herb Alpert', but Terry Swift wasn't listening at all. He was thinking about the man on the back seat and his senseless litany. It was even worse than the lyrics of some of those 'bubble gum' songs written for pre-teen rock addicts, even more baffling.

Red Indian at Viper Three?

Now what the hell could that mother mean?

CHAPTER EIGHT

'Cute,' Dell said as he studied the wiring inside the panel beneath the Crew Commander's console.

It looked like a perfectly ordinary set of cables, but, like so many other aspects of contemporary life, it wasn't at all what it seemed to be. There are many relatively harmless deceptions, such as false eyelashes and padded brassieres and breakfast-cereal packages and speeches by political candidates, but this was a lot more dangerous. That piece of green electrical cable wasn't at all like the other pieces of green electrical cable in Viper Three. It wasn't electrical cable at all. It was the trigger for another booby trap. There were so many different firing devices, and this one would set off that nasty little charge so neatly camouflaged as a circuit-breaker.

'Very cute. Hats off to the deep thinkers in Omaha,' the former major judged bitterly.

'Trouble?' wondered Falco.

'Trouble. Pressure release trigger,' Dell explained. 'The opposite of the normal set-up. Normally you set off a booby trap by stepping on or touching something that puts pressure on the detonator, but this bastard goes off if you release the pressure. If I cut the wire, it blows.'

'The VC used them a lot,' Powell remembered coolly.

Dell turned to him, sighed.

'Since you're still alive you must have figured out how to handle this sort of trigger, Willie?' he asked.

The black man nodded.

'Two ways. We sometimes rigged a hook around the wire, tied a long length of nylon cord to the hook and then jerked it loose from forty or fifty yards away,' he reported.

Dell shook his head.

'No good.'

'I know,' Powell agreed. 'We don't have forty or fifty yards, and we don't want to smash up all this equipment anyway.'

'Right. We need it. What's your other scheme? I hope it's better.'

The Marine veteran began to unbutton his blue jacket.

'It's a little more dangerous,' he admitted. 'It takes a lot of muscle and a certain amount of nerve. Two men, working together – perfect coordination. The pull on that damn thing may be anywhere from five to a hundred and five pounds. One man chops the cable with wire cutters, and the other has a grip on the cable about an inch or two above the spot where it's to be cut. He maintains the pressure – keeps it taut – until his buddy can disarm the charge itself. It's the buddy system.'

He put the jacket down, rolled up his sleeves.

'You ever done it, Willieboy?' asked Dell.

'A few times. It wasn't my favorite sport. I've seen men cut into chunks because somebody's grip slipped. The Russians have an electrical mine – the PMS – that works the same way, you know,' the ex-Marine added.

Lawrence Dell considered, decided that there was really no reason that Willieboy Powell shouldn't be just as smug and proud about his special knowledge as anyone else.

'I didn't know about that Russian mine,' the former SAC major admitted. Then he hesitated for a moment, only a moment.

'Well, buddy?' he invited as he held out the toolbox.

Powell's sole reply was to reach in and remove a pair of pliers.

The two men turned to study the booby trap itself, and after a few seconds Powell ran his fingertips over the surface – ever so slowly, ever so lightly.

'I'm looking for, *feeling* for an opening,' he explained. 'I don't think that this casing can be a single solid piece of plastic. There ought to be some small door, some opening for the men who armed the fuse on this damn thing after they hooked up the pressure cable. It would be on the bottom or the side, I'd bet. Someplace accessible but not too visible.'

His fingers wandered, probed.

'Nothing ... nothing ... nothing ... zero. Okay, I'll try it again,' he said calmly.

In the doorway, Falco grinned. It was a pleasure to work with a sensible professional who didn't rattle easily, who didn't panic in crisis.

'I'd better try the back too,' Powell muttered.

He continued his tactile patrol for another thirty-five seconds, his face immobile and his eyes focussed on something ten thousand miles away.

'Yeah,' he announced.

He pressed something on the rear of the plastic shell, and suddenly one end of the casing popped open with a click.

'Flashlight, Major?'

Dell handed him the lamp, and the two men peered in at the detonating device.

'There – on the right – that's the circuit closer,' the black man pointed out, 'and the name of the game is to keep it from closing. You'll have to wedge something in there. Nothing that conducts electricity, of course. No metal.'

'Wood or plastic, I suppose?' Dell proposed.

'I'd go with plastic, because wood may not take the pressure.'

'Are you ready, buddy?' he challenged.

'I'm ready, *Major*,' Powell replied coldly, and for a second Dell speculated on whether the ex-sergeant disliked him because he was white or because he'd been an officer or just because he found his personality unpleasant. Lawrence Dell had no illusions about his universal popularity – especially with men. More than a few of them – usually but not always those less blessed with good looks, intelligence or charm – had resented or rejected Dell.

'Here we go,' he announced as he raised the wire cutters.

He waited until he saw Powell place and close the pliers on the green cable, until he saw his 'buddy' tense and nod.

Dell squeezed the wire cutters once, then twice more before he succeeded in severing the cable. He saw Powell's muscles bulge as the man stiffened under the impact of the pressure, but Dell had no time to observe that struggle. He had his own war in which his only weapons were his reflexes, speed and two ballpoint pens. He seized the flashlight in his left hand, scooped up the plastic cylinders in his right.

'Goddam,' the former Marine grated beside him.

Dell squinted, pushed in one pen and then wedged the other in next to it.

'Ease it up – just a bit, Willie,' he advised.

Slowly – like some giant rusty machine – the powerful man holding the pliers let the cable move, perhaps a half inch.

'A *little* more,' Dell ordered with the flashlight beam focussed on the pens.

He watched the jaws of the circuit closer tighten on the plastic cylinders, heard the crunch as the pressure mounted. It would certainly be stupid to die because of two cheaply made ballpoint pens, he thought angrily, and then he smiled.

The pens had not shattered.

The explosive charge would not be fired.

'Nice work, buddy,' he congratulated his partner.

'Why, thank you, *Major*,' Powell answered.

It was very easy to admire Willieboy Powell, Dell reflected, and just as easy to dislike him intensely. Understanding him would be a lot more difficult – for anyone of any color. Perhaps – as one of the Death House guards had said about the warden – only a mother could understand that mother.

Dell's eyes swung back to the other side of the instrument complex, to the open panel in which rested the cylinder of nerve gas. Even the respirators wouldn't do much good against this GB – they called it Sarin – for you didn't have to breathe it to die. A few droplets on your skin could kill you.

'I *think* we have a problem with the gas,' he said soberly.

'For every problem there's a rational solution. All it takes is sound reasoning and leadership,' Powell replied in a voice that was almost mocking.

Falco asked what the problem was, and Dell explained it precisely.

'What do we do?' wondered the assassin.

'Something brilliant and creative like they do in the movies,' the man with the Warner Brothers face replied grimly, 'and *now*. We don't have much more time.'

There was, in fact, hardly any time at all.

At that moment, two orderlies were loading a barely conscious man onto a stretcher at the Emergency Receiving Entrance of the Great Falls Municipal Hospital while Terry

Swift watched from a few yards away. Standing beside the red Thunderbird, the long-haired singer shivered in the chill drizzle as they carried the battered stranger into the building. Swift glanced at his watch, realized that he ought to drive on because he was going to be late for his afternoon concert and reminded himself that there wasn't anything more that he could do for the man anyway. Then he sighed and walked into the hospital to tell the chunky intern on duty in the Emergency Room where and how he'd found this stranger.

'Red Indian at Viper Three – he must have said it eighty times,' the singer concluded.

'Riddles aren't my game. I'm a sutures and concussion man myself,' confided the doctor.

Then he thanked Terry Swift, and the rock singer drove away from the hospital with a small glow of righteousness and humanity that was very comforting on that cold October morning. It was going to be all right. Everything was going to be all right. The doctor would know what to do. Swift was correct – from a medical point of view. The intern did everything that he should do – from a medical point of view – and, while he was doing all these deft, sterile things, an earnest and slightly flat-chested nurse's aide was busy trying to fill out the forms. The forms were important too, and in this case answering all the questions was more difficult than usual.

Three basic questions were impossible to answer.

No, four.

The man's name.

His address.

Who to notify and where.

His blood type.

What was wrong with the anonymous stranger – medically – was a lot clearer. Dr Langer had said that 'somebody beat the crap out of him with a pipe or a baseball bat,' and she had a lot of respect for Dr Langer's judgement – medically. Of course, she couldn't write those words down on the report, but later after the patient had been treated and sent off to a room Dr Langer would dictate a proper diagnosis with words such as contusions and lacerations and maybe even multiple fractures. In addition to being unmarried, Dr Langer had a wonderful vocabulary and a blue Karmann Ghia and a way with nurses that was almost irresistible.

One of the clean, hard-working, dedicated nurses who knew this – and a good deal more – about the efficient intern was a fleshy, sensible blonde named Miss Kelleran. That was what the orderlies and nurses' aides called her, although Langer and several other young doctors referred to her either as Annie or Buster – the latter in tribute to her prominent prow. The flat-chested aide struggling with the report form was somewhat jealous of Miss Kelleran's fine figure, but she didn't mention that when the nurse entered the Emergency Room this Sunday morning.

'Good morning, Miss Kelleran,' she said for want of any better dialogue – a chronic condition since her low wages forced her to write all her own material.

'We've got a *mystery* patient,' she added in an effort to make conversation. 'No identification papers, semi-delirious and almost naked. Somebody found him crawling around out on the highway. Dr Langer says,' she confided in a whisper, 'that he's been *beaten* – maybe with a baseball bat.'

'Well, things are looking up in Great Falls,' the buxom blonde answered.

She really did remarkable things for that white uniform as she walked to the doorway of the treatment room, peered in curiously. The intern glanced up, grunted.

'What are you staring about, Annie?' he asked. 'You've seen half-naked men before.'

'Yes, this one among others. I've been out on a double date with your mystery patient, Doctor. His name's Kincaid. Roger Kincaid. He's an Air Force captain.'

'Well, somebody shot him down out on Route One-eighty-three,' announced the doctor. 'Beat the hell out of him, I'd guess, took his clothes and left him out there in the dewy dawn. He hasn't said why. He hasn't said *anything* except some gibberish about an Indian at Viper Three – whatever that is. Sounds like he's hallucinating, the poor battered bastard. He keeps repeating it over and over like a taped message.'

'What?'

The intern looked up from his patient irritably.

'The Indian at Viper Three. I told you that. No, *red* Indian at Viper Three. It doesn't make any sense at all. I don't think there are any hostile Indians around here, and not many vipers either .̇.̇. Well, your fly boy's going to live anyway – despite the dirty things somebody did to him.'

Kincaid and his head moved in a twitch.

'He's from Malmstrom, I suppose?' Langer asked.

The nurse nodded.

'You'd better let them know that he's here,' suggested the intern as he adjusted one of the bandages, 'and I suppose you ought to tell them what he's been raving about – the Indian bit.'

'You think it might be a code message – or something, Paul?'

Dr Langer smiled, showing a lot of fine teeth.

'I wouldn't know, Annie. I don't watch that much television,' he answered with almost paternal good humor.

He called two orderlies to move Kincaid out, and he watched Miss Kelleran's splendid hippy walk as she left to make the telephone call to Malmstrom Air Force Base. She was a very attractive woman, he mused appreciatively even if she was a bit over-imaginative.

Code messsages?

Ridiculous.

Somebody's jealous boy friend or husband had probably worked over Roger Kincaid for the usual righteous, nasty reasons, or perhaps the captain had gotten completely bombed on bourbon – as a good Air Force officer should on Saturday night – and then been robbed and dumped. No, no smell of alcohol. In any case, the nurse's notion of secret messages was plainly preposterous. Instead of speculating romantically about colorful plots and mysterious schemes, Annie Kelleran would do much better to concentrate on the real things she did best. Yes, the stocky intern recalled as he watched the next patient limp in, there were certain things at which Nurse Kelleran really excelled.

CHAPTER NINE

'Can I take a look?' Falco asked from the doorway.

'Why not?' Dell replied.

'I did a job once with some guys who specialized in vaults – a long time ago,' explained the executioner, 'and maybe I could figure out something.'

'This isn't anything like a vault, Stud,' the black man warned.

Falco approached the open panel warily, looked in and studied it for approximately twenty seconds before he shook his head.

'No, it isn't,' he admitted. 'Sorry I can't help.'

'Don't let it get you down,' advised the ex-Marine. 'We didn't win, but we haven't lost yet either. Even if we can't control the missiles, we're a lot safer down here than up there. Maybe we can still make a deal with them – or bluff.'

Dell shook his head.

'No bluff. Their instruments can turn off the missiles, and their control panels will show that the birds are dead.'

'So we've been defeated by the notorious military-industrial complex?' Powell said.

Lawrence Dell shook his head again.

'Not yet, not me, anyway. There's a way,' he vowed.

'Maybe we could deal, Larry,' reasoned Falco. 'We've got two of their missile boys for hostages.'

'I don't think so. A captain and a lieutenant for us – maybe, maybe not. They might go along with a deal to get us out of here,' he calculated, 'but I wouldn't bet my life on what they'd do once their damn capsule was safe.'

'The major doesn't trust the colonels and the generals, Stud,' jeered Powell.

Dell eyed him with open hostility.

'There's an old Air Force expression that seems to fit you to a "T", Willieboy,' he replied. 'You're becoming part of the problem instead of helping solve it.'

'I can't help anymore.'

'Is that why you're being so difficult now?'

Powell shrugged.

'Maybe,' he admitted. 'Maybe I'm angry that I can't. Maybe I'm scared – a little.'

The former SAC officer nodded understandingly.

'Welcome to the club, Willie,' he replied without rancor.

Both men turned to stare at the nerve-gas cylinder again.

'The Brockville bank job!' Falco announced suddenly.

They swung around curiously, hopefully.

'The Brockville bank job – the biggest vault job in history. Brockville, Ontario – just across the river from Ogdensburg, New York. Fourteen million bucks,' Falco recalled. 'Everybody heard about it. You remember, back in sixty-one or sixty-two?'

'What about it, Stud?' wondered Dell.

'Six or seven guys from Montreal, with a first-class torch man to burn open the vault. He was an ace, the best – and he had a trademark. A bucket of water. He always kept a bucket or a waste-basket full of water right next to him when he worked, just in case something caught fire from the torch. What do you say, Larry? Wanna try it?'

It was a calculated risk, for there was no way of predicting what sort of trigger had been built into the gas cylinder or how long it would take to start spitting the lethal Sarin. Two, three, four seconds?

'Get the water, Stud,' Dell answered with a gesture toward the wastebasket in the corner.

Falco returned from the toilet cubicle some ninety seconds later, set down the nearly full metal container some eighteen inches from the gas bomb.

'I'll chop it loose and you dump it,' the convicted wife-slayer told Falco. 'We'd both better put on the masks – in case the damn thing leaks. The masks won't protect us against the droplets, but if we move fast enough we shouldn't have that problem.'

They donned the masks, and Dell raised the cutters again.

'Good luck,' Powell offered from three yards away.

The twin masked faces bobbed bizarrely like those on cheap Christmas toys, and then Dell crouched over to sever the wire. He opened the jaws of the cutter wide, closed them with all his strength in an effort to hack loose the cylinder in one swift assault.

He did.

Falco scooped it up instantly like one of those Mohawk high iron construction workers tossing a white-hot rivet, plunged it into the water. The liquid began to move and churn, and both of the masked men peered at the surface urgently as they wondered whether the water would absorb or dilute or somehow stop the gas. Behind them, they could vaguely hear Schonbacher whimpering and Hoxey praying in the tunnel, but neither Dell nor the Syndicate assassin paid any attention to those sounds. Those noises were random, extraneous, potentially distracting. The men in the gas masks stared at the eddying water, stiff with desperation and barely breathing.

It finally stopped moving.

The water was calm.

You couldn't see anything different about it, Dell thought, but you wouldn't because nerve gas was colorless as well as odorless and tasteless. There was only a single way that they would know whether the water barrier had worked. Willieboy Powell, standing a few yards away. If the gas had seeped through, he'd be the first to crumple as he was the nearest of the unmasked three. In about half a minute, he would begin to cough and then he'd twitch and then the terrible convulsions would come. It might take three or four minutes more before his nervous-system controls collapsed, and at that point he'd start vomiting and defecating. In due course – thanks to the wonders of modern science – he'd die rolling in his own filth. Dell hadn't planned it this way, of course. It hadn't been his intention to use the ex-Marine as a guinea pig, but he realized that it was too late to avoid such a grim test now.

So he looked up at Powell – for some thirty seconds.

Nothing, no sign of any gas effects.

Very good.

Dell flashed the thumbs-up sign, patted Falco on the shoulder and rose from the tense crouch to remove his mask. Then Falco removed his respirator, showing a huge grin on his sweat-wet face.

'That's it?' the assassin asked, and Dell nodded.

'Aren't you supposed to say something clever at this historic moment – something quotable?' wondered Powell.

Lawrence Dell pondered, nodded.

'God bless the Brockville bank job,' he declared, and they all burst into shouts and laughter.

They'd won.

The former SAC major eyed his watch, saw that it was 8:34 A.M., Mountain Standard Time, which would make it 9:34 A.M. back in the Hole at Offutt Air Force Base near Omaha. Well, it didn't actually matter what time it was at the SAC command post anymore because from this moment on all the clocks would be set by the one here in Viper Three. They would after the telephone call, anyway.

'All right ... all right, cool it,' he told the other fugitives a minute later when their exuberance began to lose its initial hysteria. 'There'll be plenty of time to celebrate our victory over ... yes, let's use Willie's phrase ... over the military-industrial complex.'

Falco erupted with a cheerfully obscene suggestion that the 'whole goddam complex' commit an unnatural and physically impossible sexual act, an exuberant proposal that generated more laughter. Only 'Dean' Hoxey frowned at the crude indecency; even Harvey Schonbacher smiled.

'Later. Now it's time for the call to SAC headquarters,' Dell announced as he sat down at the Crew Commander's chair and reached for the telephone.

According to SAC records, that was 8.37 A.M. Mountain Standard Time – approximately two minutes after the Duty Officer at Malmstrom Air Force Base began to speak with a Miss Ann Kelleran, a nurse phoning from the Emergency Room at Great Falls Municipal Hospital. It was only 9:37 – Central Standard Time – further east in the Omaha area. This

distinction was not as petty as it might have seemed, for time --
every minute and aspect of it -- was to be crucial.

There wasn't very much of it left now.

Less than thirty-seven hours.

CHAPTER TEN

There are days and events that stick in people's minds, occasions so important that men and women who survived them cannot forget what happened or where they were when they heard the news. For middle-aged Americans, it might be that Day of Infamy in Hawaii in December 1941 and for their children it could be that other terrible day in Dallas in November 1963. The citizens of every nation – Britain, Israel, Japan, Russia, India, Cuba and the rest – all have their own memorable days of great triumph or tragedy, great crises that made headlines and dominated news broadcasts and now stand permanently in history. This is no new thing, for the Englishmen who stood fast with Harry that St Crispin's Day at Agincourt and the Atlanta housewife who wept as she watched federal troops entering the burning city undoubtedly recalled and relived those events until they died, just as those Hanoi school children will tell future generations about Uncle Ho's stupendous funeral way back in 1969.

People remember these things without effort, just as Colonel Alexander B. Franklin of the US Air Force will never forget where he was on that astonishing Sunday morning in a certain October. He was sitting at a desk in a comfortably heated bunker buried beneath the Omaha plains, exactly where he should be since he was the Duty Controller at SAC's global Command Post at Offutt. Franklin, a serious man with thinning red hair, the Distinguished Flying Cross, a wife named Arlene and a nagging suspicion that his chances of getting that general's star weren't all they might be, was an orderly conscientious person well suited to his current assignment. He was sensible, careful, well trained and utterly unlike any of those ambitious character actors who usually play Strategic Air Command colonels in films.

He wasn't paranoid, homicidal – or even stupid.

It's true that he didn't have the creativity of a Norman Mailer or the boyish good looks of Mao Tse-tung or even Joe Namath's ability to throw a football accurately fifty yards on the dead run, but he knew a lot about the Strategic Air Command and even more about the Duty Controller's responsibilities and he was cool. This morning he was also busy, a normal state for the Duty Controller here at the global Command Post. He'd just finished a routine communications check on the direct lines to all the overseas bomber bases, and in seven minutes – according to the schedule on the clipboard on the desk in front of him – he was to start the countdown for the 'surprise alert' designated Hot Harry.

He looked up at the huge plexiglass map of the world, scanned it slowly and nodded. Normal. No squadrons of Soviet bombers racing over the North Pole toward Alaska, no alarms from the Ballistic Missile Early Warning System installations in Greenland or England, nothing different from the morning intelligence briefing, no reason to expect any shift from DEFCON Five. Quiet, all quiet. There was the usual sound of some two dozen men and women going about their routine chores in the command post, but the atmosphere was calm and the situation was . . . well, quiet.

Then the telephone – the black one – rang and Colonel Alexander B. Franklin put the receiver to his head, and everything changed.

'Touchdown Duty Controller,' he recited mechanically.

'This is Viper Three,' an unfamiliar voice replied.

Viper . . . the 168th at Malmstrom, the Duty Controller recalled instantly.

'Go ahead, Viper Three.'

'I have an urgent message for the CINCSAC. Viper Three is in hostile hands. Repeat, please notify General McKenzie that Viper Three has been captured by five escaped convicts who have taken the capsule, the Missile Combat Crew on duty and the firing keys.'

Colonel Alexander B. Franklin blinked, frowned, stared and almost stopped breathing.

'What the hell are you talking about?' he demanded

angrily. 'Is this some sort of a stupid joke or silly new alert?'

'No joke, no test. This is the real thing. Red Indian. Tell McKenzie that we've got his control center and the ten birds, and we've knocked out all his inhibitors and cut-offs. We're ready to launch.'

This didn't sound like any convict.

This man spoke like an Air Force officer.

'Who is this?' the Duty Controller challenged.

'Dell, Lawrence, formerly Major Lawrence Dell . . . formerly Deputy Intelligence Officer of the 168th. Serial Number 771-33-4176. More recently attached to the Death House at the state penitentiary in Helena, Montana. Height, six feet one inch. Weight, 185 pounds. Hair, black. Eyes, grey. Small scar on bottom of left foot. Born New Haven, Connecticut, September 4, 1928. That makes me a Virgo, in case you're an astrology fan.'

'I'm not,' Franklin snapped back hostilely.

'I'm not either,' Dell confided in tones that made it clear he was enjoying himself immensely. 'I just told you all that stuff so you could check it out. It's all real, baby. I'm *really* your black-sheep missileman, and I've *really* got Viper Three and I'll *really* do something nasty if I don't hear from the CINCSAC within one hour. I've got a proposition for him, for his ears only. You got that, Duty Controller?'

'Affirmative. But in case I can't reach—'

Dell hung up, having neither any need nor desire to speak further with this faceless nameless stranger who had no identity, no reality, no meaning other than being Duty Controller. So far as Dell was concerned, the man didn't even exist when he wasn't at *that* desk with *those* phones. Even at that desk, he certainly wasn't important enough to be given the rest of the message – the 'good part'. That was to be reserved for the commanding general of the most powerful thermonuclear strike force on earth, the ex-major thought as he turned to flash a 'thumbs up' sign to his allies in the Viper Three control center.

In that other reinforced concrete 'hole' at Offutt, Colonel Franklin was earnestly reviewing the extraordinary conversation and trying to recall whether there was any operating procedure or training-manual paragraph that applied.

There had to be, of course.

Perhaps it didn't cover this unusual situation specifically, but it was reasonably relevant – and that's a great deal in today's turbulent, complex world.

First, check it out. Determine whether this situation exists as described so that the next echelon of command would have data on which to make the command decision. General McKenzie had to get an accurate picture of the situation at Viper Three – if there was a situation. Had the call actually come from Viper Three? Check it out. It would take less than nine seconds to reach the 168th at Malmstrom over this wonderfully swift and sophisticated communications network, nine seconds to find out whether anything abnormal was going on at Viper Three.

The redheaded colonel looked around the large room, observed that everyone and everything appeared wholly normal. Good. Busy and normal. Good. Efficiently pushing buttons and scanning maps and studying teleprinters and emptying ashtrays, all the things necessary for the defense of the free world. In addition – since they were human – several members of the CP staff were doing other things, internal personal things. Major St John was wondering whether his broker was right about selling the Ford stock. Husky Captain Costikyan was thoughtfully eying the imposing contours of the new blonde communications technician, patriotically calculating her brassiere size and ability to absorb vodka while a curly-haired lieutenant named P.J. Sherman – who could have answered both questions precisely – silently evaluated a number of television commercials he'd seen recently in an effort to pick an antacid for his growling bowels. None of these other considerations interfered very much with these officers' performance of duty, however. Just a tiny bit, not enough to endanger global peace or the democratic way of life.

Colonel Franklin knew the telephone number for direct-dialing Malmstrom over SAC's own lines and communications net, but he took the extra fifteen seconds to double check it in the Duty Controller's phone book because that was the sort of man he was. He hated mistakes, wrong numbers and unnecessary bloodshed.

71

'Ford Pass Duty Controller,' announced the major at the Montana headquarters.

'This is Touchdown,' Franklin began soberly in what was very close to his ordinary voice. 'We've had a call from a man claiming to be a former major named Lawrence Dell, and he says that he's one of a group of escaped convicts who have seized Viper Three. Do you know anything about this?'

'Maybe,' reported the Malmstrom Duty Controller. 'About a minute ago a nurse phoned in that a Captain Kincaid – he's one of ours – had been found out on the highway badly beaten and was now in Great Falls Municipal Hospital. According to the nurse, he's been repeating one phrase over and over again. Red Indian at Viper Three.'

'What about it?' Franklin demanded.

There was a brief silence.

'I just spoke to wing security about it, sir. It seemed completely farfetched, you understand, but I was *just about* to call the Viper Three security post to—'

'Call . . . now,' the colonel broke in coldly.

'Right away, sir,' promised the suddenly chilled major at Malmstrom.

He put down the phone, reached for another one beside it on his desk and dialed the number of the Viper Three guardhouse on the surface. He listened to the ringing – ten . . . eleven . . . twelve rings. No answer. He hung up, checked the number in his book to make sure and redialed. Fifteen . . . sixteen . . . seventeen rings. My God, he thought as he listened to the buzzing that seemed to grow louder and louder. Twenty . . . twenty-one . . . twenty-two . . . twenty-three rings.

He hung up the telephone, picked up the other instrument.

'Touchdown?'

'Yes,' Franklin confirmed.

'There is no answer,' reported the stunned Duty Controller of the 168th. 'Viper Three security post does not answer.'

Colonel Franklin considered this, absorbed the impact and meaning.

'Right. Now check the Launch Control Center below,' he ordered curtly.

'Yes, sir.'

Franklin's eyes wandered around the Offutt CP again as he waited, and he automatically noticed from the big clock over the plexiglass world map that there was less than four minutes left before he was to start the Hot Harry test alert. A light began to blink on the control panel on his desk. It was the NORAD tie line, the direct link to North American Air Defense Command headquarters buried in the mountain near Colorado Springs. If Franklin didn't pick up the phone within ten rings, the Deputy Duty Controller – at a desk a few yards behind the one where Colonel Alexander B. Franklin sat – would take the call. For every man in this important command post, there was a back-up man – and for some there were two.

'Touchdown Deputy Duty Controller,' Franklin heard the voice behind him announce.

He paid no further attention to the NORAD call, for the officer at Malmstrom was back on the line.

'Sir, the Viper Three Launch Control Center . . . I spoke to them,' said the major in Montana.

'Yes?'

'Sir, the man I got on the phone – I recognized his voice. It wasn't Captain Kincaid. It was Major Dell all right, the man who broke out of the Helena Death House last night.'

Jeezus.

'What did he say?' demanded Franklin.

'He asked whether I was General McKenzie, and when I told him that I was the Forward Pass Duty Controller he said he'd talk only to General McKenzie. Then he slammed down the phone.'

The officer at the Malmstrom CP was plainly shaken, and Colonel Franklin couldn't blame him – but they both had things to do.

'Okay, Forward Pass, you know what to do. Proceed with normal Red Indian security measures immediately, and report as soon as your team reaches Viper Three. No general alarm yet; we are not under enemy attack. Do you understand?'

'I understand. Our choppers will be airborne in less than two minutes,' promised the man in Montana.

The full gravity and complexity of the situation at Viper Three was not yet clear, so it was still a bit early for any of the

SAC senior officers to seek spiritual guidance – but General Martin McKenzie was getting it. He had no way of knowing that he was going to need it as he sat in the ninth row of pews in Offutt's simple Protestant church, listening – with more than two hundred other servicemen and their families – to Reverend Cartwright's sermon on brotherly love. It was a sincere and lengthy sermon – as usual – and it made a good deal of sense even if it wasn't particularly original in either conception or language. It could have made more sense to McKenzie if the CINCSAC had been able to keep his mind off the B-91 figures and the Senate committee.

'But brotherhood is not and cannot be an abstract thing,' said the minister. 'Not in America today, not in this troubled world. Brotherhood must be part of our daily lives. I ask you . . . each one of you . . . what about brotherhood in *your* life?'

The thing in McKenzie's breast pocket – the miniature receiver that resembled a pregnant grey fountain pen – issued a low clear beep . . . beep . . . beep, and the CINCSAC stood up immediately. He was a courteous and considerate person, especially with clergymen, small children and members of Congress, but he rose unhesitatingly right in the middle of the sermon. Actually, it was not too far from the end of it, but when that little radio sounded Martin McKenzie couldn't wait. There was an emergency, a significant SAC emergency – not just a bomber down somewhere or a routine phone call from some Assistant Secretary of the Air Force.

Beep . . . beep . . . beep.

Mrs McKenzie looked up anxiously; she knew the general had been seated on the aisle – his usual place because it permitted instant departure – and now, without a glance or a word, he was walking quickly toward the door. The minister saw and recognized the CINCSAC leaving, and for a moment the clergyman hesitated and almost stumbled in his flow of simple, effective, moral rhetoric. He knew too, but he drew upon his spiritual resources and sense of responsibility to the other worshipers and he continued resolutely. A few of the colonels and majors in the church exchanged brief uneasy glances as they silently speculated, and then they lowered their eyes and hoped that the power of prayer wasn't overrated.

As McKenzie closed the big door behind him, the wind hit at his face and his eyes moved to the parked staff car. The radio signal was coming from an FM transmitter in that vehicle. Sergeant Dickey, the burly thirty-year-old driver, had pressed the red button built into the dashboard, and now Dickey would explain why he'd triggered this emergency signal. McKenzie hurried to the blue sedan, reached it as the chauffeur rolled down the window to speak.

'What is it, Sergeant?'

'Urgent message from the Duty Controller, sir; he's still on the phone.'

The general nodded, slid into the rear compartment and picked up the radio-telephone.

'McKenzie here,' he announced as his eyes scanned the multi-colored Mondrian-like mural formed by the mass of cars in the church's parking lot.

'This is Colonel Franklin, sir – the Duty Controller. We have a rather peculiar situation at Viper Three.'

'I'm listening,' goaded the CINCSAC impatiently.

'General, I think we'd better go to scrambler,' Franklin suggested.

It was bad. It had to be bad if a cool, experienced officer such as Franklin would discuss it only over a scrambler phone that would inhibit electronic eavesdropping.

Of course it was bad.

The goddam beeper never sounded for birthday parties or weddings, only for trouble. The whole job was crisis and trouble, and newspaper cartoonists and night-club comics who made jokes about the paranoia of senior commanders. Yes, it was easy enough to get paranoid or at least ulcerous – or perhaps just constipated like Brigadier General Hammond in Intelligence, the CINCSAC reflected. With this sour thought in mind, General McKenzie flicked the scrambler switch and wondered what the bad news would be.

'Okay, let's have it,' he ordered.

'Red Indian at Viper Three,' Franklin blurted – and then regretted saying it.

Even with the scrambling equipment to break up the words into fragments, could you be completely sure that there wasn't *somebody else* – with an unscrambling device – listening?

'Where else?' demanded McKenzie.

Here we go, World War III on a nice Sunday morning.

Apocalypse in October.

SAC had failed. The mighty multibillion-dollar nuclear deterrent had not deterred, McKenzie thought bitterly – for about two seconds before he refocussed all his attention on the problems of coping and retaliating. Everything was in readiness for *instant* retaliation, of course. *Massive* retaliation, of course. Missiles, planes – big planes and little planes with big nuclear weapons and little nuclear weapons, and more missiles in submarines were all cocked like some gigantic pistol, and there were several detailed plans. There was Ajax Victor Ajax in case the Russians attacked but the Chinese didn't and Jolly Green Giant in case the Chinese struck and the Russians didn't and Waterloo Blue Seven in case both Communist powers attacked – with atomic and hydrogen warheads. Of course, if either or both struck with conventional weapons or in months ending in 'r' or on an Easter Sunday when it was raining, there were other retaliation plans – elaborate and meticulously researched schemes that covered hundreds of pages – for that too. These were all fresh new plans, all updated every six months by the Strategic Targets Board and the Plans Division of the Joint Chiefs of Staff.

'Nowhere else. Only Viper Three, sir, and that's all it's going to be. It isn't *them*, General. Not either of *them*.'

Crazy. If it wasn't the Russians or the Chinese, who could it be?

Franklin spoke again before the CINCSAC could ask.

'General, I think that it would be better – a lot better – if you came to the CP as quickly as possible. I really don't want to discuss this by radio phone, not even on scrambler. Everything else on the board is clean. Not a single sign of anything abnormal, so it can't be a major strike. It's just Viper Three, and it's weird.'

It had to be weird. If the attack on Viper Three wasn't the work of either of the Communist nuclear powers, it was something weird all right. It might even be freaky. 'Freaky' was a word that General McKenzie had acquired from his sixteen-year-old son, Peter, who frequently tried to explain the re-building of jalopies and the temper of contemporary American youth to his father. Freaky or not, it was undoubtedly important because Duty Controllers were carefully picked men of stability and sense whose professional judgements had to be respected.

'I'll be there in fifteen minutes,' promised the CINCSAC.

He was there in twelve, and as he entered the underground CP his eyes moved to the large map of the world. Normal. Everything looked normal. He glanced around the big room, saw that everyone seemed to be going about the routine chores with the usual calm efficiency. The only thing at all out of the ordinary this Sunday morning was the presence of Major Douglas Winters at the Duty Controller's desk, and McKenzie guessed that Franklin had probably summoned him on the premise that the CINCSAC might want his aide nearby in this crisis.

This weird crisis.

'Okay, who is it?' McKenzie asked bluntly as he reached the two officers. 'Who is it and what is it, and what's so weird?'

Franklin told him about the two telephone conversations.

'This is all for real?' wondered the general.

The redheaded colonel nodded.

'I'll play you the tapes, if you want, sir,' he offered.

McKenzie considered, decided. Everything said over the Duty Controller's phone was tape-recorded routinely, and it might be useful to listen to these two brief conversations. The three men walked to the tape-unit console, Franklin rewound the plastic ribbon and they heard his exchanges with Dell and the Malmstrom Duty Controller.

'Well, what would you say, Doug?' McKenzie asked his frowning, taciturn aide. Winters, who wasn't actually that tight-mouthed by nature but had learned to cultivate this skill at the Air Academy, took a deep breath before he replied.

'I'd say we're in trouble, sir – and not only at Viper Three. The Red Indian at Viper Three is extremely serious, but what bothers me just as much is that the system is defective. If some-body can take *one* of the Snakepit holes, then maybe somebody else can take *others*. These holes are all *systems*-engineered as a complete unit, with primary emphasis on security. The *system* has apparently failed. It will obviously have to be redesigned.'

Obviously.

But also later.

'We'll get to that tomorrow, Doug,' the practical CINCSAC agreed, 'but today – right now – I want to be sure about Viper Three. This bastard Dell might not have taken the installation at all, you know. Maybe he's just knocked out their phones and cut into the line himself somewhere, somewhere ten miles away. An eyeball inspection by that security team flying out of Malmstrom – an on-the-spot report of what they actually *see* – is the only way for us to be sure.'

They returned to the Duty Controller's desk, and the red-headed colonel dialed the CP of the 168th.

'Forward Pass, this is Touchdown again,' Franklin announced. 'Have your choppers reached Viper Three?'

'I'll check by radio. Shall I patch you into the board so you can hear it directly?'

'Please do, Forward Pass.'

Franklin gestured toward the extension phone on the next desk, pressed a button on his instrument as General McKenzie lifted the other one to listen.

'Fast Charlie, this is Forward Pass,' they heard. 'Fast Charlie, this is Forward Pass. Have you reached target area yet? Repeat, have you reached target area yet?'

The commander of the lead helicopter replied immediately, and despite a little static his words were remarkably clear.

'Forward Pass, this is Fast Charlie One. We are approaching target area at nine hundred feet. Still about a mile and a half out because of headwinds. Visibility poor. There's still some patchy mist and drizzle up here. . . . Should be in sight very soon. We're closing at an air speed of ninety-five.'

At ninety-five m.p.h., it was only a matter of seconds – thirty or forty.

'Two o'clock,' announced another voice. 'Fast Charlie Three to Fast Charlie One. Target area ahead at two o'clock. See it?'

'Radio tower ahead at two o'clock,' the pilot of the lead copter confirmed. 'Yes, I see it. Stand by to circle area and touch down.'

Routine. They'd fly around Viper Three once just to make certain there was no ambush waiting, and then two of the compact Bell transports would land to disembark armed APs while the third rode shotgun at four hundred or five hundred feet.

'Fast Charlie One to Forward Pass. Target area directly ahead. Charlie One and Charlie Two going in for landing and security inspection. Three will cover from airborne position in accord with standard procedures. . . . Going down. . . . There's the perimeter fence. . . . Car. . . . No, it must be a wagon . . . station wagon, parked inside near the guardhouse. Gate closed. . . . No visible damage to fence. Fence appears intact . . . two hundred feet . . . no signs of intrusion or Red Indian . . . one hundred feet. Here we go. . . . Landing about twenty yards from the front door. . . . Touchdown. Go!'

That last word was a command to the Air Police, and McKenzie could visualize exactly what was happening. The two whirlybirds on the ground with their rotors still spinning noisily, the eight APs jumping down from each and then spreading out in a wide skirmish line – a 'U' that would ring the guardhouse on three sides. They'd 'go' quickly, with their carbines and machine guns ready.

'Forward Pass this is Fast Charlie One. No sign of any activity yet. No sign of any personnel, friendly or hostile. I don't like that. Two of our APs are checking out the station wagon now. Looks like a regular SAC wagon. . . . Just a second, one of them's coming back to say something. . . . No, wait a minute . . . Forward Pass, it's a Red Indian all right. Two Air Police lying in the wagon. Our team recognized them – Sergeant Russell and corporal Mendez. Mendez is dead. Unless you order otherwise, our team will enter the guardhouse now.'

McKenzie nodded.

'Touchdown to Forward Pass. Affirmative,' announced Franklin.

They heard the Malmstrom Duty Controller echo the authorization, add his own postscript advising caution. Then they waited, each man silent, alone, taut, troubled and well aware that he should expect the worst. Of course, Martin McKenzie had long expected the worse – every morning he awoke with that assumption. McKenzie faced every day with the confidence that something terrible was likely to occur. Although he was dedicated to science, efficiency, standardized procedures, meticulous maintenance systems and the triumph of reason, the CINCSAC had also absorbed – over the years – a certain quiet acceptance of the twin facts that this was not the best of all possible worlds and that the Existentialist philosophy of random absurd occurrences related to the human condition much more meaningfully than any Pentagon planner would admit.

Of course, the CINCSAC reminded himself sensibly, this wasn't the worst of all possible worlds either. It could always get worse. Murphy's Law. Murphy's Law was an old Air Force truism. If anything can go wrong – it will. Now, brooded McKenzie, something that couldn't go wrong had done so.

And what would Senator Baylor Caldwell say about *that*?

The hard-running Presidential candidate who fancied himself a friend of the American armed forces would undoubtedly say a great deal, mused the CINCSAC, and none of it would be constructive – but it would sound righteous.

'Stupid bastard,' muttered McKenzie.

'What's that, General?' the Duty Controller asked anxiously.

'Nothing, nothing.'

'Yes, sir.'

The Air Police were in the guardhouse now. They had to be. In a minute or so, there would be a radio message on what they'd found – but McKenzie had no illusions about what it would be. It would be bad, and the only question was just how bad. The answer came some half a minute later with a report from Fast Charlie One that another corpse had been discovered, and two bound and gagged cooks – hysterical with incoherent tales of armed invaders – had been found in a closet. There was no one else in the guard house.

'Tell them to try the Launch Control Center on the intercom,' McKenzie instructed.

Then the general turned to his aide as Colonel Franklin passed the order, and McKenzie sighed.

'We'll know in about eighty seconds, Doug,' the CINCSAC estimated.

'Yes, sir – but I don't understand *why* they'd do this. Why would escaped convicts attack a presumably impregnable missile base instead of heading for the hills – or even the Canadian border?'

McKenzie sighed again.

'We'll know in about . . . about fifty-eight seconds,' he replied. 'They're not crazy,' he added. 'I can tell you that – they're not crazy. This wasn't pulled off by any bunch of loonies or hairy Yippies. According to what I heard about this Dell when he was convicted, he's very smart and very practical. He was on his way up; the Air War College was his next assignment. Since he's done all the talking on the phone, I suspect he's in command down there – and he's no nut.'

'I'm sure you're right, sir,' Winters fenced politely, 'but a man who commits murder isn't exactly Mr Normal. There's got to be something wrong, wouldn't you say?'

Those Screen Actors Guild psychiatrists on the TV medical dramas had really gotten to Winters, Martin McKenzie realized gloomily. Mr Normal? Who the hell was Mr Normal? A lot of noble-minded Americans and Britons and Japanese wouldn't think it was very normal for a decent man to devote his life to megatons and massive thermonuclear *re*taliation (let alone taliation) – a man such as neat, clean, crewcut Douglas O. Winters, who never violated traffic regulations or other people's wives and who genuinely liked those cookies the Girl Scouts sold door to door. General McKenzie had long suspected that those homey tidbits were actually produced in a huge Japanese plastics factory that was completely transistorized, but there'd be no point in telling Winters *that*.

'Fast Charlie One to Forward Pass,' crackled the now familiar voice of the helicopter pilot. 'Fast Charlie One to Forward Pass. Lieutenant Sheldon just talked to the Launch Control Center on the intercom, as ordered. He says he got a man named Dell, who claimed that Captain Towne and Lieutenant Canellis were prisoners and said he held the capsule. He said "we" – so I guess there are other people down there with him. He said he'd explain it all to General McKenzie on the phone, and he told us to pick up our dead and injured and get the hell out. It's a Red Indian all right.'

'Sounds like it,' judged the cautious Duty Controller at Malmstrom.

'*Sounds* like it? You ought to see the sergeant they gunned. Damn near cut him in two with some kind of automatic weapon. . . . Listen, Forward Pass, Lieutenant Sheldon wants further orders. Do we pick up the hot and cold bodies and get the hell out, or don't we?'

It was a very good question.

There were a number of possible answers, the commander-in-chief of the Strategic Air Command calculated, but they were all bad.

CHAPTER ELEVEN

McKenzie spoke directly to the major at Malmstrom.

'Forward Pass, this is Spider Biter. This is Spider Biter,' he announced – using the code name for the CINCSAC so the Duty Controller in Montana would know that the highest authority in the Strategic Air Command was taking responsibility for the decision.

'Forward Pass, notify Fast Charlie to follow Dell's instructions and to evacuate all personnel from Viper Three surface installations,' McKenzie ordered. 'One chopper is to stay behind, flying an airborne surveillance pattern at five hundred feet but cruising outside the perimeter fence. Is that clear?'

'Roger, Spider Biter,' assured the tense Duty Controller, who'd never spoken with the august CINCSAC before.

'After you've done that, I want you to move about fifty Air Police out to circle Viper Three – and you'd better send along a couple of armored cars. Your security force has armored cars, doesn't it?'

'Affirmative, Spider Biter.'

'Good. Keep them at least a couple of hundred yards from the fence, but make sure nobody goes in or out. Nobody. One more thing, I don't want word on the Red Indian to spread – for obvious reasons. When your Fast Charlie choppers get back, put everybody – the APs and the pilots and the wounded and the bodies – in the isolation ward at your base hospital. Seal it off – tight. No phone calls in or out. This is absolutely crucial. Is that clear?'

'Affirmative. Absolutely clear.'

McKenzie hesitated, glanced at his aide.

'Anything else, Doug?' he asked.

'Maybe we'd better seal off Malmstrom itself – just as a precaution, sir.'

Sound.

'As soon as you've passed the word to Fast Charlie,' said the general, 'put me through to your Base Commander.'

It didn't take very long to get Brigadier General Stonesifer on the line.

'Stoney, this is Spider Biter. There's something freaky going on at Viper Three. Red Indian – sort of. Your Duty Controller will explain the details; I don't have time.'

'Yes, Spider Biter.'

What the hell was it? wondered the one-star general.

He didn't say that, or anything else.

The CINCSAC was in a hurry, and when four-star generals are in a hurry one-star generals listen – intently.

'It's a mess, Stoney, and it could cause a bigger mess if word got out now. I'm ordering you to seal up Malmstrom. Plug it. Ram the cork in, and don't pull it until I personally authorize it. Nobody leaves Malmstrom without your personal okay. No outgoing phone calls. Nothing. Zero.'

'I'll declare a special security exercise immediately,' promised Stonesifer. 'That way there'll be a lot fewer questions, sir.'

You could count on Stonesifer.

It was true that he suffered from a slight resemblance to Sterling Hayden, but you could count on Stoney to cope.

'Good deal. I'll talk to you later.'

When McKenzie put down the phone, his eyes moved around the large room and its staff. They didn't know about Viper Three – yet. Now the CINCSAC glanced over at his lean young aide and found himself wondering whether Winters was still thinking about the flaw in the system. That was the way they trained them these days, McKenzie realized, and it was probably good – but there was more. Suddenly, for no apparent reason, Martin McKenzie remembered the big fire-bomb raid on Tokyo. He'd been in command of a B-29 squadron then, flying the lead ship and looking down at one hundred – or was it one thousand – fires. Then they'd begun to merge into larger blazes, shooting up great gusts of hot updrafts that rocked the bombers. Thousands of *people* had been dying below them, and that was a great deal more important than any system.

Nobody talked about people or cities anymore, just *targets*.

It wasn't even simply targets, but the even more abstract phrase 'target *areas*'.

Almost everyone in the Pentagon spoke and thought that way now, especially all the bushy-tailed majors and colonels who'd never seen a city burn. Some of the older commanders, including Pete Crane, who was Air Force Chief of Staff, still remembered and you could talk to them, but in another five or ten years the computer kids would be running the whole show. They had most of it already. It was funny. There was a generation gap all right, but it was the scientific younger men who accepted mass destruction so dispassionately while the older ones remembered. It was funny, but not at all comical.

'I'd better talk to him,' McKenzie told the Duty Controller quietly. 'Put me through to the Viper Three capsule, please.'

This time Franklin direct-dialed.

'Hello, is that you, McKenzie?' somebody asked.

It was a crisp, confident voice, the voice of a well-educated Easterner who might have taken an acting course or two at some Ivy League college. It wasn't that flat prep-school snob sound – just sure and clear.

'This is McKenzie,' the general said – and then he didn't say anything more for some two minutes.

Dell did all the talking, explaining what his group had done and could do and would do – unless its terms were met. The terms were, like those of everyone else nowadays, non-negotiable. The former major then hesitated, obviously waiting for the CINCSAC to object and hoping he would – so Dell could put him down harshly. No, that game wasn't for Martin McKenzie, who didn't feel guilty and hardly qualified as a middle-class white liberal anyway. As a general, he was ineligible by definition. He remained silent.

'You still there, General?'

'Yes.'

'Okay, this is the deal. It's a package deal,' the rogue major announced as a preface to his statement of terms. There were three parts, all stated simply and explicitly.

'You're crazy,' McKenzie answered.

It wasn't a wise thing to say, but the terms were so fantastic that he couldn't help articulating his shock. Actually, the deal

85

wasn't crazy at all – from the convicts' point of view. It was very clever, incredible and bold and clever.

'Flattery will get you nowhere,' Dell mocked, 'and *your* opinions of me or the deal don't matter. There's only one man who can make the deal, and you'd better call *him*. No tricks. Call him *now*.'

And then Lawrence Dell did what a lot of men in the armed forces had dreamt of: He hung up on a top general.

McKenzie was breathing heavily now, still reacting and absorbing behind a face that was as blank as he could keep it.

'Son of a bitch,' he whispered – and he felt a little better.

Only a little.

'Sir?' asked Winters.

He wanted to know. No one else had been listening on any extension, so it wasn't surprising that Colonel Franklin and the general's aide were staring at the CINCSAC expectantly.

McKenzie shook his head, considered what had been said and what had to be done.

Son of a bitch.

It was brilliant.

Obscene, terrifying and brilliant.

That bastard Dell would have made a damned good general.

Son of a bitch.

'Doug,' the CINCSAC said, 'I want you to call General Stonesifer at Malmstrom.'

He explained the orders to be related, and then turned to Franklin.

'Colonel, I want everything in the command post to continue on an entirely normal basis. There is to be no alert, and you are not to discuss this with anyone – not even your deputy. I don't want any word of this thing to get outside this CP; that's important.'

What thing?

What had Dell said?

'What about when the shift changes at sixteen hundred, sir?' Franklin asked. 'There'll be a new Duty Controller coming on this afternoon.'

'No, there won't,' decided the CINCSAC. 'Well, he can take over but you are not to leave this bunker. That's an order. And tell the replacement that any calls or messages relating to Malmstrom are to come to me – and only to me. That's an order; put it in the log book – in writing.'

What the hell had Dell said?

'Sir, my wife—' began the redheaded colonel.

'Phone her that you're on a special job and that you won't be home for . . . for a day or two. Keep it casual, routine. I don't want any questions or rumors starting.'

Telephone in hand, Major Winters interrupted with a polite 'Sir' and a grim look.

'Sir, I've passed your orders to General Stonesifer – and he's going to attend to it immediately. He also gave me a message for you.'

'Yes?'

'They've tested – and it's true. The inhibitors controlling the Viper Three birds have been knocked out or sabotaged, sir. The control circuits are dead, all dead. All readings zero. Any further instructions?'

McKenzie shook his head.

'I'm going to the Battle Staff area,' he announced as he turned toward the stairs leading to the second level, where SAC's senior commanders would sit in crisis or war. 'Come on up when you're finished,' he told his aide.

It was bad, the CINCSAC admitted to himself as he reached his desk on the upper level. He glanced at the phones, sat down and sighed.

It was bad, and it was going to get worse – very soon.

CHAPTER TWELVE

This would not surprise Martin McKenzie, for he had long suspected that there was a corollary to Murphy's Law. If Murphy's Law provided that anything that could go wrong would do so, then it was McKenzie's Law that anything that went wrong would get worse. With this affirmative view of life, a wise and patient wife who genuinely loved him and an historical perspective that Roman generals had taken just as much crap from their Senate in their day, McKenzie had been able to survive thirty-two years in the military air services of a great power without losing his hair, honesty, commitment to the democratic process, respect for living creatures and ability to limit his alcohol intake to one brandy after dinner. Well, sometimes two – when on leave or talking budget with some influential bureaucrat or legislator.

Such philosophy usually comes with age, so younger people are generally more prone to be surprised. Dr Paul Langer, for example, was surprised some twenty-five minutes later when he received a telephone call from the Great Falls Municipal Hospital's Medical Director informing him that another intern would take over the Emergency Room in ten minutes – at which time Dr Langer was to report to the Medical Director's office.

'What's up, Paul?' asked freckle-faced Don Borden when he arrived to take over. Dr Borden, who was still buttoning his white jacket as he entered the Emergency Room, was a capable physician but his dialogue was rather ordinary.

Langer shrugged, unwilling to admit that he didn't know either. It was a trifle embarrassing. The Medical Director seemed even more embarrassed when Langer reached his office, but the older man tried to make the best of it. His ability to make the best of things was one reason Dr Irwin Fiske was Medical Director.

'Dr Langer, these two gentlemen are from the Air Force. I should say *with* the Air Force,' he corrected himself.

The intern was surprised for a second time, since neither of the two strangers on the Medical Director's couch was in uniform. Dressed in sport jackets and slacks and knit shirts, they looked like any thirty-year-old Great Falls junior executives en route to an afternoon of weekend bowling or casual visiting with the neighbors.

'Captain Drew and Lieutenant Werth,' announced the Medical Director without saying which was Drew and which was Werth. Both were eying Lange thoughtfully and one of them tried to smile, but he didn't quite make it. Still, the effort counted for something, Langer concluded.

After all, the previous President of the United States had scored heavily in all the public-opinion polls by presenting a 'low profile' to avoid controversy, and there wasn't anything much more noncontroversial than 'yes.' It had a nice positive ring, and it couldn't offend anyone.

'They'd like to ask you something, Doctor,' continued the graying Medical Director.

'Yes?'

'Dr. Langer,' began Captain Drew or Lieutenant Werth, 'we'd like you to help us – voluntarily.'

It had to be the captain, because the higher-ranking officer would naturally do the talking, and it had to be something unpleasant if it was to be done 'voluntarily.'

'Of course,' agreed the intern with a show of that direct sincerity that he knew the Medical Director wanted.

'It's a very delicate security situation – *national* security,' explained Captain Drew.

'Of course,' Langer acknowledged just as if he had the slightest idea as to what Drew was discussing.

'That injured man who was found out on the highway – Captain Kincaid,' Drew said.

The intern looked over at Lieutenant Werth, wondering whether he was a mute or was simply forbidden to talk. Werth tried to smile again, failed. He wasn't even close this time.

'You treated Captain Kincaid, and you reported some things that he was saying in his delirium,' declared Drew.

'Yes, I did. Maybe an hour ago. It didn't make much sense.'

The two officers in civilian clothes exchanged meaningful glances, vaguely irking the intern, who hated to be left out of things.

'Doctor, I know this sounds odd but we've been informed that it would be in the interest of national security if you came with us – to Malmstrom,' said Drew.

It was easy to tell Drew once you put your mind to it, Langer realized. Drew was the one with the bushier eyebrows.

'These fellows actually are Air Force officers?' the intern asked warily.

'Oh yes, they are,' assured the paunchy Medical Director briskly.

'You can inspect our credentials – if you wish,' offered the one who had to be Captain Drew.

Any patriotic American wouldn't have considered such a thing, but Dr Langer had seen a lot of British spy movies and he'd never looked at any security officer's credentials, so he figured what the hell?

'Sure,' the intern replied cheerfully.

It was probably all some kind of a joke.

The two strangers passed him small plastic folders and he examined the twin sets of credentials, and neither looked like a joke.

'You want me to go to Malmstrom *now?*' he asked as he returned the identity cards.

'If you please.'

Drew was courteous as well as neat. Langer had never seen a more carefully combed head of hair, and not a bit of dandruff. This was somewhat reassuring, for in the commercials the good guys -- the ones who score with the blondes – never have dandruff.

'Is that all right with you, Dr Fiske?' Langer said to the Medical Director.

'Of course. National security. We'll get someone to cover your shift today and tomorrow.'

Tomorrow?

'You'd better pack a toothbrush and pajamas,' suggested Drew helpfully.

Tomorrow?

'I haven't done anything and I don't know anything, nothing that relates to national security,' protested the intern.

The captain shrugged sympathetically.

'We're just following orders, Doctor, and these orders come *direct* from General Stonesifer. He'd certainly *appreciate* your cooperation.'

'Voluntarily?'

'Yes, sir.'

'I'm not arrested?'

'Certainly *not*, Doctor. You haven't done anything illegal,' Drew answered with a smile. It wasn't a bad smile, and maybe by the time that Werth got to be a captain he'd be able to smile too. There was probably a course they gave them along with the Escape and Evasion training and the Cold Weather Survival routine – Intermediate Smiling and Personal Hygiene. This Drew probably graduated in the top tenth of his class.

Despite the smile, the intern still couldn't quite believe it.

'You're sure this isn't a gag?' he persisted. 'I'm not on "Candid Camera," am I?'

'That show isn't even on the air anymore,' Werth erupted.

He could talk.

'It isn't on the network, but it might be in syndication,' Langer fenced.

'This ... is ... for ... real,' declared Captain Drew earnestly.

Paul Langer led the way to his small room, loaded his overnight gear into a United Air Lines bag and then started toward the stairs that would bring them to the rear parking lot where Captain Drew said they'd left their 'vehicle.' This thing was clearly linked to what Kincaid had said or what he might have said, and the intern recalled that Anne Kelleran knew about it too. For a moment he considered mentioning this to them, but there was no point in dragging her into this, so he refrained from involving her and made small talk until they reached the tan Chrysler sedan.

'Hello, Doctor,' she said primly.

Nurse Kelleran was seated by the rear left window, with her own airlines bag – Northwest Airlines – at her feet.

'You know what this is all about?' she asked.

'National security. Secret stuff. I'm not allowed to talk about it,' he lied unhesitatingly.

'Testes,' replied the pragmatic blonde.

'She's too proper to say "balls," ' Langer explained to Captain Drew.

'You got me into this,' accused the nurse.

'Testes,' answered Dr. Langer as he sat down beside her. 'She's a bit scared, I think,' he told Drew in man-to-man tones.

'There's nothing to worry about, Miss,' soothed the captain mechanically.

The intern studied Drew's face, grinned as he guessed that the competent captain probably didn't know what was going on either.

'They didn't tell you? Good old Stonesifer didn't tell you *either*, did he?' challenged Langer.

Drew ignored this provocation.

'Let's go,' he said to the lieutenant.

A few moments later, the tan Chrysler rolled out of the parking lot and turned left toward the highway that led to Malmstrom. Some sixty yards behind, a blue USAF ambulance followed and Dr Paul Langer knew – knew beyond any doubt when he first glimpsed it in the rear-view mirror – that Captain Roger Kincaid was in the rear compartment.

CHAPTER THIRTEEN

It was snowing, and the armed men who stood on either side of the door to the eighty-story gray building behind the Bakhrushkin Theatrical Museum on Zatsepsky Val stamped their boots as the cold wind grew stronger. They were wearing the standard winter uniforms, including the three-finger brown mittens and *shapkaushanka* caps with ear flaps and *shinel* single-breasted overcoats – attire necessary in October this year because the frosts had come early. The weapons slung over their shoulders were the familiar 7.62 millimeter Avtomat Kalashnikovs, the AK 47 submachine guns that were standard issue.

There were other men armed with those same guns inside the building, including a pair guarding the entrance to Soyuzov's office on the fourth floor. Aleksei Soyuzov did not frequently work on Sundays, at least not during the past three years in which he had been assigned to a high post on the *stavka* here in the capital. As the Glavnyi Marshal Bronetankovikh Voisk – the Chief Marshal of Armored Troops – he was always on call, of course, but the calls rarely came on weekends. This evening, he was actually waiting for a call or a message. It would probably come in writing, and the Red Army Chief of Staff had instructed barrel-chested Aleksei Soyuzov to be at headquarters waiting. Foreign intelligence agents might well be watching the building, Marshal Barzinko had explained to his old comrade in arms, and they might suspect something if the Chief of Staff himself were to come in on a Sunday evening.

That would eliminate the surprise, and the operation had been drafted by the Plans Division with surprise in mind. Barring some major mistake by somebody in East Berlin or some master stroke by one of the NATO countries' intelligence

93

organizations, the operation should be a surprise all right – for whatever that was worth, Marshal Soyuzov reflected.

In his opinion, the entire operation might be politically sound, but it didn't make much sense from a military point of view. Of course, the decision had been made by those clever types on the Central Committee of the Party. The Orders came to the Chief of Staff from the Minister of Defense and he got his instructions from the Council of Ministers, but Soyuzov knew that the real power – the power to move entire tank armies and launch air fleets and occupy countries such as Hungary and Czechoslovakia, *and others* – rested in the Central Committee. It was in those secret debates and crafty maneuvers within the Central Committee that the doves and the hawks, The Stalinists and the moderates, the supporters of violent revolution everywhere and the more cautious types, formed national policies.

It was the Central Committee that had called for Operation Yamshchik – Coachman in English. That's what the Americans and the British would call it if their espionage services were efficient, Soyuzov told himself as he puffed on the Cuban cigar, but of course there was no reason to expect that theirs would be any more precise or competent than the Red Army's GRU. All this cloak-and-dagger business was rubbish, for it was the combat units that counted. It was the combat units that would pay if this operation misfired.

The marshal paced up and down slowly, favoring his left leg – the one with the steel pin that always reminded him of the final smash into Berlin when the weather was bad. He looked out the window at the snow, and he thought about burning Tiger tanks with swastikas on their sides in that other winter.

'Long time ago,' muttered Soyuzov as he realized that he'd be sixty-two on Thursday.

'Unsound,' he added as his thoughts shifted to Yamshchik. It was militarily unsound because it involved a larger risk than the prize was worth, surprise or no surprise. He wouldn't say all this aloud, though, for there was still the possibility that the Komitet Gosudarst Besopasnosti – the sly, snoopy Committee for State Security – had bugged Red Army headquarters again. That civilian counterespionage *apparat* was always trying to suck up to the Central Committee of the Party, furtively trying to grease back into authority by showing up the Red Army.

'Unsound,' the marshal repeated defiantly in an even louder voice.

Then his damaged leg hurt again, and he mumbled a crude soldier's oath more befitting a paratroop sergeant than the Red Army's Chief Marshal of Armored Troops. Soyuzov returned to the desk, and it was as he was sitting down that the courier from the Kremlin arrived with the order. The typed message was concise, clear.

As planned, the operation would begin at 0300.

Soyuzov studied the signatures, noted that the order bore the handwritten approvals of both the Minister of Defense and the Chief of Staff.

Good enough.

It was *their* responsibility.

He rang the bell that summoned Lieutenant Colonel Belski.

'Podpolkovnik Belski,' the marshal began – and he tapped the piece of paper on his desk – 'the operation is on. Notify the units in Germany to proceed with Yamshchik as planned.'

Some moments later after Belski had left, Marshal Soyuzov turned in the big chair to look out into the square. The snow was coming down more heavily now, and at this rate Soyuzov estimated there would be at least three inches on the streets before morning. For a moment he again wondered what the reaction to Yamshchik was going to be in Washington, that remote city across a continent and an ocean – so far that it was still only Sunday afternoon there.

Would the Americans yield this time, or would they resist?

It was difficult to predict.

CHAPTER FOURTEEN

1600 Pennsylvania Avenue NW, Washington, DC.

No postal zip code necessary.

'Good morning, Mr President,' the hawk-faced man with a gold star on each shoulder said pleasantly as he entered the large sunny room.

Brigadier General Vincent M. Bonomi spoke the ritual words in the same amiable, courteous and *something more* tone that he'd used to start this daily meeting for the previous three years, nine months and two weeks. The *something more* was *knowing*. Bonomi and the man he addressed had known and trusted each other for a long time, all the way back to the Korean War when they'd flown as a team in an F-86 squadron. Now Bonomi was a US Air Force general 'on loan' to the Central Intelligence Agency, a lean, shrewd man who was quietly amused by the awareness that he'd have been retired as a mere colonel forty-one months earlier if the Air Force and the CIA hadn't discovered his close friendship with David T. Stevens. David T. Stevens, an articulate and broad-shouldered Ohioan whom everybody said was almost as handsome as the martyred John F. Kennedy, was now the President of the United States. It was Vincent Bonomi's job to present the President's daily briefing, the concise CIA summary of 'world conditions' – all top secret, of course.

Stevens listened to Bonomi's standard greeting, nodded as the general closed the door behind him.

'Good morning, you son of a bitch,' the President of the United States replied.

This too was part of the ritual, something that had started at a windswept fighter base in Korea when Captain D. T. Stevens had confided to his wingman and best friend his dream of becoming the Chief Executive of the United States. It was only a dream, a secret and unlikely but not entirely impossible dream. Captain V.M. Bonomi had promised not to divulge the secret and he'd kept his word – but each morning as they hurried to their jets at 6:45 A.M. he'd greet his flying partner with a furtive but cheery 'Good morning, Mr President' and Stevens would reply 'Good morning, you son of a bitch.' Some two decades later, this aviators' exchange still retained some of its jet-jockey jest – but it also reminded the two men who they'd been and what they were. Nobody else spoke to David Stevens quite as honestly as Vince Bonomi, for everyone else wanted something from the President – and he knew it. He accepted that as the natural order of things, but he didn't like it. As an intelligent and realistic politician it shouldn't have bothered him at all, of course.

It did.

It still did.

This Sunday morning he liked it even less, for he was weary from campaign traveling and troubled by the latest Harris Poll results and just a bit headachey from two glasses of champagne too many the previous evening. It might have gone if he'd been able to sleep late, but the American people and the hypocritical *news media* – God, how he loathed that pompous phrase – and Ray Gumbiner expected the President of the United States to check in with the Lord at least once a week. Ray Gumbiner, chairman of the party's National Committee, often pointed out that the previous Chief Executive had cannily 'spread his trade around' by worshiping with a different faith every other Sunday – but David Stevens wasn't going to imitate that cheap performance. Stevens had done a number of things that he wasn't too proud of, but he wasn't cheap. He wasn't particularly pious either, but he had gone to church as usual this morning – a fortnight before the election.

'Shall we proceed to affairs of state?' Brigadier General Bonomi asked as he placed the black leather attaché case on the end table.

This case, like General Bonomi and the job he filled, was special. It was lined with steel, and its combination lock was connected to a small incendiary device. If the proper four-digit combination was not dialed the first time, the special contents of this special container would be incinerated in five seconds.

'I hear you had an elegant affair of state right here last night,' Bonomi continued. 'Frolicking until nearly three A.M., according to the trusty *Washington Post*.'

'Another state dinner for another Arab king,' Stevens confirmed as he refilled his coffee cup. He glanced at the silver pot and then at his friend, who shook his head.

'Don't look to me for sympathy,' Bonomi teased gently. 'As far as I'm concerned, you see one Arab king you've seen them all. They're like Chinese dinners. Half an hour after you're finished with them you can hardly remember them.'

'You used to make that same remark about twenty years ago, Vince,' Stevens reminded his former wingman, 'only then you said Korean whores instead of Chinese dinners.'

'They told me I shouldn't talk dirty in front of the President.'

David Stevens sipped, put down the half-empty cup and sighed as he heard the sounds of the demonstrators picketing outside the White House. Who was it this time? There were so many groups protesting so many things out on the sidewalk so often that all the chants were beginning to sound the same.

'That bother you?' Bonomi asked.

'Not anymore, and *that* bothers me. A President should be bothered – just a bit anyway.'

'Ah – the awesome loneliness of command,' joked the general. 'I can't take your grumbling too seriously, Dave. After all, nobody forced the job on you. You fought like a bastard to get it, and you're doing the same thing again to keep it. Admit it.'

The President smiled, nodded.

'You like the job, Dave. Admit that too.'

'I do,' Stevens confessed.

'So stop feeling sorry for yourself you ambitious, power-crazy bastard. You like it, and you do it well. Besides, there are plenty of things that bother you. This Arab king bit bothers you, doesn't it?'

'It bothers the hell out of me, Vince. They've got me in the middle, boxed in tight,' erupted the President. 'Gumbiner says

98

I'm risking the Jewish and liberal vote by seeing King Achmed two weeks before the election, and the boys at State say I've got to talk to him now to show he's got US support – to prevent a coup by fanatics in his country. The CIA – your people – agree.'

'Horse shit, Mr President. My people are running a chain of pizza parlors in the Bronx, with the exception of my kid brother, who's a surgeon up in Pittsfield, Massachusetts. My people? Why, if you don't get re-elected, Dave, I'll be retired by *my people* about eight minutes after you leave office. Don't try to crap your old buddy, Dave. The king's here for tanks and planes, not talk. You know it and I know it and those bright boys over at State know it. The Israelis know it too, and you can bet your Chief Executive ass that they're sweating a lot more than you, Dave.'

'You still talk like a fighter pilot, Vince.'

'I never pretended to be much more – and I was good at it.'

'Very good,' Stevens recalled.

Vince Bonomi had saved his life – perhaps a dozen times – in dog fights with MIGs, but neither of them ever spoke of that. It would have embarrassed both of them, and it was unnecessary.

'Okay, you were pretty good yourself,' Bonomi admitted, 'and you've been a pretty good President. You're a little tired and a little scared right now – with that punk Caldwell closing in on you – but I'm betting that you're going to be a pretty damn good President to the last minute of the last day you're in office.'

'Thanks for the pep talk, Vince. '

The ex-wingman grunted.

'For chrissakes, let's get on with the briefing. Okay, Mr. President?'

'Okay, General.'

Bonomi opened the case, removed a sheaf of papers – five pages of double-spaced typing – and sat down to start reading aloud what the Central Intelligence Agency had to report to the Commander-in-Chief.

The prospects for another French devaluation and an evaluation of Red Chinese guerrilla activity in Thailand.

Composition and political analysis of the new Czech cabinet to be announced next week.

The deteriorating health of the President of Argentina, the source of the arms being smuggled to rebels in the Sudan, the significance of satellite photos of the new Russian industrial complex near Kamyshlov – a missile plant to produce the big SS-16s.

The probable outcome of the British By-elections scheduled for December, the re-equipment of the North Korean Air Force with MIG-23s, French weapons sales in the Near East and – finally – a funny anecdote about Fidel Castro's sex life. Being aware of President Stevens' sense of humor, the CIA team that wrote these TOP SECRET summaries liked to end on an amusing note. In accord with the old show-business adage, they tried to 'always leave 'em laughing.'

'Is that all, Vince?' the President asked.

'All for today. What else did you have in mind?'

'Well, I'd like a progress report on Wet Suit,' Stevens replied. Bonomi smiled, for Wet Suit was a secret and slightly controversial CIA operation in Egypt that hadn't been mentioned for some weeks now and the Air Force general suspected that the CIA probably would have preferred that the Man in the White House forget about it. But this Man in the White House had an excellent memory.

'And what about that Red Summit meeting scheduled for November eighth in Bucharest?' continued the President. 'I'd like something more than a list of their hotel reservations, dammit. State says the Chinese may be coming. Yes or no? What about the agenda? What about that rumor about Mao's wife?'

'I'll put it all on the shopping list,' Bonomi promised.

'Good. Say, Vince, about King Achmed—'

The telephone rang, and both men turned toward the desk near the window.

They stared.

The sound was coming from inside the desk, from the drawer that housed the special 'hot line' phone to Strategic Air Command headquarters outside Omaha. It had a loud distinctive ring, much more powerful than the ordinary bell on the ordinary telephone.

Stevens walked quickly to the desk, sat down and took up the red phone.

'Hello. . . . Yes, General McKenzie, this is the President,' Bonomi heard him say. 'Yes . . . what? . . . I thought that was impossible.'

David Stevens looked as if someone had punched him in the stomach. Bonomi had never seen his face like this, never.

'Let's have the rest of it. . . . Right. . . . Right. . . . And whom do they want? . . . That's crazy. . . . They can't be serious. . . . Who are they? . . . No, the names don't mean anything to me. I want a full report on them within the next hour. . . . General, I want to make sure that I've got this absolutely straight. You'd better repeat it.'

The President of the United States listened for a full minute, visibly disturbed by what was being said.

'All right, I'll get back to you as soon as possible,' he promised the CINCSAC. 'Does anybody know about this? . . . Who else? . . . I see. Yes. . . . No, I'm not blaming anyone – not yet, anyway. . . . What's the situation out there now? . . . I see. . . . That makes sense, even if nothing else about this insane thing does. General, you know this set-up and I respect your judgement. Do you have any suggestions? . . . Is there any way to dig them out? . . . Thanks for laying it on the line. . . . Right. I'll phone you as soon as we've decided.'

Stevens hung up the red phone, shook his head.

'Something wrong?' asked Bonomi.

'Vince, what do you know about the Minuteman capsules and their defenses?'

The former fighter pilot pondered, shrugged.

'Not a helluva lot more than you'd read in the papers or some aviation magazine. I was never a rocket man, you know. The missile boys say that those holes are practically blastproof, just about impregnable to anything less than a direct hit with a nuclear warhead.'

The man whom some people said was almost as handsome as John F. Kennedy sighed.

'Not quite impregnable,' he announced grimly. 'I just heard something fantastic from McKenzie, maybe not so fantastic but certainly ... what's that phrase we used to use – scary and hairy.'

The President was deeply disturbed, shaken.

'At least it'll take your mind off that Arab king,' Bonomi said in an effort to brighten the atmosphere.

'What Arab king?'

Then the President told him what the CINCSAC had reported, and as Stevens spoke his authority and sober strength grew firmer with each word.

'It's scary and hairy all right,' Bonomi agreed.

'Now I know how Kennedy felt when they first showed him those U-2 pictures of the Russian rockets in Cuba,' mused Stevens slowly.

For several moments neither man spoke.

'Two o'clock. Meeting here at two o'clock,' David Stevens decided. 'Grosvenor, Darby, Crane, Michaelson – Bill Frost too. You'd better stick around, Vince. This may be an historic meeting, and I wouldn't want you to miss it.'

His old friend smiled.

'Yes, Mr President – although I can't see what good a lousy one-star general could do with all those great men present.'

Stevens shrugged.

'Vince,' he replied as he reached for the black phone, 'a mature man who has the nerve to say "horse shit" to the President of the United States can always come in handy.'

'I wouldn't say it to you in front of anyone else, Dave,' protested Bonomi.

The President did not answer.

He was already speaking into the telephone, issuing the instructions for the two-o'clock meeting.

Some 1800 miles to the northwest, Lieutenant Philip Canellis was beginning to moan. It wasn't exactly a moan that was issuing from his bruised, puffed lips, for Dell's judo blow to the neck had affected the young missileman's larynx. The prisoner who lay in the bunk made the hoarse hurting sound again, and Falco walked across the Launch Control Center to see what was happening.

'He seems to be coming to,' judged the assassin.

'Is he all right?' Dell asked from the red swivel chair of the Crew Commander.

'Take a look. I'm no doctor.'

The former Deputy Intelligence Officer of the 168th rose, lit a cigarette and then joined Falco.

Canellis moved, as much as he could with his wrists and ankles bound. There was clotted blood at one corner of his mouth, and for a moment Dell wondered whether the first blow – the blow with the gun to cut off any shout at the hatch – had broken the young officer's jaw or teeth. That would have been entirely unnecessary, most unfortunate. Dell had nothing against either of the missile crew, nothing against the other men whom the fugitives had overwhelmed on the surface either. Like everyone else in America today – including members of the Black Panthers, the Chicago Police Department and the defensive squad of the Minnesota Vikings – he regarded himself as a basically good person who rarely used more violence than was necessary. Of course, sometimes a certain amount of force was required because other people – less wise or noble – got in the way and interfered with his legitimate efforts to enjoy life, liberty and happiness. Any top executive, student militant or philosophy professor would have understood that.

Canellis stirred again, and one eyelid flickered.

'He'll be all right,' Dell predicted.

Hoxey, who'd been watching and listening from a few yards away, smiled. 'Deacon' Hoxey might burn churches and shoot police, but he certainly didn't want to hurt anybody. He wished well to everyone, with the exception of those evil, corrupt individuals who were resisting God's will so sinfully. There were so many of them, so many. It was a nightmare. And there were so many others who were dupes or atheists, who wanted to fluoridate water or worship false deities or watch filthy movies. These people often made Hoxey sad, sometimes even angry.

Now the other captive groaned in the next bunk.

'Deacon' Hoxey nodded sympathetically, walked to the toilet sink and returned with two paper cups filled with water. He reached down, gently raised Canellis' head and carefully, almost tenderly, poured a few sips of liquid into the lieutenant's

mouth. Then he repeated the same process with Captain
Towne, the Crew Commander whom Falco had clubbed.

'That was very thoughtful of you,' Lawrence Dell said.

The madman smiled modestly, resumed his humanitarian
pouring.

CHAPTER FIFTEEN

Arthur Renfrew Grosvenor, Harvard '42 OSS '46 and an almost perfect size 38 according to the custom-tailoring department at Brooks Brothers, was the first to arrive. He was also the Secretary of State responsible for the foreign relations of a great power, a tall serious man with considerable intelligence, an excellent fluency in French and Spanish, less hair than anyone else in the Stevens Cabinet and a reputation as a connoisseur of medieval art. Some of the younger men at the Department of State had spread a mischievous rumor that Grosvenor was a medical marvel born without sweat glands, but that was completely untrue. The lanky balding Secretary of State did ... perspire ... on occasion, although no one in the Department had ever seen it. The fact that no one at State had seen it meant nothing, of course, for they'd never witnessed him in bed with Mrs Grosvenor (Bryn Mawr '47) and there were four children. The Secretary of State wasn't perspiring this Sunday afternoon as the limousine drew up to the White House, although he was a bit puzzled as to why the President had suggested he arrive by the little-used East Gate.

He was also somewhat curious as to why the President had summoned him, but Stevens would explain that shortly. Perhaps it had something to do with King Achmed's visit, which was going quite well. 'I'll have to tell the President that,' Arthur Renfrew Grosvenor reflected when the chauffeur stopped the black Cadillac at the East Entrance. The White House door – the side door – opened immediately, and Grosvenor saw one of the junior military aides waiting.

That, like this unscheduled Sunday meeting, was odd.

It seemed clear that the President didn't want the press, who kept a collective eye on the Pennsylvania Avenue main entrance, to know about this meeting. The chauffeur opened the car door and the young captain gestured, almost impatiently, and the Secretary of State entered the building immediately. The implied urgency seemed rather peculiar, for if there was any crisis anywhere – anywhere in the world – the matter would have been reported to the Department of State by the nearest US Embassy. It was too bad that the public didn't realize how efficient the Department's new global tele-communications system was, Grosvenor brooded as he followed the Army captain – Captain Hartung, according to the name plate on his tunic – toward the stairs.

Secretary of Defense Robert Guthrie Darby, MIT '48 and Lockheed Aircraft '70, reached the White House a few minutes later – but not by the East Entrance. He came in through the tunnel from the Executive Office Building next door, accompanied by General Peter Crane. Crane, who normally wore four stars as befitting the chief of Air Staff, understood why they were arriving furtively and why he'd been asked to come in civilian clothes. The President had authorized McKenzie to report the basic situation to Crane, and now the general – unlike Arthur Renfrew Grosvenor – was definitely damp in the armpits. As a matter of fact, he felt terrible all over – in part because the President was probably going to blame the Air Force.

Evan Michaelson, wearing his usual horn-rimmed glasses and bow tie, was the next to enter the building. The Director of the Central Intelligence Agency, a Civil Service hero because he'd worked his way up through the ranks to the top post, arrived via the South Gate. He'd been cooking Sunday brunch – cooking was his hobby – when Bonomi had called that the President wanted to see him. Michaelson didn't particularly like Vince Bonomi – or, to be accurate, Michaelson was annoyed with his own miscalculation about Bonomi, for the former fighter ace had turned out to be the President's man rather than the CIA's. It wasn't supposed to work that way – not according to the logic of a career bureaucrat, but any professional politician could have predicted it. A civil servant's loyalty is to his agency, bureau, department. Loyalty – personal loyalty – was hardly a quality that the international intelligence community took very seriously in any case, but Michaelson was nagged by the thought that he should have judged Bonomi more carefully. After all, Evan Michaelson was the first social psychologist (Ph.d., U. of Chicago) to head America's largest espionage organization.

He wasn't supposed to misjudge, and he was supposed to know.

The fact that he didn't know why the President had summoned him so peremptorily – well abruptly and presumably urgently – added to his suppressed discomfort, and he bit down on the new meerschaum as he entered the white House and saw Bonomi approaching down the corridor.

'Sorry to break up your Sunday,' the general apologized in tones that were almost perfunctory, 'but something's hit the fan.'

Hit the fan? Bonomi still used those archaic Air Force phrases, some of them going back to the prehistoric era of World War II.

Michaelson shrugged with the philosophic resignation of a cold War veteran who'd endured many crises, wondered whether Bonomi would explain. He didn't.

'Big party?' tested the CIA director.

'No, just a select few. You, Grosvenor, Darby, Pete Crane and Bill Frost. Here he is now.'

William Lee Frost, a curly-haired Chicagoan whose substantial legal skills were matched by his talents as a political fund raiser, looked much too young to be the Attorney General of the United States. His disarmingly innocent face reflected the unseamed serenity of a man barely thirty, and it was only the few gray strands just beginning to appear and the occasional *something* in his eyes that hinted at the tough worldly wisdom of the mature forty-four-year-old male within that body. He had style, not the predictable style of the Episcopalian aristocrat that Secretary of State Arthur Renfew Grosvenor featured but a somewhat lusher and charismatic style – the style of a much traveled international banker, perhaps one of the French Rothschilds. Grosvenor was rich old Yankee, but Frost – much more relaxed and tolerant – was the scion of one of the not so old but equally affluent families of the Midwest. His father had come from Russia at the turn of the century, acquired the new name of Frost somewhere and constructed a real-estate empire in the six-plus decades that followed. Now the senior Frost sent generous checks to charities, played poker and pinochle with his cronies and boasted with expert modesty about 'my son the General.' It amused him that the approved form of address for the Attorney General of the United States was 'general' – and it delighted him too.

'Good afternoon, General,' Frost said to Bonomi.

'Good afternoon to you, General,' the Air Force officer replied.

'Evan,' Frost said in pleasant acknowledgement of the CIA director.

'Afternoon, Bill. Coming to our party?'

Bonomi controlled his impulse to smile. *Our* party? It was, alas, typical of the intelligence types to hint that they knew much more than they did. *Our* party? It was laughable, for Michaelson had no idea as to why the meeting had been called. It was the President's party and a grim one at that.

'Yessir, when the Chief Executive calls the Attorney General puts down the Sunday *Times* and comes a-running,' Frost admitted. 'Not that much in it anyway. Another in-depth report on drug addiction in suburban kindergartens, the latest on what air pollution is doing to those bears in Yosemite, an article on the Women's Liberation movement by Gore Vidal and the regular weekly rat count in nine typical American ghettos. Three more university presidents quit, and the Ford Foundation has given nine million dollars to the Rockefeller Foundation – a move that the entire Yale Divinity School basketball team has denounced as racist.'

Michaelson nodded, resigned to the Attorney General's odd sense of humor. You couldn't be entirely sure that *everything* he'd just said was sophomoric whimsy – with the state of the world being what it was – but most of the account sounded like the sort of creative fiction normally encountered in *Mad* magazine, the Los Angeles *Free Press* and the *Congressional Record*.

'You seem to be in good spirits, Bill,' the CIA director observed noncommittally.

'And you look as grim as ever. I ought to send over some of

those dirty books that the Supreme Court won't let us keep out of the mails; they might cheer you up.'

In fact, Frost wasn't feeling nearly that jolly and hadn't been since he saw Michaelson a few minutes earlier. A shrewd and practical man, he'd guessed that something was wrong – something significant, something that would cause Stevens to summon at least two Cabinet members to an emergency meeting. It wasn't civil rights, politics, air pollution, inflation or the budget for the National Arts Council either – not if Michaelson was present.

'Gentlemen, the President is waiting,' Bonomi reminded – and thereby terminated the exchange.

They headed for the elevator. In the White House 'operations center' down in the basement, teleprinter circuit 1 – the 'secure' line to the Pentagon – was clattering noisily. Petty Officer 3rd Class Harmon D. Dukes walked across the room, scanned the roll of yellow paper that was steadily emerging – and frowned. The words that were marching inexorably across the paper – the individual words made sense all right, but the message didn't seem to have any relevancy to the White House.

SECRET AND URGENT. FOR IMMEDIATE DELIVERY TO CYCLOPS. DELL LAWRENCE. CONVICTED MURDER FIRST DEGREE MARCH 18TH. VICTIM WIFE DIANA MAVIS DELL AGED TWENTY-NINE. HOMICIDE METHOD STRANGULATION. SITE FAMILY APARTMENT MALMSTROM AFB MONTANA. BIOGRAPHICAL DETAILS FOLLOW. LAWRENCE DELL CAUCASIAN PROTESTANT NO PREVIOUS CRIMINAL RECORD, NO PREVIOUS MARRIAGE, NO KNOWN EMOTIONAL OR PSYCHIATRIC DIFFICULTIES. DELL BORN NEW HAVEN CONNECTICUT SEPTEMBER 1938 SON OF DOCTOR AND MRS RICHARD DELL. OLDER BROTHER RICHARD DELL JUNIOR. YOUNGER SISTER ELIZABETH. . . .

The message kept unspooling as the machine stuttered on and on, but Petty Officer Dukes couldn't understand why this information was being rushed to Cyclops – the code name for the President of the United States. Perhaps it had something to do with some appeal for a pardon, the communications technician speculated.

'Good afternoon, gentlemen,' David Stevens said and as they chorused 'Good afternoon, Mr President' he gestured to the chairs and leather couch. 'That stuff come in from McKenzie yet, Vince?' he added immediately.

'I'll check.'

Stevens nodded toward the desk phone, and his former wingman dialed the communications room.

'Coming in now. Be up in five or ten minutes,' Bonomi reported.

The President nodded.

'You all know General Bonomi?' he asked in a voice that communicated that he really didn't care whether they did or didn't. 'Okay, we'd better get down to business. This is an emergency meeting. We've got an emergency – a serious one and a strange one. It affects both national and international security. I have deliberately chosen not to assemble the entire National Security Council because this matter is so secret that I don't want a single person who doesn't have to know to hear a single word about it. Is that clear?'

He paused only to catch his breath, expecting no reply and leaving no time for one before he resumed.

'You know about this, General?' he asked the Chief of Air Staff.

'Yessir,' Crane confirmed. 'McKenzie called me. He said you'd authorized it.'

The Director of the Central Intelligence Agency bit down angrily on the $40 pipe his wife had given him for his birthday, annoyed that he too hadn't been properly 'put in the picture.'

'Viper Three,' said the Chief Executive, 'is the SAC designation for one of the Minuteman capsules buried in the plains of Montana. Malmstrom, the 168th Strategic Missile Wing. Last night or rather very early this morning, five convicted murderers – one a former SAC major who'd been with the 168th – broke out of the Death House at the state penitentiary in Helena. Later this morning, they jumped a missile crew on its way to Viper Three and stole their station wagon and uniforms. Sometime after that, they managed to overpower the security team on the surface at Viper Three and then — some-how — succeeded in seizing the capsule itself. I don't know how.'

'That's impossible,' muttered the Secretary of Defense.

'No. It's supposed to be — but it isn't. They did it,' Stevens corrected coldly.

The head of the Defense Department glanced over to Crane, who nodded in grim confirmation.

'They're inside now,' continued the President. 'That big steel door is locked, and they've succeeded in disconnecting all the cut-off devices that would have permitted men in other capsules to neutralize the ten missiles controlled by Viper Three. In simplest terms, they can fire those rockets whenever they want to — and they're threatening to do so.'

The Secretary of State looked puzzled. The Director of the CIA wore an expression of earnest concern, the Secretary of Defense appeared to be wavering between righteous oratory and vomiting, and General Crane seemed to be blinking and swallowing much more than usual. They were shaken but not puzzled. Arthur Renfrew Grosvenor, a sober, civilized man who never rushed or lost his head, was puzzled.

'I don't understand,' he announced in that fine Brahmin voice of old New England. 'It doesn't make any sense.'

'Jeezus Christ,' said Darby.

Grosvenor frowned, disassociating himself from this emotional vulgarity.

'Mr President,' Michaelson interrupted with the rational cool that one might expect of the head of the CIA, 'What did you mean by "threatening"? Is there some price, some deal?'

'They have something in mind,' Stevens answered.

Grosvenor's going to wet his pants when he hears this, Vince Bonomi thought.

'The Government of the United States doesn't make deals with murderers,' declared the Secretary of State.

The President turned to the Attorney General.

'You got anything to say, Bill?'

Frost shrugged.

'I'm still listening — and I'd bet you're still talking, Mr President,' he replied.

'Let's all listen,' countered Stevens.

Thirty seconds later, they heard the phone amplifier on the SAC hot-line instrument grinding out the tape of Dell's call.

They listened tensely to Dell's announcement that the convicts had control of Viper Three and its ICBMs, his declaration that the raiders were ready to launch the missiles unless the Government met the fugitives' terms and his flat statement that these terms were non-negotiable. 'It's a package deal,' they heard the ex-major warn – and they all sat up stiffly as they waited to discover what the 'package deal' might be.

'Three parts. First, money. Cash money. There are five of us – all decent American capitalists – and we want one million dollars apiece. That's five million dollars in used currency – a bargain price.'

Secretary of Defense Darby sat shaking his head.

'Second, out. We want *out* – out of the United States. Transportation to another country on a jet transport – a very comfortable and very special jet. It won't cost you anything to charter it, because you own it. I'm talking about Air Force One.'

General Crane had known this was coming, but he winced anyway.

Air Force One was the President's personal plane.

'Third, safe conduct,' Dell continued. 'It's not that we're unpatriotic or lack faith in our Government, but we don't trust you – any of you. Nothing personal, you understand, but the leaders of so many countries have lied and betrayed and triple-talked so often that we've lost our Boy Scout faith. You might try to trick us or kill us once we get out of this rocket hole. You might even slip an altimeter bomb into the money bags to blow up our plane – like those Arab terrorists did to the Swissair transport. We want a hostage to go out with us, to go all the way.'

This ought really to tear Grosvenor up, Bonomi anticipated.

'The hostage is to be the President of the United States.'

CHAPTER SIXTEEN

That tore it all right.

Michaelson almost dropped his pipe and Darby stood up under the impact, and General Peter P. Crane – holder of two Distinguished Flying Crosses, eleven other US medals and nine decorations bestowed by NATO powers whispered an oath that wasn't entirely audible but one word was definitely 'bastards.' McKenzie hadn't mentioned the question of the hostage, and now the Chief of Air Staff knew why. The CINCSAC hadn't dared to speak of it, even over the scrambler.

'Preposterous,' judged the Secretary of State unhesitatingly.

'Ridiculous,' he added a moment later.

He's going to say 'outrageous' next, calculated the President.

'Outrageous,' Grosvenor fumed.

Arthur Renfrew Grosvenor was a very able diplomat, Stevens thought, but he was wholly predictable.

'*Momsers,*' the Attorney General judged.

The Chief Executive of the United States nodded. He'd heard Frost use the Yiddish expression before. It meant 'bastards' – in spades.

'The man's insane,' Grosvenor insisted.

At that moment, McKenzie's voice sounded again on the tape.

'You're crazy.'

'Flattery will get you nowhere,' answered the former USAF major, 'and your opinions of me or the deal don't matter. There's only one man who can make the deal, and you'd better call *him*. No tricks. Call him *now*.'

And General McKenzie did just that,' Stevens announced. 'He called me, and I've called you.'

The President picked up the telephone.

'Thank you,' he said to the man in the bunker near Omaha.

'We'll get back to you shortly, General, and of course you'll phone immediately if there are any new developments.'

Then he hung up the red instrument, turned to the men in his office.

'As I see it, there are three problems – one legal, one political and one military,' Stevens reasoned. 'That's in an ascending order of importance, I'd say. And an ascending order of difficulty, I suspect. Bill, if it should turn out that we *have* to do business with this man Dell and his gang, what's our legal position? Can we do it? *Can* we pay off these criminals and help them escape?'

'Mr President, the Government of the United States cannot do business with murderers,' Grosvenor protested.

Stevens sighed.

'Arthur, you know that this Government and a lot of other Governments – the British and the Russians and a hundred more – have been doing business with all sorts of unsavory dictators and homicidal tyrants for a very long time,' he said patiently. 'We're not particularly proud of it and we hope that someday – soon – it won't be necessary, but let's not get pious now. And let's not interrupt the Attorney General, our senior legal expert. Bill?'

Frost shrugged.

'*You know* the answer, Mr President,' he noted frankly, 'but I'll say it anyway because I gather you want me to – for the record, I suppose. All right – *for the record* – since the Constitution provides that the President is responsible for the conduct of foreign affairs, and since the firing of those missiles would undoubtedly affect our foreign affairs, my legal opinion is that you can deal with these *momsers*.'

'And the money?'

'Mr President, there are certain funds annually appropriated by the Congress for the Chief Executive to expend at his discretion – funds that certainly exceed five million dollars,' Frost replied. 'In an emergency of this sort, I'd say that you'd be *entirely* within your authority to expend those funds. I'd imagine that the CIA pays out more than that each year to even more unsavory types – including a few assassins – so you can too.'

Michaelson considered answering the snide remark, decided that he'd settle the score some other time.

'Let's not play games,' the Attorney General added bluntly. 'If we can't stop these criminals any other way, we'll pay and I'll produce a fifty-page legal memorandum justifying the whole thing. I'll get out the old one that they used for the Bay of Pigs operation and copy the same footnotes.'

Now both the Secretary of State and the Secretary of Defense were scowling angrily.

'This is no time for such levity. It isn't funny,' protested Arthur Renfrew Grosvenor.

'I know. I'm not laughing,' Frost acknowledged. 'I'm too scared to laugh,' he confessed, 'and too embarrased to cry.'

No crap, Bonomi thought. There was no pretense, no crap about Frost.

'I'll keep that carefully reasoned legal opinion in mind – just in case it should ever come to that,' Stevens announced. 'I hope it won't. Now, what about the political implications?'

'Impossible,' warned Grosvenor. 'Absolutely impossible. It might be more accurate to say catastrophic. We can't let anybody – not even our closest allies – know about this. It isn't like the Cuban missile crisis at all. This is, after all, entirely our fault. All the blame lies on our own armed forces.'

'Garbage,' Bonomi challenged. 'Part of the responsibility belongs to the Air Force – okay – but the Air Force didn't create the goddam mess that made missiles and thermonuclear warheads necessary. Grow up, Mr Secretary.'

Right.

Bonomi was right, the Chief of Air Staff told himself, and it was time that *somebody* straightened out these sanctimonious civilians who blamed everything on the military.

Yes, the ex-fighter pilot had said exactly what Pete Crane would have said – if he hadn't controlled his temper.

'We can parcel out the blame later,' interrupted Stevens, 'and I'm sure that there'll be enough for everybody. To continue with what you're saying, Arthur, we can't let this out because it would hurt us badly. And what if it reaches the ears of the Soviets or Chinese?'

'They wouldn't believe it,' Michaelson replied quickly. 'I can say – categorically – that they'd assume that it was some trick, and they'd immediately escalate their defense readiness to prepare to counterattack. No, Mr President, I think that every man in this room realizes that there isn't a chance in the world that we could tell Moscow or Peking that some of our ICBMs might be coming their way soon – but we don't mean them any harm. We'll be in the middle of World War III about eleven or twelve minutes after those missiles leave Viper Three, since they're certainly aimed at Red targets.'

Stevens nodded, glanced at Crane.

'Would you have any ideas as to what the specific targets of the Viper Three rockets are?' the President asked.

The general reached into his pocket, took out a folded sheet of paper.

'I checked as soon as McKenzie called me. Target One, Soviet naval base at Kronstadt right near Leningrad. Target Two, the Voroshilov plant that makes their SS-11 missiles – which happens to be in Sverdlovsk, which has a population of eight hundred and eighty thousand. Target Three, the big dam at Magnitigorsk. Target Four, Soviet Air Force headquarters in Siberia – outside Vladivostok. Target Five, the Ukraine city of Kharkhov – population approximately one million one hundred thousand. Target Six – oh, Six, Seven and Eight are mainland China. Six is—'

'Don't bother. That's enough,' Stevens broke in grimly. 'I think that the picture is quite clear.'

'They're all *legitimate* targets, Mr President,' Crane pointed out, 'and all designated by the Strategic Targets Board.'

'Tell that to the people in Kharkov and Sverdlovsk,' the Attorney General suggested sardonically. 'They'll feel a lot better knowing that they're dying *legitimately* in a properly authorized holocaust.'

'The Air Force didn't pick these targets, dammit,' Crane argued. 'It was an interdepartmental group, including CIA – if anybody's interested.'

Michaelson put down his pipe.

'Pete, nobody's blaming the Air Force for the targets,' the imperfect but intelligent head of the Central Intelligence Agency said in tones of sober reason, 'or for the lousy state of the world either. Yes, Mr President, I agree that the implications of this target list are quite clear.'

There was an unpleasant moment of silence.

'World War Three,' said the President.

'World War Three,' Michaelson concurred.

More silence, even more unpleasant.

'You,' Grosvenor said as he pointed his finger at Darby, 'you've *got* to get those criminals out of there. There must be a way. You have troops, planes, napalm, atomic warheads.'

'I don't know,' the Secretary of Defense replied cautiously. 'I understand that those Minuteman bases are supposed to be impregnable, or close to it. There's that big steel door into the Launch Control Center and all kinds of alarms and security gear to prevent a surprise attack.'

'Gas? How about gas?' peace-loving Arthur Renfrew Grosvenor was surprised to hear himself ask.

'These holes are gasproof. They've got air-purifying equipment that kicks on automatically if the sensors sniff any gas,' Crane answered.

'Cut off their power,' urged the New Englander.

'Each hole has its own emergency generator.'

'That kicks on automatically?' Frost tested.

The Chief of Air Staff nodded.

'The missiles? Can they be reached in their . . . their silos?' Grosvenor questioned hopefully.

'Each covered by a seventy-ton steel-and-concrete lid that can only be raised from inside by a compressed-air gadget. That lid is a solid slab, engineered to be as close to blastproof as possible.'

'What about an air strike? suggested Darby. 'Could TAC fighter bombers hit the ten silos at the same time – with atomic bombs?'

Crane looked at him, then to Stevens.

'Maybe. Theoretically, yes,' he answered, 'but I can't be that sure. The commander of TAC– *he'd* say he was sure that his boys could do the job – but that's mighty goddamed perfect bombing. Super pinpoint bombing – only one shot at the targets and ten different targets.'

'One shot?' Grosvenor wondered.

'If we don't knock all ten birds out on the first try, you can bet your ass that those hoodlums down there will launch whatever they've got left. What the hell have they got to lose? They're all dead men anyway. No, I couldn't recommend an air strike,' the senior USAF commander concluded.

'We've got to do something,' insisted the Secretary of Defense.

'Maybe – but an air strike, even one with the best pilots TAC can muster, is one helluva gamble,' Crane reiterated. 'You flew fighter-bombers, Mr President,' he recalled, 'and you know what the odds are against ten direct hits out of ten low-level attacks on small targets.'

For a moment, Stevens and Bonomi remembered those wild days in Korea some two decades earlier.

'General Crane's right. The possibilities of human error – pilot error – even down to three hundred to four hundred miles an hour, are just too dangerous. No, I can't buy the air strike.'

The President had decided, but the conversation was not finished.

'We have enormous military power,' Darby argued, 'and it certainly should be enough to cope with five jailbirds hiding in a hole in Montana.'

'I don't know,' Stevens reflected. 'It wasn't designed for that situation. It ought to be able to cope with just about anything on earth, but it wasn't such a howling success in Vietnam. It wasn't designed for that situation either.'

'To draw a crude analogy,' Frost concurred, 'These five hoodlums have attempted to mug the United States – and you can't stop a mugger with a bombing plane.'

Stevens turned to his former wingman, stared the question.

'Mr President,' Bonomi answered in deliberately controlled tones, 'there are a number of possible military solutions that we may have to explore very soon. We'll probably want the Army Chief of Staff over here if that's necessary, but there's something else we might try first.'

'Go on, Vince.'

'Why don't you talk to Dell? What have you got to lose? You're a clever arm-twister, a sharp bargainer and a damn fine politician. You've made a lot of deals with a lot of difficult people in the last twenty years or so,' the one-star general reminded, 'and maybe you can make some kind of a deal with this crowd. I'd bet you've had worse types to lunch – here.'

Stevens could think of half a dozen immediately, most of the chiefs of state in 'friendly' countries.

'Nothing personal, Mr President,' Bonomi added.

Good afternoon, you son of a bitch.

'I understand that, General,' David Stevens replied.

Of all the others in the room, only Michaelson could sense that there was some private message – some unspoken dialogue – in this exchange. It was, of course, another subtle statement of that personal intimacy and loyalty that defied lines of command and official channels of communication.

'What do you think of the idea, Evan?' Stevens tested.

Michaelson hesitated, calculated and nodded.

'It might be useful,' he admitted cautiously.

'Bill?'

'Why not, Mr President? I understand you've had lunch *and dinner* with worse types,' Frost answered.

He's probably talking about King Achmed, speculated Grosvenor. The Secretary of State had no illusions about Frost's views on the Arab-Israeli situation, for even though the Attorney General didn't meddle in international affairs he didn't often bother to hide his feelings either. There was really no room for feelings in the shaping of the foreign policies of a great power, for enlightened but firm self-interest had to prevail over emotion as it always had – and the national interests of the United States precluded any indulgent sentimentality. Most political leaders in Washington and London, in Paris and Moscow, in Peking and Tokyo understood this sort of thinking, the Secretary of State knew, and it was disappointing to find men as impractical as Frost in high places.

The President's next question interrupted this train of thought.

'Bob?'

The Secretary of Defense had no objection, since efforts to negotiate, real or false, successful or otherwise, might buy time for the Army and Air Force to prepare their counterattack. Crane supported this position with a silent nod, and then

Arthur Renfrew Grosvenor solemnly announced that he always preferred peaceful private negotiations to force. It was a matter of historical record that such 'conversations' could be 'quite fruitful', concluded the Secretary of State knowingly.

'I don't know how far my negotiating talents will go with these convicts,' warned Stevens, 'but I'm more than willing to try.'

'You can use the SAC hot line and go through the Offutt bunker communications set-up,' Crane suggested. 'It's the most direct and most *secure* way.'

The President picked up the phone that was linked to McKenzie's subterranean command post.

As he did so, Marshal Korbynin began to speak into another telephone at the field headquarters of the Soviet Forces Group – Germany – thirty-four miles from East Berlin. The 76th and the 99th were to move out immediately, and the MIG-23 squadrons were to be prepared to take off just before dawn. By the time the sun rose, the first waves of fighters were to be in the air corridors. The radio and radar jamming was to start precisely five minutes before the supersonic interceptors left their runways, and Marshal Vladimir Korbynin would personally make certain that any officer who failed to keep to the timetable would be punished.

Chief Marshal of Armored Troops Soyuzov had made it very clear that coordination and timing were important in this operation, for Yamshchik had been conceived and planned by the Central Committee – the Central Committee of the Party – as a swift and perfect surprise. Whether the operation would succeed was not entirely certain, Marshal Korbynin realized, but one could be quite sure as to what would happen to a senior field commander – even a Red Army marshal – who irritated or failed the Central Committee. One could also be certain that if Yamshchik did not succeed, the blame would be pushed onto the field commander. Aleksei Soyuzov was a decent fellow, but he hadn't risen to such a high post on the Red Army *stavka* without learning how to shift the blame for failures to someone else.

Good old Aleksei Soyuzov wasn't going to take the blame himself.

That was entirely natural – in this army and others.

In Soyuzov's position, Marshal Korbynin wouldn't take it either. If all went well during the next three or four days, Korbynin might eventually rise to that position – that comfortable headquarters spot in Moskva. It was the consciousness of what might happen if all didn't go well that caused the commander of the Soviet Forces Group in Germany to speak so unpleasantly into the field telephone.

CHAPTER SEVENTEEN

'The keys,' Dell said suddenly.

'We forgot to get the damned keys,' he explained.

'What?' mumbled Schonbacher.

Sweaty-faced and looking extremely uncomfortable, the porky sex criminal seemed to be perspiring even more than before despite the fact that the capsule's air-conditioning system was delivering an even sixty-eight-degree temperature. That part of the System was still functioning perfectly, but Harvey Schonbacher was perspiring nevertheless. If he weren't so lazy, vain or stupid, Dell thought, the idiot would remove the stolen coveralls that were plainly too small.

Or it might be fear.

That was all they'd need, one of their five men at the clammy edge of panic.

'You all right, Harve?' the former missile officer asked with calculated nonchalance.

'Sure. What about the keys?'

'The firing keys?' Powell interjected.

'That's right,' confirmed Dell.

'What about those goddam firing keys?' challenged the sex killer testily.

Deacon Hoxey frowned, offended by the improper use of the Lord's name.

'I don't like that talk,' he announced.

'Oh, for chrissakes, shut up,' Schonbacher jeered. He saw the hatred glow in the madman's bright eyes, and he stepped back nervously.

'Harvey didn't mean any disrespect, Deacon,' assured Dell, who'd noticed the same surge of internal fury. 'It was just a figure of speech, a bad habit. You've got to watch that, Harve. That's an *awful* way to talk to decent people, you know.'

Falco nodded in admiration.

You really had to hand it to Larry.

Smooth, and very fast.

'I'll watch it, Larry,' Schonbacher pledged hastily. 'I'm sorry I said it. I'm not feeling too well,' he apologized. 'Maybe it's something I ate. My stomach's a mess. I'm not a well man, you know.'

Fear.

It was crude sour fear, Dell judged – and immediately felt depressed.

'I think Harvey's got an ulcer,' Powell contributed to ease the tension, 'so let's not be too hard on the poor fellow, Deacon. Forgiveness is one of the great Christian virtues, I seem to recall.'

The rage in Hoxey's face began to subside.

'As I was saying, we forgot to collect the two firing keys,' Dell continued briskly, 'and without those keys we don't have much muscle at all. We can't launch the birds without those keys, can we, Sandy?'

Captain Sanford Torne didn't answer.

The yellow-haired Crew Commander of Missile Combat Crew 889-C was awake and ungagged, and he could have replied. He'd had a few sips of water and his head didn't hurt quite as much as it had when he'd come to an hour earlier, and there were a lot of things he could have said. Even though the back of his skull still throbbed and the bindings at his wrists and elbows chafed, there were a number of things that Towne could have said. He glared at the enemy from the bunk, remained silent.

'Aren't you going to say anything?' Dell pressed.

No answer.

'Not even "My country 'tis of thee"?'

Towne didn't reply.

Lieutenant Canellis did.

'Traitor,' the younger officer said bitterly. 'You're a goddam traitor, Dell.'

Falco shook his head in exaggerated reproof.

'We just went through *that*, kid,' he reminded. 'That kind of evil talk is out.'

'They'll hang you, Dell. They'll hang all you bastards,' Canellis vowed.

The professional assassin sighed. 'I just hope he doesn't say "you'll never get away with this." I must have seen that picture a *million* times on TV – at least a million times.'

'You won't get away with it! They'll hang every one of you!'

Falco's eyes narrowed.

'I thought they'd shoot us,' he confessed. 'The Army doesn't hang people, does it, Willieboy?'

The ex-Marine looked thoughtful.

'As I remember it, firing squads are the bit – although it might be different for treason. That's if we're caught and convicted. I think we could beat it on temporary insanity.'

'I come from a broken home myself,' Falco concurred slyly. 'Terrible childhood. I'm all mixed up, very nervous.'

'Emotionally insecure?' suggested the black.

'That's it. I still suck my thumb – when no one's watching. What about you, Larry?'

'My mommy never loved me. How about you, Willie? I'd say that you were definitely a victim of racial oppression, ruined in the ghetto.'

Was he jesting or sneering?

'Between the ghetto and those bleeding hearts in the poverty program, I've developed some terrible antisocial attitudes,' Powell answered. 'I have this sick inferiority complex that makes me want to hurt all white people, especially officers.'

'I won't turn my back on you,' promised Dell.

'I wouldn't, Major.'

Was Powell playing or threatening?

'Where *are* the firing keys?' Schonbacher demanded impatiently.

'Ask the lieutenant,' Dell suggested. 'He seems to be the talkative one. My friend Sandy's sulking, I guess.'

Schonbacher walked to the bunk, peered down at Canellis.

'Okay, Lieutenant, where are the keys?' he questioned.

'Screw you.'

It was adolescent, stupid and ridiculous.

That was the thought in Dell's mind.

Something else was troubling Willieboy Powell.

The former SAC major had spoken of the plan and the capsule many times, but he'd never mentioned the firing keys.

Why?

'Screw you,' Canellis repeated defiantly.

Schonbacher raised his pistol, and before anyone could stop him struck the young officer in the pit of the stomach. Then the rapist lifted the gun again.

'I'll shoot you, Harvey,' Dell said quickly in loud, angry tones. 'Once more and I'll shoot you.'

Surprised and uncertain, the fat man hesitated.

'We need those keys,' he blustered.

'*He* can't deliver them. Put the gun down, you idiot – *now*.'

'The major isn't kidding,' Falco judged. 'He's going to gun you, Harve.'

Breathing heavily and sniffling, Schonbacher slowly lowered his weapon and then skipped back two steps. Lieutenant Canellis was gasping and heaving; he might vomit at any second.

'That was a stupid stunt,' Dell said harshly, 'and I'm about fed up with your stupidity, Harvey. First you wanted us to kill that guard who stuck his head into the car – when it wasn't necessary – and then you turned chicken when I told you to move up the tunnel ahead of me – which was necessary. Now the senseless violence on a defenseless man who doesn't even have the combination.'

'Bad form, Major? Poor sportsmanship?' Powell taunted.

Dell shook his head.

'No, just stupid. Only the Crew Commander knows the combination of the safe in which the keys are kept – *that* safe.'

He gestured with the machine gun toward a small red box set on brackets that jutted from the wall near the Crew Commander's chair. The metal rectangle was perhaps seven inches wide, five inches high and ten inches deep. A combination dial was built into the face.

'When the crews change, the Commander of the one going off duty turns over the log book and the combination to that safe to the Commander of the new shift,' Dell explained.

'He's saying you hit the wrong guy.' Falco chuckled. 'I did that once myself in New Orleans. The local boys got real sore about that, wouldn't pay me until I came back to town a couple of weeks later to hit the right one. They looked a lot alike.'

'You might say dead ringers,' suggested Dell, who knew that 'hit' meant 'kill' in underworld slang.

'Yeah, you could say that,' the assassin agreed. 'Anyway, Harve, you should have belted the other one – the captain. Maybe you can kick the combination out of him.'

'I'll take care of that,' the former Deputy Intelligence Officer of the 168th interrupted in authoritative tones.

At that moment, Canellis began to throw up in shuddering convulsions.

'Shit,' the underworld executioner grumbled. 'It's going to stink up the whole place.'

'I didn't—' Schonbacher started to reply.

'You clean it up,' Dell ordered. 'You made the mess, so you clean it up. Get paper towels from the toilet. I'll talk keys to Captain Towne.'

The telephone rang, and they all turned to the sound.

'Get the towels, Harvey,' Dell said as he walked to the Crew Commander's chair.

He sat down, picked up the instrument.

'Yes, General McKenzie?' he said coolly, very coolly.

'This isn't General McKenzie. This is the President.'

Even though he'd been half expecting this call, he braced under the impact of that familiar voice.

'Yes, Mr President?' he replied.

'Jeezus,' Falco whispered, 'the *President*?'

The ex-major managed to smile.

'With whom am I speaking?'

'My name is Dell, Lawrence Dell, Mr President.'

Stevens glanced at the teletyped biography on his desk, continued.

'Major Dell,' he began, deliberately avoiding 'Mr' because there might still be some leverage for the Commander in Chief in reminding this murderer that he'd been an Air Force officer, 'I understand from General McKenzie that you're in command of the men who are currently occupying the SAC base designated Viper Three.'

'That's correct. We hold the Launch Control Center, and we've dismantled the inhibitors that could prevent us from firing the missiles. They're Minutemen-2, with thermonuclear warheads of approximately one megaton yield.'

The son of a bitch was laying it right on the line, Crane thought as he listened to the exchange over the desk amplifier.

'I've been informed of that, Major.'

'These aren't the latest models, Mr President. The Minuteman-3 has multiple warheads so each can hit several targets,' Dell explained blandly, 'but these ten missiles can only take out ten targets – one each.'

The bastard's trying to get Dave angry, Bonomi judged.

'I understand,' Stevens replied evenly, 'and I understand that you and your companions escaped last night from the Death House at the state penitentiary in Helena.'

'That's correct. We're *desperate* men – capable of *anything*,' Dell acknowledged in a voice tinged with mockery. 'If we weren't so desperate, we'd never have attempted anything as *dangerous* as assaulting a SAC base.'

'I think I can understand that, Major. Men facing death will try anything to stay alive. I used to be a fighter pilot in an F-86 outfit during the Korean War, and I can appreciate the survival instinct. I've been afraid myself, many times.'

'I'm *glad* that you understand, Mr President. It isn't that we've got anything against SAC – or the Government of the United States. We'd have seized any country's missile base. Yours just happened to be handy.'

'Is that supposed to be a joke, Major?'

Dell sighed.

'I'm afraid so. Not very good, was it? Perhaps I'd better stick to breaking out of escapeproof prisons and seizing impregnable missile bases.'

Stevens paused for a few seconds to organize his presentation.

'Major Dell, this is a much more serious matter – serious for the entire nation, perhaps for the world – than you may realize. Frankly, I don't understand how a man of your intelligence and education could do something like this. It's one thing to flee from a state prison but quite another to attack an ICBM base. This isn't some cheap gangster movie, you know.'

'I know. It's a big-budget production, Mr President. It's

going to cost five million dollars to get this show on the road – and I assume you want it on the road as much as we do. You wouldn't want it to stay at Viper Three for one minute more than necessary, would you?'

It was not going well.

'General McKenzie told me that you'd mentioned some such figure, and he reported that you'd also made some rather melodramatic threats, but—'

'No buts and no threats and no bargaining,' Dell broke in curtly. 'Pay our price – the full price – or we launch the missiles.'

'I can't believe that you'd say that if you knew what the targets of those ICBMs are,' Stevens countered.

'I don't have to know. *You* know. You know and you're scared witless. I know that the targets aren't Disneyland or the London Zoo. They're somewhere in Russia or China – maybe both. I don't care, and my friends don't either. All we care about is our money and our lives, and our futures in safety outside the United States. We don't want to live here anymore. It's too dangerous with all the air pollution and crime in the streets, riots, drug addicts – not to mention police brutality and the shocking decline in sexual morality. If you add the falling quality of television programming, the logic of our decision should be apparent to anyone. Don't you agree, Mr President?'

General Crane's frown reflected his puzzlement.

What the hell did the quality of TV programming have to do with it?

'Major, I don't see how either wisecracks or polemics can help us reach a mutually satisfactory agreement,' David T. Stevens persisted. 'As you yourself said, we all want the same thing – to get you out of Viper Three. If we keep this common objective in mind, we can talk sensibly about possible ways – realistic ways – to accomplish this. There are several routes we can explore. I might speak to the Governor of Montana, for example.'

'About what? We've got Viper Three; he doesn't.'

'Well, Major, I could ask him to consider the possibility of executive clemency on the previous homicide convictions. Since it was your human self-preservation instinct that drove

128

you men to this extreme measure, I might urge Governor Wilcox to commute the death sentences – to reduce them to five or ten years in jail.'

Now that was creative thinking, the Attorney General mused – but too creative unless Dell was stupid. Wilcox belonged to the opposition party, and even if he went along with Stevens' request he'd leak the whole thing to his friend Caldwell about ninety seconds after the convicts left Viper Three. It might save Viper Three, but it would blow the election.

'No deal,' Dell announced. 'We're not going back inside – not for five minutes let alone five years. That Wilcox is a louse anyway, a louse and a liar. Only an idiot would trust him.'

'I'm asking you to trust the President of the United States.'

Next he'll whistle a few bars from 'The Star-Spangled Banner', the ex-SAC officer speculated.

'Not a chance. We don't trust anybody anymore, Mr President. We don't trust Santa Claus or the United Nations or even John Wayne. Pay up, or we launch.'

'What the hell are you talking about?' Stevens demanded in a voice reflecting his tension. 'Who the hell are you to make such threats? You're not talking to some fat-cat oil millionaire about a ransom for his nine-year-old daughter, you know. You're playing around with millions of lives, tens of millions of lives. This is no clever armored-car robbery or bank stickup, dammit. This could be World War III, maybe the end of civilization.'

'What civilization?'

'Now you listen to me. You're playing with something that's terribly dangerous – nuclear blackmail. That's what it is, Dell – nuclear blackmail.'

'Exactly – and you ought to know all about it, Mr President,' the fugitive with the film star's face replied. 'That's exactly what you and the righteous Russians have been doing to each other and the whole damn world for nearly twenty years. Well, we're following your example – only we're putting it on a paying basis. We're small-businessmen, so we're only asking for a small profit. Actually we're selling you this base and its missiles for a fraction of their cost – maybe twenty percent. It's our going-out-of-business sale, and you'd be a damn fool to miss it because it's never going to be repeated.'

'Major Dell, as a career Air Force officer and a SAC missile specialist you must have a fairly clear picture of what a nuclear war could do.'

The man in the Viper Three capsule ignored the appeal.

'Thirty-six hours, that's what you've got,' he warned. 'You'd be crazy not to buy at this price, and we're throwing in two slightly used SAC officers as a bonus – free. Buy the base, and get the missile crew without paying a single penny more. Any sensible businessmen would jump at such a bargain, and any economy-minded congressman would urge you to consider the great savings to the already burdened taxpayer.'

'Spare me the social satire, Major,' Stevens responded. 'I think you do better with the threats – as unrealistic as they are. Even if you consider this situation from a wholly selfish point of view, you must realize that World War III wouldn't improve your health either. You and your friends could end up just as charred as the women and children.'

'Balls – Mr President. We're down in a deep radiation-proof hole, and we can stay for two weeks after the war begins. The fire storms should be over by then and the radiation levels down by more than two thirds, and the devastation and confusion ought to make it a lot easier for five healthy, ruthless and well-armed men to escape. If any women or children or major contributors to your campaign get incinerated, it's going to be *your* fault. You can avoid the whole thing for a pittance, less than Americans spend on mouthwashes and deodorants in a day. Don't be cheap; it ruins your image as a great statesman.'

Stevens glanced across the room to Bonomi, shrugged.

'Major Dell,' he said slowly, 'I hope that we can talk this out rationally. One of my associates has suggested that you are, in effect, trying to mug the United States. The Government cannot and will not permit that. If we cannot prevent it by negotiation, we will have to consider using the enormous military strength and resources at our disposal. Despite what Senator Caldwell has been babbling during this campaign, we're still the greatest power on earth.'

'Now who's threatening?'

'This is no mere threat, Major. As Commander in Chief, I'll do what I have to do.'

'Get the money and the plane – that's what you have to do – and by eight P.M. tomorrow night.'

It wasn't going anywhere.

David Stevens knew that when a discussion – with the chairman of a Senate committee, the head of a foreign power or your wife – wasn't going anywhere it was often wise to recess before things got worse, to stop talking so that both sides could reflect and, hopefully, contemplate compromise.

'I'll think about what you've said,' he announced, 'and I'll get back to you later. I trust that you, as a reasonable man, will give serious consideration to what I've said, Major.'

Dell laughed.

'I'm *not* a reasonable man, Mr President. I'm a cashiered Air Force officer, a dishonored ex-gentleman, a convicted wife-killer and a hunted fugitive from the Death House. None of the rules – your rules, the old rules – apply to me anymore. I have no further stake in your system, the system that was going to kill me. Do you really think that we speak the same language?'

Now it was starting to slide downhill into bitterness, and the President realized that he had to stop this dangerous descent immediately.

'Discuss this with your friends,' he advised, 'and we can talk more about it later.'

He hung up the phone, turned to face his advisers.

'Not so good,' he admitted.

'The man's irrational, a mad dog!' Grosvenor declared angrily.

'You think he's a mad dog, Bill?'

The Attorney General shook his head.

'Not really. There are probably seven states where a man with his ideas and rhetoric could be elected Lieutenant Governor,' William Lee Frost estimated.

Michaelson puffed on his pipe, eyed the Secretary of Defense.

'Any way you look at it, this Dell is disturbed,' judged the CIA chief in a voice that was demurely pompous. 'Psychological testing should have screened him out a long time ago.

He'd never have been passed by *our* psychologists, I'll tell you that.'

Darby ignored the provocation.

'We'll have to dig them out,' he said to Crane. 'STRIKE alert battalions, tanks, short-range missiles, helicopter gunships.'

'Maybe those TAC fighter-bombers too,' the Chief of Air Staff thought aloud.

It was much less painful to talk about hardware than to face the fact that it was some flaw or flaws in his own service had made this crisis possible.

'Good try, Mr President,' Brigadier General Bonomi said consolingly. 'You know, I almost thought you had him with that man-to-man talk about fear and self-preservation. He sounded interested for a minute.'

'He's smart,' Stevens answered. 'He's not as witty as he thinks he is, but smart. And he's bitter-mean, nasty-mean. No, I don't think I was even close.'

'Good try though.'

'Good try but no brass ring, Vince,' said the Chief Executive of the United States.

His former wingman shrugged sympathetically.

'I think it may be time to move up the Army and the Air Force – just as a precaution,' announced the President.

'Very sensible,' confirmed the Secretary of Defense with a purposeful gleam in his eye – and then he started speaking rapidly. There was no trace of uncertainty or fear in his voice as he briskly explained the units, weapons and operations that he had in mind. He made an excellent presentation.

As he spoke, a blue ambulance escorted by a jeep and two light trucks filled with Air Police pulled up at the rear entrance to the base hospital at Malmstrom. A minute later, two orderlies carefully unloaded a stretcher.

'Don't drop him,' Captain Drew ordered. 'We had enough goddam trouble finding him out there in the fog, so don't drop him now.'

The Air Intelligence officer was irritable, tense and wet. The two-hour search along both sides of the highway had done that, and mopping his face with a handkerchief didn't help much.

'Get him inside, dammit,' Drew goaded.

The face of the man on the stretcher was puffed, bruised, streaked with caked blood. The orderlies carried the stretcher into the building, followed Drew to the third-floor door marked Isolation Ward. Armed guards flanked the entrance, but neither of the orderlies dared to comment on this unusual sight. This was obviously no time for casual conversation; Drew's entire manner had made that clear since the search force had left Malmstrom some 155 minutes earlier.

'Restricted area, sir,' one of the guards said.

'I know, I know. General Stonesifer's orders,' Drew replied curtly. 'The general wants this man inside,' he added with a nod toward the stretcher.

The AP nodded and opened the door to permit the orderlies to carry the injured man into the Isolation Ward.

'Who's he?' asked Dr Stanley Bigelman.

Dr Bigelman — a plump young captain who'd arrived at Malmstrom only a month earlier — hadn't been in the Air Force long enough to know that he wasn't supposed to question intelligence officers.

'Witkin — Lieutenant Harry O. Witkin,' Drew intoned. 'They'll be bringing up another man, a Sergeant Rienzi, in a minute.'

'What's wrong with this one — Witkin?'

'I think he's pregnant,' Drew snapped. 'For chrissakes, can't you see what's wrong with him?'

'No, I can't. I'm a doctor, not a magician. His face looks as if he went four rounds with Godzilla.'

'The rest of him looks even worse,' Drew answered. 'Lieutenant Witkin has been violently, viciously and illegally assaulted. He requires immediate medical attention. So does Rienzi. That's all I can tell you.'

Dr Bigelman nodded.

'Has this got anything to do with the other one you brought in earlier?' he asked as he leaned down to study Witkin's battered head and face.

'That's none of your business. You stick to the doctoring, and don't ask questions. I've already said that I can't talk about this case.'

Big shot, Bigelman thought. Big shot and his big deal.

133

Typical Air Force nonsense. Ridiculous. Nobody tells anybody anything, and nobody listens either. Stanley J. Bigelman M.D. had made it absolutely clear when he took the commission that he was interested in obstetrics and wanted to be stationed near Miami, where his brother Harold was practicing law. Instead these shmucks had sent him up to the frozen wastes of Montana. Some SAC efficiency. Some way to treat the top man in his class at Cornell Medical School.

Bigelman pulled down the sheet, pursed his lips to whistle.

'He's in worse shape than the other one,' he judged.

'Then fix him. Tender loving care is what he needs, Doctor,' Drew advised as he turned.

The intelligence officer left as Rienzi was carried in, and Bigelman had the orderlies put the new arrival on a treatment table in the next room. Bigelman was just starting to work on Witkin when he noticed the civilian resident from the Great Falls hospital watching from the doorway.

'I think this one goes with the other who came in with you,' Bigelman speculated. 'This one is a lieutenant named Witkin.'

'The other one is a captain named Kincaid,' Langer replied.

Bigelman worked on his patient for several minutes.

'You know what this is all about, Doctor?' he finally asked.

'Not really. Only a little of it. They told me not to speak about it – national security.'

Dr Captain Stanley Bigelman grunted.

'They say that about everything in SAC,' he complained. 'If a colonel has hemorrhoids, that's classified too.'

'This isn't hemorrhoids,' announced the blonde civilian nurse who was now standing beside Langer.

'And it isn't the work of Godzilla either,' Langer added.

The Air Force physician looked up, admired Miss Kelleran's fine figure and yellow hair and wondered whether she 'belonged' to the resident from Great Falls Municipal. No time for that now, the bespectacled captain concluded gloomily as he returned to the process of helping Witkin.

'You know there's something crazy going on here, Doctor?' he challenged Langer. 'They won't let anybody out of this ward, and they've closed off all phone calls out of the base. You know there's something really crazy going on here, don't you?'

Langer nodded and discreetly – when Bigelman wasn't watching – patted the blonde nurse with a certain reassuring but proprietary affection. He patted her exactly where gentlemen of taste and sensibility normally pat attractive young ladies with reassuring and proprietary affection, and Ann Kelleran was modestly reassured by this thoughtful gesture.

'Yes,' Langer answered, 'I know that there's something really crazy going on here – but I'd guess that General Stonesifer is the only one around here who knows what it is.'

'It's got something to do with an Indian – a red Indian,' said the nurse who was just a trifle annoyed at being ignored – treated like a second-class citizen by these men.

That seemed to catch Captain Bigelman's attention.

He'd been in SAC for only a few months, but he recognized the phrase.

'A red Indian and a viper,' Miss Kelleran explained triumphantly.

That *really* got his attention.

'Does she know what the hell she's talking about?' the Air Force physician asked.

'Generally – yes,' Langer admitted. 'In this case she – and I – don't know exactly what those words mean, but we heard Kincaid say them and we've heard he's a missile crewman. This red Indian and viper bit – is it *that* bad?'

Stanley Bigelman hesitated, wondered why he hadn't joined the Navy instead.

'Bad? I'll tell you how bad this could be,' he responded in grim tones. 'It's so bad that I can't tell you how bad it is. I don't *dare* to tell you how bad.'

'That bad?' wondered the nurse, who was getting a bit nervous about what she'd said.

'Worse,' Bigelman replied as he reached for the antiseptic once again.

It was sunny and lovely this time of the year down in Florida, he brooded, and the girls looked great on the beach in their bikinis. They would appreciate an intelligent young doctor who played good bridge and had graduated first in his class and had excellent prospects. Stanley J. Bigelman frowned as he considered the implications of what the nurse had reported, of Captain Drew's attitude and the sealing off of this ward and the whole base. You didn't have to be that smart, you didn't have to be the top man in your class to understand the implications of this thing.

This could ruin his entire medical career.

CHAPTER EIGHTEEN

There are certain kinds of things that certain kinds of people do well.

British journalists are absolutely tops in sneering at every aspect of American life, a skill acquired through generations of breeding, poor dental service and acute envy of the wage scales negotiated by the trade union that represents US reporters.

Danish girls are exceptionally gifted at simulating sexual acts, a talent on which an entire and highly profitable national film industry has been constructed.

China regularly produces top-notch table-tennis champions and mathematicians, and France is hard to beat at sauces, wines and obscure novelists – as well as dress designers. Germany excels in symphony conductors, brewmasters, airline stewardesses and people who were never Nazis, and India has this flair for borrowing money and increasing its population that cannot be denied. It is probably something in the soil that gives Spain pre-eminence in bullfighters, Cuba a lock on cigar rollers and Egypt such superiority in creative writers of military press releases. Russia has long been known for its ballet dancers, violinists and defectors. There are several Asian nations that have traditionally set the fashions in political invective, random diplomatic obscenity and arson, but they no longer dominate these fields so completely since American college students have made great strides in these sports in recent years.

The USA has also made considerable progress in another field of contemporary endeavor – cleaning up messes. Whether these are messes made by foreigners or American citizens, the US Government has developed the skills, organization, resources and cheery spirit that it takes to deliver one thousand tons of food and medicine to Mexican flood victims or to put ashore a Marine division in Lebanon. There is even one branch of the US armed forces that has been created especially for emergencies that require quick reaction, a euphemism for clearing up some mess that seems to demand rapid military intervention. Well, military *assistance*. It's the other side that does rotten things such as military *intervention*. This interservice US organization that stands ever vigilant to assist – with airborne battalions of paratroops, and task forces of cargo planes and fighter bombers – is familiarly known as STRIKE Command. If that name doesn't seem too familiar to you, it's certainly familiar to the residents of Tampa, Florida, since the global headquarters of STRIKE Command is located at nearby MacDill AFB. STRIKE is actually an acronym like CORE and WASP, and the public-information officer at MacDill would be quite happy to tell you that the name was created because this force is prepared to deliver Swift Tactical Reaction In Every Known Environment. This may seem like poor copywriting, but the Air Force can't compete with Madison Avenue salaries, so it makes do.

STRIKE Command has a lot of excellent radios and some wonderful plans and the authority to call upon certain US air, sea and land units that are maintained in a very high state of readiness. STRIKE also has some great quick-thinking and hard-nosed and clear-eyed staff officers, including a three-star USAF general named Kermit O. Warsaw who is the most quick-thinking and hard-nosed and clear-eyed of all. For more than thirteen months – that is, since he became the STRIKE commander, Lieutenant General K. O. Warsaw had been training and planning and running test exercises but there hadn't been any important crisis that required STRICOM (STRIKE Command) to call on CONARC for the STRAC troops or to assemble TAC C-130 transports and F-105s in a CASF – a composite air strike force.

Now – on this fine Sunday afternoon – it happened.

It wasn't as big as *it* might have been, but *it* was very clearly important and the Joint Chiefs had recognized that only STRICOM could handle this emergency. The JCS chairman himself had telephoned Warsaw from that 'war room' buried under the Pentagon and alerted him that something had 'hit the fan out in Montana' at a SAC base.

138

'It'll be banging in over your printer in about six minutes, K.O.,' the head of the Joint Chiefs of Staff predicted, 'but I wanted you to know first. This one comes right from the White House, and the security's so tight that only you and your Ops Director are supposed to know what the hell's happening. You'd better crank up your fire brigade fast, the Alert Battalion at Fort Lewis and a company of armor out of Hood. If Rucker can spare some gunships, you'd better get them moving north too.'

'This is no exercise?'

'Hell, no. The real thing. We may need a squadron of TAC fighters for a missile strike, and you tell them it's no game. Live ammo all the way. Solid gold.'

Solid gold was the current code phrase for nuclear warheads.

Only the President of the United States could authorize the use of such weapons.

'Did *he*—'

'He did,' the JCS chairman confirmed. 'I've got it in writing. You'll get the verification over your teleprinter circuit, all neat and official. You'd better move your butt, K.O.'

'Malmstrom?' Warsaw asked.

'Malmstrom. One more thing. We're probably dumping DEFCON Five in a couple of hours. I've recommended that we go to Four, just as a precaution, but the Secretary's dragging because he's afraid that the change in global alert status could get a lot of people nosy.'

'It would get me nosy,' admitted the general in Florida.

'Don't get nosy, K.O. – get cracking.'

Lieutenant General Kermit O. Warsaw assembled his key Plans and Ops commanders, and they were all at their stations in the MacDill h.q. seven minutes later when the orders clattered in over the Pentagon teleprinter circuit. When the message had been decoded a little later, STRICOM began sending out its own messages over the direct lines to the Tactical Air Command and the Continental Army Command. The Alert Battalion of paratroopers at Fort Lewis in Washington (not DC) began loading its assault gear into trucks, and the maintenance crews at the nearby airfield finished pumping fuel into the big transports. Down in Texas, even bigger transport planes opened their yawning cargo doors for medium tanks and klaxons were sounding at a fighter squadron headquarters on a Nevada air base.

A stream of coded instructions flowed from MacDill over the excellent communications network created for just this purpose, and men and weapons started to move toward the USAF base near Great Falls, Montana. The men had no idea as to why they were going to Malmstrom, and the officers whom they asked didn't know either. Some of these captains and majors considered asking a colonel or a general, but when they warily questioned the senior officers it turned out that they couldn't or wouldn't say. All that anybody knew was that the orders had come from STRIKE Command and that it wasn't a test or swift-reaction exercise.

'You'll find out when you get to Malmstrom' was the most that anyone would offer.

And while the greatest military power on earth prepared to raise its mailed fist, five defiant criminals in a hole in the ground were focussed on a small red metal box. They had finished discussing Dell's conversation with the President, and now they were concentrating on the problem of getting physical possession of the firing keys that were in the safe on the wall. To be precise, Falco, Powell and the ex-major were focussed fully on this but moist Harvey Schonbacher was still pouting and sulking about having been forced to clean up the vomit and Deacon Hoxey was off somewhere in a better world where there was an enormous amount of cleanliness and Christian piety, a wonderful sense of pervasive guilt but none of those awful nightmares – and unlimited numbers of blue-eyed virgins who never exposed their legs and always sang psalms in perfect soaring twelve-part harmony.

Marvin Hoxey genuinely hungered for a better world, certainly one better than the miserable one he'd known. He was the son of an alcoholic Arkansas farmer and the slightly feeble-minded daughter of a small-town grocer, a rather sweet woman who'd turned to the Lord very early in a married life dominated by poverty, migraine headaches and beatings at least three times a week. Marvin Hoxey's older sister, Linda Lou, could not be considered a sweet woman by the most charitable of Christians, however, and had last been heard of working as a $10 prostitute in Hot Springs or was it Fort Smith? She was a living blue-eyed symbol of the terrible sin that tormented her boney brother so mercilessly, that sent him reeling from religious sect to religious sect on an anguished quest that finally convinced him that all clergymen were mealy-mouthed hypocrites who were 'soft on evil' and unwilling to punish sinners with the hell-fire and damnation they deserved. So Hoxey drifted into his own fiery faith, selling Bibles from door to door and occasionally burning a church or two when the Lord told him to. Unlike a lot of other people, Marvin 'Deacon' Hoxey meant to do only good. Like a lot of other people, he did a great deal of harm and refused to admit it.

Harvey Schonbacher certainly refused to admit – even to himself – that he'd done a great deal of harm. Even at his trial, he had primly pointed out that he was a licensed pharmacist and a college graduate and a native son of Helena – and men such as that simply don't go around raping and stabbing. Why, Harvey Schonbacher was a respected forty-two-year-old taxpayer who always flew the flag on the Fourth of July, wore a clean shirt every day and gave to both the Red Cross and the Community Fund – and he never stocked any of those obscene paperback books in his drugstore. It wasn't actually *his* store – he managed it for his uncle – but that hardly mattered. What mattered was that people had always been jealous of his good grades and intelligence and business sense, and some of those envious ones had mocked his weight and spread lies about his private life. Under normal circumstances, a pillar of the community such as Harvey Schonbacher would have retained a good trial lawyer and that counsel might have gotten him off with six to ten years for involuntary manslaughter. But his uncle had refused to advance a penny for legal fees after discovering the doctored ledgers and the missing $2,880, so Harvey Schonbacher had been defended by a rather inexperienced attorney and convicted of first-degree murder. It was true that he'd always been clumsy and unsuccessful with girls, but he staunchly denied his guilt on these heinous criminal charges – three rapes and a homicide – even after they put him in the Death House.

'My conscience is clean,' he swore in a letter appealing to Governor Wilcox for clemency.

And it was too, despite three rapes and a murder.

He had a wash-and-wear conscience.

He refused to face who and what he was, and continued to reassure himself that he was a misunderstood but superior person suffering from the enmity of the less intelligent, the less successful, the less respectable. One court psychiatrist had concluded that Schonbacher was psychotic and the other leaned in favor of paranoia, but since they couldn't get together they finally found a middle ground in their mutual dislike of the accused and wrote a report that concluded he was 'legally sane' because he 'probably understood' what he'd been doing. There are some very sound people in the state of Montana, perhaps not as hip as those glib Easterners and maybe a bit unsophisticated in appreciating contemporary films and foreign wines – but quite practical in a way that Barry Goldwater would understand even if Dustin Hoffman wouldn't.

Actually, Schonbacher wasn't that difficult to understand. Impossible to like, but not that hard to understand. Dell understood and disliked him, but was much too busy at the moment to waste any time contemplating the grimy personality problems of his unpleasant associate.

'I don't think we've got too much time now,' he said to Powell, and the former Marine nodded in comprehension.

'Time before what?' wondered Falco.

'Before they come,' the black man replied.

'They'll be coming all right. It may take them an hour or three, maybe five at the most,' Dell predicted, 'but they'll be coming. They won't just roll over simply because we threatened them. They'll react.'

'They always react,' Powell confirmed.

'Who the hell is *they*?'

Dell sighed.

'Stud, *they* is the big brass – the big boys, the generals and the top civilians, the people who advise the President on big decisions such as this,' he explained. 'They're not used to being pushed, and they're not about to give in to five convicts without some kind of a struggle. They've got a lot of muscle, a lot of power – military power that cost two or three hundred billion dollars to put together, and a record of not being too reluctant to use it whenever they feel justified.'

'And they're probably sore as hell,' judged the assassin.

'Yes, but they're not stupid – despite what the college kids say. They may not be the brightest bunch in the world, but they're not the dumbest either. They'll try to figure out some stunt – some sneaky trick, and then they'll hit us.'

'That's why we need the keys,' said Powell.

'Isn't that right, Major?' he challenged a moment later. 'Or don't you trust us with the keys? We were good enough to help you break out and then to take this place, but maybe you wouldn't want to share the control of those precious keys with us? We're just a bunch of cons, and you're—'

'Stick it,' the former SAC officer interrupted.

'The major gave an order – my, my.'

'I said stick it, Willieboy, and if you don't know where I'll show you.'

'Show him later,' urged Falco. 'Let's get those goddam keys now.'

The Negro opened his mouth, but Falco wouldn't let him continue the argument.

'Later for you too. You can do your whole number – including the Gettysburg Address and the birdcalls – later, okay?'

Powell glared, finally shrugged in acquiescence.

'Okay, Larry, now it's your turn,' said the underworld executioner. 'How about getting the combination from your buddy?'

Dell walked to the bunk where Captain Sanford Towne watched.

'You all right, Sandy?'

The yellow-haired prisoner didn't answer.

'You'll be all right,' Dell predicted. 'Just take it easy, and you'll be home in bed with your wife in a day or two. It'll all be over in a day or so, and we'll be on our way.'

Towne remained silent.

'You heard what I explained to the President, didn't you?

It's simple enough. Just a simple reverse on the advertisements. Pay now and fly later.'

'He won't buy it, Larry,' Towne replied.

Then the young captain saw the tension in the faces of the others.

'Of course *you* knew he wouldn't buy it, Larry,' Towne continued craftily. 'You've had enough experience to understand that. What did you bring *them* here for?'

Dell recognized the tactic.

'Oh, the captain's being clever.'

'Larry,' Towne pressed in a lowered, confidential tone, 'why in the world did you bring them here? You trying to make some sort of deal for yourself?'

Powell and Schonbacher were staring suspiciously, and the amused look on Falco's face was the same one the assassin had worn after machine-gunning the Air Policeman through the window.

'Maybe you *could* buy yourself a pardon by turning them in,' Towne speculated.

'You're getting to be a pain in the ass, Sandy,' sighed the former major.

'I think he's trying to split us up,' Falco estimated. 'What do you call it – divide and conquer?'

Dell nodded.

'He's very clever, Stud, and very patriotic.'

'Shit, I know the words to "The Star-Spangled Banner" myself – but this is money. This is big money, and my ass too. Let's stop all this crapping around, Larry. Either he gives us the combination or we hurt him till he does. It worked with those guys in the station wagon.'

The man with the movie star's face shook his head.

'No, not him. It won't work with him.'

'What is he, some kind of a fanatic?' Falco wondered.

'Worse than that. He's the son of a general. He really believes in mom's apple pie and the Stars and Stripes and the honor of the US Air Force. A born hero, that's our Sandy.'

The assassin's brow furrowed.

'I didn't know there were any of those left, Larry,' he muttered.

The former Deputy Intelligence Officer of the 168th pointed at Towne.

'He's one of them. There aren't too many, but he's one of them.'

Falco turned to the ex-Marine.

'Yes,' Powell confirmed, 'there are some like that. I saw them in Vietnam. They were ready to die, and some of them did.'

'And some came home with the Navy Cross,' Dell added.

The black man looked at him angrily, wondering how he'd found out about the medal. Willieboy Powell hadn't told any of these men about that Navy Cross or the two wounds that preceded it. Falco saw the glare, guessed.

'You got the Navy Cross?' he asked admiringly.

'I got athlete's foot and a sixty-five Ford too. So what?'

Falco would not be deflected.

'That's something, Willie, the Navy Cross.'

That bastard Dell, Powell brooded.

That tricky bastard would do anything to show how smart he was.

'What about the keys, Major?' he demanded brusquely.

'I'm thinking.'

'Can we bust the safe open?' suggested Falco. 'Maybe we don't have time for all this deep thinking, and maybe there's something in that toolbox we could use.'

'And maybe the safe's booby-trapped,' the ex-sergeant added.

Yes, bitter as he was Powell was the best of them, Dell thought again.

'Maybe we ought to get out of here?' Schonbacher asked suddenly.

'Shut up, Harvey,' Dell replied.

'No, I won't. I heard what you were all saying. The Government's going to send troops to attack us, some kind of sneak attack. They'll *creep up* on us and wipe us out.'

'Nobody's going to *creep up* on us.'

'I don't believe you, Larry,' challenged the rapist. 'They'll try something tricky. I say let's get out of here before they catch us by surprise.'

'How are we going to do that, Harve?' Powell asked softly.

'The Air Force station wagon. With a little luck and those uniforms, we might make the Canadian border in a few hours. It's only a hundred and fifty miles. We could claim political asylum – or say we're against the draft.'

'You against the draft, Stud?' Dell asked wryly.

'Hell, no – I told you I was patriotic. I'm against Harve though,' the underworld executioner added cheerfully. 'That's because he's chicken and he's stupid. Nothing political. He's getting on my nerves.'

'What do you think we ought to do about Harve?' questioned the former major.

'Maybe we ought to drown him in the toilet,' Falco responded.

Schonbacher stepped back defensively.

'You don't scare me. I say this place is a trap,' he defied.

'You think we ought to drown Harve in the toilet, Willie?' Dell asked.

'No, we're going to need the toilet.'

'Very sensible, Sergeant. Now listen, Harve, and listen carefully. We couldn't get two hundred yards now, because – beyond any doubt – there are Air Police up there surrounding this whole base. They'll have the highway blocked too,' Dell explained. 'Beyond any doubt. I'll show you.'

He walked to the Crew Commander's chair, flicked a switch. A small glass panel built into the console – it was perhaps three inches by five – glowed, and a moment later the fugitives were looking at the area between the Viper Three guardhouse and the front gate.

'All the comforts of home. Closed-circuit TV,' announced the man who'd handled launch-site security for the 168th. 'A little extra something so guests can't drop in unexpectedly. It rotates too – if I turn this other dial.'

'Then why didn't they see *us* coming in?' Schonbacher demanded.

Now the black Marine veteran looked at him pityingly.

Maybe Falco's idea was sound.

It might be worth giving up the toilet.

'The crew didn't see us because of the fog and rain,' Dell reasoned, 'or maybe they didn't have it on.'

He started to rotate the control knob, and after a few seconds stopped.

'There. See that? There's somebody over there – on the left – just outside the fence. . . . And there's some more of them,' he pointed out after he'd turned the camera another forty degrees.

'I can't make them out in this drizzle – just figures, that's all,' complained the rapist. 'How do you know they're Air Police?'

'Oh shit, Harve,' scorned Falco, 'who the hell else would be hanging around out there in this weather? It sure isn't the Great Falls Chamber of Commerce, you idiot.'

'Maybe they're Indians,' Dell suggested. 'After all, this used to be Flathead country, as I recall. Maybe the Flatheads are rising again. You keep an eye on them, Harve, while Stud and Willie and I work on the keys.'

With Schonbacher occupied and out of the way, the three men returned to the problem of the safe.

Logically.

They could torture Towne, but it was extremely unlikely that he'd tell.

There was no point in hurting the lieutenant, because he didn't know the combination and no matter how loudly he screamed Towne wasn't about to betray the keys just to save his deputy. Maybe this sort of thing worked in the pre-1950 movies, but that sort of compassion wouldn't move a resolute patriot such as Captain Sanford Towne in the grim 1970s.

Towne was the tougher of the two, but only Canellis could be broken.

'Wait a minute, wait a minute – there has to be a back-up system in case something happens to the Crew Commander,' Dell recalled. 'Right, an emergency procedure. The Deputy Crew Commander doesn't have the combination, but he knows where to find it if the Crew Commander goes crazy or drops dead of a heart attack. It's written down somewhere, maybe in one of those.'

He gestured toward eight fat loose-leaf binders on a shelf, each bulging with at least one hundred printed pages of technical instructions, standing orders or maintenance procedures.

'Or maybe somewhere else,' he admitted.

'Larry, I think you'd better let me reason with this kid,' Falco proposed. 'I could get it done a lot faster. The people I work with run into this problem all the time, and they've got ways to lean on guys – nasty ways that work. Of course the guys they lean on this way may never be the same again,' he continued in a voice loud enough for Canellis to hear, 'but usually they dump what's left in a lime pit or maybe shove the leftovers into one of those big compressors that squeeze car bodies into scrap.'

Dell nodded his assent, and the assassin moved across the chamber to the lower bunk where the lieutenant lay listening. Powell and the ex-SAC officer saw him lean over to speak softly to the Bostonian.

They couldn't hear what he said, but they saw the shock on Canellis' face. After some thirty seconds, Falco walked back to join them.

'You got a screwdriver in that tool kit?' he asked casually.

Then he winked, and Dell translated instantly.

'Sure, Stud,' he answered, 'and there's a good pair of pliers too.'

Falco found the tools, hefted them.

'Going to be some bleeding,' he announced in the matter-of-fact tones of the women who tape the weather reports for the telephone company.

'First-aid kit on the wall,' the former major responded with a nod.

'Fine, fine. Would you get it, Willieboy?' requested the assassin. 'With all your combat experience, I'd bet you know something about tourniquets and that sort of jazz. Of course, you can't tourniquet an eye – but you'll think of something.'

As Powell opened the metal box, Falco returned to the double-decker bunk and said something more to the lieutenant. Canellis replied with a terse obscenity that had no effect at all.

'Okay, he'll probably look good with a dog anyway,' Falco said.

Then he pulled a cigarette lighter from his pocket, flicked the switch and carefully seared the metal tip of the screwdriver with the blue-edged butane flame. A moment later, he stood up and plunged the screwdriver into Towne's right shoulder. The

148

captain in the upper bunk screamed in shock and pain, then screamed again.

'I'll finish the left one next,' Falco promised as he showed Canellis the red-stained tip of the tool.

'Under the seat! Under the seat of the Crew Commander's chair!' the younger officer cried out shrilly.

Dell crouched down, looked and found the small envelope taped beneath the bottom. He tore it, extracted the file card and carried it to the safe.

Captain Towne was still gasping and moaning and Lieutenant Canellis was cursing and raging, but Dell ignored all this to concentrate on dialing the combination. 8 R, 27 L, 16 L, 11 R.

Click.

The door opened under his tug, and there were the two stainless-steel keys.

'Very good, Stud,' Dell complimented. '*Very* good. You certainly have a way with people.'

'Bastard!' shouted Canellis.

Powell was busy with the injured captain, ripping open the coveralls and pulling down the right side – tugging urgently. Then he jerked Towne half up, twisted at the crimson stained sleeve and finally exposed the gashed shoulder.

'He'll live, nothing serious,' judged the ex-Marine as he tied the tourniquet.

'You blinded him, you bastard!' screamed the lieutenant.

Falco smiled broadly, wiped the screwdriver on his trouser leg.

'I told the kid I was going to poke old Sandy's eyes out,' the underworld executioner confided. 'I figured that might shake him up pretty good, you know.'

'You're a real psychologist, Stud,' Powell said sardonically, 'but not much of a surgeon.'

'I never actually went to medical school,' Falco responded, 'but I watch all those doctor shows on TV.'

He looked down at Canellis again.

'Listen, kid, I just stuck it into his shoulder to get the holler and the blood,' he explained. 'I didn't take his eye out. Just a little hole and a lot of blood.'

Dell nodded in confirmation.

'Scout's honor, sonny,' he vowed. 'You didn't really think that Mr Falco would do a terrible and barbarous thing such as that, did you?'

'That's for weirdos,' Falco declared. 'I'm no bishop, but I'm no weirdo.'

Now the impact of what he'd done hit Canellis, and he moaned.

'Mr Falco does not go around maiming people,' Dell continued. 'He may kill a few now and then – but only in the course of his business. He's one of those backbone-of-America small businessmen, asking no special favors or subsidies from the Government. He's not one of those dirty long-haired bomb throwers.'

'He even makes a point of tearing the excise stamps when he opens a pack of cigarettes,' Powell contributed as he finished the tourniquet.

The lieutenant was shuddering and making gasping noises that indicated he might be on the verge of tears.

'And I don't litter either – or throw rocks at cops,' Falco announced, 'and I don't bad-mouth my country.'

'It's the Eastern liberal press that's given Stud such a terrible reputation,' Dell declared solemnly. 'All those sneaky radicals who resent his old-fashioned American patriotism.'

'Larry,' Captain Towne called.

Dell took the keys from the safe, held them aloft.

'Rest easy, Sandy,' he advised. 'Nobody's going to hurt either of you. As I once said to the lovely daughter of the British ambassador, just lean back and relax.'

'Put them back in the safe,' pleaded the Crew Commander.

Dell glanced up, saw Powell and Falco and Schonbacher eying him earnestly. Then he noticed Hoxey staring from the doorway, wearing that same look of suspicious concern. No, Dell couldn't relock the keys in the safe if he wanted to – not unless he wanted to risk his command and probably his life.

'You going to put the keys back in the safe?' the ex-Marine asked with his hand resting on his gun.

Dell flashed his best, warm, fake smile with all those good teeth.

'Don't be silly,' he chuckled suitably as he dropped both keys in his coverall pocket. 'What am I, a damn fool?'

'I say we're all damn fools to stay here,' grumbled Harvey S. Schonbacher. 'Keys or no keys, I say let's make a run for the border.'

Even as the sex murderer whined and fretted on, Lawrence Dell could see that Powell wasn't satisfied. The black man had noticed his moment of hesitation in deciding, and Willieboy Powell would be watching and waiting. His distrust was plain, almost tangible, and the only thing that might dissolve it would be to give him one of the keys.

No.

The former Deputy Intelligence Officer of the 168th wasn't ready to do that, to take that chance.

What chance?

It was difficult to say, but it was a chance and Dell hated to take more than were necessary. No complications – that was his slogan.

Schonbacher was still arguing that Viper Three would be a trap when Captain R. V. Gunderson, Jr, punched 'Yamschik' into the CIA computer-retriever in the basement of a huge building in Virginia. The basement itself was enormous, and the $29,000,000 computer-retriever and its display screens were the largest that the Radio Corporation of America made. If there was any other reference to or data on an operation named 'Yamshchik' in the vast microfilmed CIA files, it would be projected on that three-by-five-foot screen within two minutes. To get a print-out in the form of a six-by-nine-inch photocopy, Gunderson would simply press the orange button marked 'print' and he'd have it within ninety seconds. It was a very costly but efficient piece of technology, but all it produced this afternoon was the fact that the National Security Agency – the code-breaking and electronic eavesdropping branch of the US intelligence community – had overheard some six previous references to 'Yamschik' during the previous month. Now NSA reported four more in a single evening, but still no clue as to what the operation behind the code name might be.

Whatever it was, 'Yamschik' was heating up rapidly.

Captain R. V. Gunderson, Jr, would have to mention that in his morning report, he decided, for there was always the chance that it might be something important.

CHAPTER NINETEEN

'Of course, the data isn't conclusive and it's somewhat unsatisfactory working solely with secondhand sources,' Dr E. Z. Pinney said in the soft accents of Atlanta.

'Definitely unsatisfactory, Mr President,' ratified Dr Helen Osgood.

These were Michaelson's people. The CIA Director had recommended the baby-faced Georgian and the tall woman with the good legs as 'the best in the business' – which might not be saying too much as it was a rather specialized business. The two doctors – both in their late thirties, General Bonomi estimated – were staff psychoanalysts attached to the Central Intelligence Agency, but they didn't treat CIA personnel. No, they spent their time preparing 'personality profiles' of key foreign political and military leaders. They went over every article and interview, every film clip and radio tape about a 'subject' – devoting months to a single man or woman before submitting a lengthy and detailed estimate of the personality and what it might do in certain types of situations or crises. Stevens remembered their remarkably accurate 'profile' of the Polish Prime Minister.

'Working at this speed is quite a gamble,' Pinney pointed out in a tone that was modest without being apologetic, 'since the job ought to take – well, a lot more than three hours.'

'Instant salvation isn't our bag,' said the sensible woman, 'and we really can't tell how sound or comprehensive the diagnoses of those Montana court psychiatrists were. They're almost all we have to go on, Mr President.'

Cleveland, Stevens guessed. It was after six P.M. and he was both tired and hungry, but he speculated that she came from either Cleveland or Akron.

'Excuse me, Dr Osgood,' Stevens apologized, 'but you're from Cleveland, aren't you?'

The tall woman smiled pleasantly.

'Akron, Mr President.'

'Sorry to interrupt what you were saying,' the man with the last traces of a champagne headache replied.

She nodded to her colleague, who was presumably the senior in either age or Civil Service rank.

'Dr Pinney has some thoughts about this Falco,' she said by way of introduction.

She was smart but not pushy.

Not aggressive, to use her own terminology.

Not passive either, and – as the ring on her left hand indicated – married.

Perhaps a mother.

What would it be like to have a CIA psychoanalyst as your mother? Stevens wondered.

'Would you like some more coffee?' Bonomi asked.

He was still flying wingman, still protecting a weary David Stevens.

'No thanks, Vince. Please proceed, Dr Pinney.'

'James Falco would appear to be a glossy modern version of the classic criminal psychopath,' the Georgian began in placid, measured tones. 'That means – in the simplest of terms – that he either doesn't know or doesn't care about right or wrong. Actually, such considerations don't occur to him. Some criminal psychopaths are filled with a rage-hostility toward everyone and erupt in violent acts – indiscriminate violent acts – against other individuals or society in general.'

'The Texas sniper?' Stevens suggested.

'Exactly, Mr President. Yes, that sort may explode in an apparently unpremeditated orgy of pointless homicide. James Falco is not that sort. If the police records and the trial summary are correct, Falco has killed a number of people but always on a "contract" and always for money. What's more, he's only killed members or former members of some organized criminal group. He's never shot a policeman or a bank guard, which might reflect an attitude or perhaps just very careful planning on his part. Despite his notorious and compulsive

154

sexual activities, Stud Falco is neither indiscriminate nor undisciplined.'

'Even after he kills, he never steals from the victim – not even when he has plenty of time,' the other analyst noted.

'That's correct,' Pinney continued smoothly. 'He's no thief. There's an unsubstantiated report that he may have worked with a team of safecrackers ten or twelve years ago when he was only twenty-four, but for at least seven or eight years he's been as assassin for hire. The police talk about sixteen or seventeen murders he may have done, but it could just as easily have been thirty. That's one of the incongruities in this personality. Falco has no trade-mark, no standard way of killing. No M.O., as they say on television. He's quite resourceful, shaping his tactics to each situation. In New York, he's supposed to have murdered a man with a sniper rifle and in New Orleans they believe he used a bomb wired to the ignition of the victim's Cadillac.'

'That man was a narcotics dealer – a wholesaler who'd been cheating his importer,' the woman from Akron filled in tidily. 'Falco himself is not known to use drugs. He does drink, but rather little when he's working.'

'And when he's not working he relaxes in resort areas such as Las Vegas or Puerto Rico where he can gamble,' the Atlantan continued, 'but he never plays for large sums. He goes to those places for the sun and the women, show girls or hat-check girls or sometimes call girls. His sexual appetites are extraordinary, and the nickname Stud would appear to be wholly justified. One might speculate that these unusual drives are related to his childhood, of course. He had no mother. To be more precise, his mother died in childbirth and his father was crippled in a construction accident three years later. Falco was sent to live with an aunt in Buffalo, but he ran away when he was eleven and again at thirteen. He was in a school for wayward or incorrigible boys for four years, and then escaped. After that he worked for some numbers racketeers in Philadelphia, and we don't know anything more for certain until he was arrested in a stolen car in Youngstown in 1958. He jumped bail, disappeared. In 1961 he did the same thing in Phoenix when he was arrested for carrying an unlicensed revolver.'

Stevens sighed.

'That's all interesting, but what is this man likely to do *now* – in this situation?' he asked.

'Whatever he thinks will best suit his comfort and survival. He's only served two years behind bars – for assault – and while he was a model prisoner, presumably to impress the Parole Board, he told the warden on leaving that he'd never serve another term in any prison.'

'Would he launch those missiles?'

'Yes, Mr President, he is capable of doing that – for his own comfort or survival. This man has no connections, no identity. He's nothing like the standard Mafia stereotype you read about in the papers. He has no religious feelings, no link to any particular Cosa Nostra "family", no loyalties, no fixed residence. Yet we hear that he has a good sense of humor, spends freely, is generous with his women and gets along easily. He has no free-floating hostility toward society – since he seems to be outside society – but he doesn't really care about anyone else.'

'Not vicious but deadly?' Bonomi asked.

'You could say that, General,' Pinney agreed. 'It might be linked to an Oedipal fixation caused by deprivation of his mother at—'

'Never mind, Doctor,' the President interrupted. 'What about his father or other relatives? Would they have any influence with him?'

'His father died in 1967, and Falco hasn't had anything to do with the others in years. Maybe I haven't made myself clear. This man *has no family*, not even the Family of Man. I don't know whether you read contemporary fiction, Mr President, but Falco is the ultimate in alienation. He's a mobile lone wolf, sort of a hit-and-run driver for hire who kills and drives on without a care in the world. To quote his own words, he believes "strictly in Number One" – and in keeping his commitments to his employers. When he takes a contract to kill someone and accepts the down payment, he always delivers.'

'Professional pride?' wondered Bonomi.

'Probably, but self-preservation too.'

'Powell?'

'Very different, Mr President. Perhaps Dr Osgood would want to comment on him.'

They had quite a neat little routine, working like a veteran night-club act and sharing the spotlight with a smooth dignity that had to be admired.

'Willieboy Justice Powell,' the woman began, 'is one of seven children. Yes, Justice is actually his middle name. His mother was a cleaning woman in the Baltimore municipal court building. His father worked in a hospital garage, still does. Powell is a high-school graduate with good grades, and he was an excellent athlete. Captain of the football team and – this is interesting – president of the chess club. As a matter of fact, he helped found the chess club.'

'And he writes *haiku* poetry?'

'No, General, not that we know of. But he had the IQ and the academic skills that would have made him college material,' she emphasized, 'and he wanted to go. He wanted to make it inside the System. No money though. This was back before it became fashionable for colleges to give scholarships to bright blacks – so he joined the Marine Corps. He did two hitches, saved his money and built an impressive combat record on a tour in Vietnam. Two Purple Hearts and a Navy Cross. He was a sergeant – a very good sergeant. The man who was his company commander out there – I got him on the phone in Quantico about an hour ago – says that he was one of the best, aside from his attitude toward officers. Powell didn't like officers; he was courteous to them but they could tell that he resented them.'

'Why?' asked the President.

Dr Osgood shrugged.

'Nobody seems to be sure. In terms of intelligence and leadership skills, he seems to have been officer material himself – even if he didn't go to college. Perhaps he felt he was as good or better than they were, or perhaps it was some submerged racial feelings about being ordered around by whites – or perhaps it was just some entirely personal problems with authority.'

'Powell has some history of resenting authority,' the Georgian reported, 'and a need to make his own decisions. Even back at high school, when the coach sent in plays Powell didn't always use them.'

Stevens frowned.

'How did you get all this in a few hours, Doctor?'

'Mr President, the Agency has had ninety people doing research on these five men from the minute the Director left you. The entire Special Projects Unit at our R. and A. group has been mobilized.'

Yes, you could count on Evan Michaelson to do that sort of thing.

'Please go ahead, Dr Osgood.'

Powell had left the Marine Corps in sixty-eight, started college in Helena on the GI Bill and quit at the end of his freshman year. He'd married a secretary, taken a job as an auto mechanic. It wasn't clear why he'd dropped out of school. It had not been any academic difficulties, for all his grades were A or B. In 1969, he'd become the father of a son and received a $25 a week raise. In 1970, his appreciative employer had given Willieboy Powell another raise in recognition of his good work. All this was known, but nobody was certain why the ex-Marine had been in *that* bar *that* night. The trial transcript indicated that the man Powell had killed, a welder named Rex Oppen, had a reputation as a brawler and the Negro had sworn that Oppen started the fight. The jury apparently believed the testimony of Oppen's two drinking companions – one a city fireman – and convicted Powell of murder.

Powell was not known as a heavy drinker.

He had no criminal record.

He'd apparently never been in that bar before.

He'd told the court psychiatrist that he expected to face an all-white jury and to be convicted, and he had been convicted by an all-white jury.

'Of course there aren't many blacks in Helena, Montana,' Dr Osgood added factually.

The President shook his head, twice.

'At the risk of sounding cold if not cruel, it hardly matters at this moment whether the jury was right or wrong,' he said slowly. 'Justice always matters and social discrimination always matters, of course, but right now I can't even feel indignant or sorry. What matters, I'm afraid, is whether Willieboy Powell thinks he got a fair trial and how this may affect him. What matters is what this bitterness might do to his decisions, his attitudes toward one question.'

'I can't give you an absolute answer,' she replied. 'Only Willieboy Powell knows. He resents authority, distrusts what some people call the Establishment and believes that it has unjustly condemned him to be executed – probably for reasons that are largely racist. He's no psychopath like Falco or holy madman like Hoxey, but he ended up in the same Death House with those two. He has reasons to want to get even – all the reasons that a lot of minority people have – plus some others that are his very own.'

'You're not saying that all Negroes would launch those missiles,' Stevens summarized, 'but you're suggesting that this particular black man – this complex individual – might be capable of doing it?'

'That's the crux of it, Mr President,' she confirmed as she crossed those sleek legs. 'He's angry enough to do it. He was a good warrior and he killed for his country and got medals for it, and now he believes that he's being crucified for the accidental slaying of one barroom brawler. I'm not apologizing for Powell, you understand.'

'We understand,' interjected Bonomi, 'or at least we're trying to understand. I don't think that the President has to defend his—'

'Never mind, Vince. This is no time for campaign speeches on human dignity and civil rights. I don't care whether either of the doctors vote for me.'

'Mr President,' she protested, 'I didn't mean anything like that.'

He almost yawned. He was that tired.

'Dr Osgood, there are times when the President or the head of any country may find himself compelled to be some sort of a son of a bitch,' David Stevens confessed, 'but I'm not that kind of a son of a bitch.'

'I don't think you're a son of a bitch at all,' she said calmly, 'but I wanted to make it clear that I don't think that Willieboy Powell is a son of a bitch either. Nor is he a hero, not anymore.'

'There aren't many left, except on television,' said Bonomi.

'We only need a couple, Vince, just a couple. Let's get back to Powell. What sort of appeals or pressures might reach him, Doctor?'

She considered for fifteen or twenty seconds.

'Perhaps his wife and son,' she suggested tentatively.

Then she reconsidered.

'Yes, perhaps he'd be moved by them,' she reasoned, 'so perhaps he'd respond to them – depending on how you mean to use them. Are you contemplating some appeal by them to him, or do you mean to use them as hostages?'

Stevens blinked.

'Are you kidding, Doctor? Do you really think that I'd hold a woman and a two-and-a-half-year-old child as hostages?' he asked.

'It's a great idea,' Bonomi mocked. 'We could torture them, and let Powell hear the screams over the phone.'

'Cut it, Vince. . . . Dr Osgood, do you really believe I'd do that?'

She was totally unintimidated.

'Your humanitarian attitudes are well known, Mr President,' she acknowledged calmly, 'but I assumed that you would do whatever the President of the United States had to do to protect the nation – the two hundred and seven million citizens of all ages, sexes, colors and ideologies – from annihilation. It may be unpleasant at times, but the Chief of State is primarily responsible for the many – especially their lives. I'm sure you know that, Mr President.'

'Of course making such decisions is never easy,' soothed her colleague, 'but that goes with the assumption of power. The electorate presumably views the President as an all-wise and resolute father image and is delighted to leave these difficult matters in his capable hands. If the larger-than-life father has to do something tough or ruthless to preserve the family, the family would rather not share the responsibility for such acts – even though these were necessary acts. The President does what he must do, and if he's prudent he'll probably tell as few people as possible.'

Beyond any doubt, these were Michaelson's people.

'How long have you been with the CIA?' Stevens asked him.

'Four years last June, just eleven months longer than Dr Osgood. We were both on the staff at Austin Riggs up in Stockbridge, Massachusetts before that, and I was at St Elizabeth's here in Washington before that.'

At that moment, Bonomi interrupted to point out that it was 6:50 and the President would probably want to eat dinner soon – an exit cue that both Stevens and the CIA pair welcomed discreetly. The President needed a break after all these hours of intense pressure, and the two physicians were getting hungry.

'Can you be back at 9:30 to resume the briefing,' the general asked them, 'or would you rather have dinner here?'

Dr Osgood shook her head, smiled maternally.

'I'd rather eat with the children,' she said sweetly. 'Sunday evening, Sunday dinner – it's a family custom.'

The two psychoanalysts were almost at the door when Stevens asked his last question.

'Dr Osgood, I don't mean to pry but I'm curious as to what sort of work your husband does.'

She smiled again, quite pleasantly.

'Why, he's an analyst too – with the Agency,' she answered as she took Dr E. Z. Pinney's arm with an unmistakable intimacy.

Stevens and Bonomi exchanged glances when the door closed behind the departing visitors.

'They're probably very decent, Vince, and nobody's saying that about you, General.'

His former wingman chuckled.

'Hell no, Mr President. I'm one of those ruthless butchers in the heartless military establishment who spends all his time polluting the environment and abusing nonwhites and people with long hair, sir. My hobby is trampling flower beds, you know.'

Stevens' mind returned to what the analysts had said.

'Those nice serious people – the ones who think that the President of the United States ought to be capable of anything, including infanticide and cannibalism – may have given us a lead, Vince.'

'Powell's wife and child?'

Stevens nodded.

'I wouldn't count on it, Dave. I'm not very big on Dr Freud myself, and maybe Willieboy isn't either.'

The President began to pace.

'Vince, this isn't a question of psychoanalytic theory,' he reasoned. 'What else did those doctors give us? Schonbacher is a self-pitying horror and moral incompetent who's basically a weakling, not a policy maker or a leader in any sense. And Falco is totally alienated, so much an outsider that he doesn't care about the rest of the world.'

'And Hoxey's out of his tree, the classic religious nut whom they should have caged a long time ago. An authentic kill-for-Christ freak,' Bonomi summarized grimly.

'That leaves Powell.'

'We haven't talked about the murderous major yet, Dave.'

'He'll be the most complex, the most difficult. I'd bet on that.'

The general ground out the stub of his cigar.

'It ought to be one helluva bet, Dave,' he replied. 'You'll be shooting dice for sixty million or eighty million American lives – and God knows how many Russian or Chinese.'

Those were the classified estimates – sixty million to eighty million US fatalities as a result of the Soviet's first thermonuclear strike.

'That ought to make you the highest roller in history,' Bonomi observed.

'That's why I'm thinking about Powell and his wife and son,' Stevens explained. 'To put it simply, right now they're all we've got.'

'You're not counting much on Darby's plan or those STRIKE units?'

'Would you?'

'No, but I don't have to. You have to make that decision, Dave. As one of your predecessors put it so succinctly, this office is the end of the line – the place where the buck stops. Everybody else passes it up and up, and it ends here. That's the price for getting your name in the history books, Mr President, but I don't have to remind you of that.'

David Stevens shook his head twice.

No, nobody had to remind him of that.

'Vince, get McKenzie on the phone. Tell him to call the base commander at Malmstrom. They've got to find Mrs Powell and the boy as soon as possible.'

'That's a job for the FBI, isn't it?'

The President shook his head again.

'Normally, but not this time. I can't risk involving any more people or agencies, not even the FBI. No, tell McKenzie that he's got to use SAC security agents – in plainclothes. By midnight, I want a phone number where I can reach Mrs Powell. That's an order.'

The tone of voice left no room for argument.

'Okay, Mr President, I'll get right on it. May I use the red phone, sir?'

Stevens gestured toward the desk.

'For chrissakes, Vince, don't get difficult,' he asked as he started for the door. 'I've got enough trouble. I'm sorry about that "order" bit, but I don't have much time and the pressure hurts. I'm counting on you to help, Vince. There aren't that many people around whom I can trust,' he added frankly.

Trust – that was the word that did it.

'Okay,' the former wingman replied, 'and you're probably right. It can't hurt to talk to Mrs Powell. I'll get McKenzie moving while you push on for dinner. If I recall Amy's Sunday timetable, you should have been at the table half an hour ago. You don't want to get her mad at you too. You can't afford to lose any votes, you know.'

Amy Desiree Stevens, who didn't dress as badly as one previous First Lady or ride horses as well as another, was already rather edgy if not irritable. The endless strains and crises of the campaign had frayed her usual poise and equanimity, and now the sensible attractive daughter of the fourth richest man in Minneapolis – she was still attractive and sensible after more than two decades of marriage – was simply hanging on and trying to cope. She was a gracious hostess, a superior mother, a canny political adviser, a resolute spokesman for the American Indian – and normally cheerful and/or passionate, depending on the room and the company. These days, she was also worried about the man and the country – *her* man and *her* country. She genuinely detested Senator Baylor Caldwell.

But she liked Vince Bonomi, and that was one reason that the President invited him to join them at dinner. It was not the merriest of the meals that the Stevens family had enjoyed in the White House, but it would have been worse if the old friend hadn't been there. Of course, Amy Stevens sensed that something was wrong – something serious. Of course, she didn't ask what it was, for if the President of the United States wanted to discuss the something he would. It probably wasn't the campaign, she calculated as she chewed abstractly on the Rocky Mountain trout, for if the problem was political the dinner guest would be Ray Gumbiner or Bill Frost, or that courtly, cunning Senator from Kentucky.

Of the five people at the table, only the two hungry teenagers enjoyed the meal. By all the laws of American politics, the Stevens children should have been named Billy and Nancy or Tom and Barbi or Ted and Tricia. In fact they were christened Douglas and Sallyanne but they were just as nice as if they bore any of those other wholesome names – and they were heavy eaters.

The men eating at Viper Three were not impressed by the frozen dinners that Dell showed them how to heat, but the fugitives were honest enough to admit that the food was clearly superior to that served in the Death House. Despite all the folk legends, the meals served to condemned men in Montana and the cuisine at roadside diners catering to truckers are – like the people who perpetuate such legends – hearty but undistinguished. The cooking might have improved if someone had complained or if the culinary inspectors of the *Guide Michelin* came by more often, but by some oversight not one of *Michelin*'s Gallic gourmets had ever visited the Montana State Penitentiary.

Powell was the first to finish, and as soon as he was done he walked to the commander's console to turn on the TV scanner for another routine check. The black man was pleased to observe that the drizzle had halted and the fog lifted, but the rest of what he could now see so clearly was disturbing. He rotated the camera slowly. There they were, what he should have expected.

It was a large force.

'Oh oh,' Willieboy Powell told his partners in loud, bitter tones, 'there goes the neighborhood.'

CHAPTER TWENTY

Dell stood beside him a moment later, staring at the screen.

Troops.

Scores of soldiers spread out just beyond the fence, and they were setting up heavy weapons.

105-millimeter recoilless rifles.

50-caliber machine guns, mounted in fours on what looked like light tanks.

More troops, and a cluster of trucks behind them.

'Son of a bitch,' the former major said.

'Malmstrom?' asked Powell.

'No, they're not local. Too much heavy equipment for any SAC security outfit.'

He was right.

These were paratroopers, the alert battalion from that airborne unit at Fort Lewis.

'They're all over the place,' announced the ex-Marine as he began to rotate the camera again.

More soldiers.

More vehicles, including at least six tanks and some self-propelled howitzers on tracked carriages.

Men setting up searchlights.

Men talking into walkie-talkies. There'd be a mobile communications center somewhere nearby, a van crammed with radio and teleprinter gear. There'd be a command post too, and probably a field kitchen. With all these goddam troops – there were at least three hundred or four hundred visible – there'd be medics, engineer units and the other support specialists.

Dell was correct, even if his estimate of the size of the encircling – no, besieging – force was low. Of course, he didn't know that much about the Army and he couldn't see a number of the enemy's units – the rocket batteries and the launchers for the ground-to air missiles, among others. The actual number of troops deployed within two miles of Viper Three was 1,900, 1,897 to be precise, because three had been injured in a jeep accident just outside the air base.

'You ever in the Army, Stud?' asked Dell.

'No, I didn't like the clothes, so I did a number for the draft-board psychiatrist and they decided I wasn't a wholesome American boy.'

'Well, in case you don't see a lot of war pictures, here's what you missed, Baby,' Powell announced, 'so come take a look.'

The assassin walked forward with sniffling Harvey Schonbacher to study the scanner.

'Jeezus, it looks like John Wayne's birthday,' Falco declared in tones of awe and admiration. 'There must be hundreds of them. Look at 'em. Busy little bastards, aren't they? Hey, Willie, what's that?'

'Medium tanks.'

'Fabulous. Just fabulous. This is really the big time, isn't it? I've always thought I was a pretty hot pistol,' Falco confided, 'but I never thought anybody would send *tanks* to get *me*. They didn't even use tanks on Dillinger or Capone. I kind of like it. It shows respect.'

'You'll have your name in lights next,' the black man predicted wryly.

'Why not? I might even make the Ten Most Wanted list,' Falco mused.

'You're already on the Five Most Wanted list,' said the ex-major as he resumed the rotation of the camera.

The visibility was exceptionally good for this time of night, but that didn't surprise the man who'd handled launch-site security for the 168th. He knew about the infra-red attachments that permitted this TV camera to see as well in the dark as in daylight. He also knew from Schonbacher's bulging eyes and anguished expression that the rapist was on the verge of panic.

'Easy, Harve,' he advised. 'Don't get all sweaty. It's only what we expected, after all. The entirely predictable and, if I do say so myself, predicted reaction of the dull military mind.'

'We should have run for the border!'

Dell shook his head, patiently but wearily.

'No, Harvey. If we'd tried that, we'd be dead. D-e-d-d.'

'I love your spelling, Major,' complimented Powell.

'My penmanship's even better. Now listen to me, Harvey. We did the smartest thing and the only thing we could do, and it's still our ball game. Those kids up there don't mean a thing. They probably don't even know what the hell is going on.'

Schonbacher turned to Falco.

'Don't you think we ought to run, Stud?' he appealed.

'Didn't your mother teach you not to talk in the middle of the picture?' reproved the assassin, who was still staring at the screen. 'Christ, you're ruining it for everybody else. Show a little consideration, will you?'

'More tanks arriving,' the ex-Marine observed coolly.

'Stud, you can't—'

Falco spun, hit him and sent him sprawling.

'Shut up, Harve,' he told the fat man on the floor. 'You're getting on my nerves,' he continued, 'and I don't like that.'

Then he drew his revolver.

'Not another word now, Harve,' he said.

'There go the lights,' Powell announced as several powerful beams suddenly stabbed at the guardhouse.

Falco turned back to the screen, and Dell walked across the small chamber to help Schonbacher to his feet.

'He didn't scare me,' insisted the pharmacist.

'Of course he didn't,' Dell agreed obligingly. 'Why don't you fix that lip and get yourself some coffee, and we can talk about it later.'

Schonbacher knew that he was lying. This pretense at friendliness didn't deceive Harvey Schonbacher for a moment, since he was well aware that they all disliked him. No, he couldn't trust any of these thugs. Their apprent courage was merely camouflaged stupidity, and Harvey Schonbacher was shrewd enough to realize that he'd have to make his *own* plans and decisions if he was to survive this mess. He'd apply his intelligence and education; he'd think out a way to escape by himself. Buoyed by this furtive hatred, Schonbacher walked to the table that supported the first-aid kit.

'Well, *they've* reacted, Major,' the former sergeant noted, 'so what do *we* do?'

'We communicate.'

Dell dropped into the commander's chair, picked up the telephone and dialed the SAC Command Post at Offutt.

'McKenzie,' he said curtly.

The CINCSAC was on the line within thirty seconds.

'This is Dell at Viper Three.'

'What is it?'

'It's quite a show, General. I thought I'd let you know that. We're watching the whole thing on TV, and it's the biggest thing since Ed Sullivan had those two hundred and twenty-two Polish dentists drilling in unison.'

'What are you talking about?'

'General I'm talking about all those troops that just moved in on the surface. The troops and the rockets and the tanks and the portable Mark-88 latrines, the whole package. They moved in right in the middle of dinner, you know.'

'I hope they didn't ruin your appetite,' McKenzie replied.

'Not a bit. I rather expected some troops, but I expect that you knew that. Was this your idea?'

'No.'

'No, it was probably that clown Stonesifer,' the renegade major speculated. 'No, the decision was made higher up, I'd bet. What's the point of such a big force, General? I'm asking because I'd hate to think that you were planning anything stupid – such as an attack.'

'The President has ordered that the area immediately adjacent to Viper Three be sealed off as a security measure,' McKenzie answered.

It wasn't quite a lie and it wasn't the entire truth either.

It was something in between, product of one of the skills that a man must cultivate if he's to become a senior general or top executive. Aleksei Soyuzov or the head of any major cultural foundation could have told Dell that and McKenzie could have too – if he desired. He didn't.

'Whose security?' challenged the former intelligence officer.

'The security of the United States ... and of these negotiations.'

Dell considered this reply.

'All right,' he conceded, 'I guess neither of us would benefit from getting this into the newspapers. It would certainly ruin the stock market. Yes, the end of the world should really shake up those financial wizards at the mutual funds and the big brokerage houses. Wouldn't you say so, General?'

The flawed fugitive was trying to be provocative, Martin McKenzie observed without much rancor, and he was succeeding – to a small degree. As a rational and purposeful commander, McKenzie couldn't afford to permit himself to be deflected from the main issue, the goal of the operation, the target.

'You could say that, Dell,' he replied aloud, 'or you could say what you called about.'

'I've already done that, but I'll repeat it in case you're dense – sir. We can see what you're doing, and we don't believe your story at all. No tricks, because we're ready to launch. Is that clear?'

It was hardly surprising that Dell was suspicious.

He too had made his career in the booming trade of institutionalized violence where pious platitudes were cheap and the pre-emptive strike all important.

'Clear.'

'Roger. Over and out,' Dell concluded in parody of Air Force radio argot.

Falco spoke as he put down the phone.

'I didn't know anybody really talked like that, Larry,' he confided, 'except on TV shows or old movies.'

'You're right,' Dell agreed, 'but Air Force officers have a lot of time on their hands between wars and they love to watch those old flicks. After all, film is an American art form like birth control and pinpoint bombing – right?'

'I never thought of it that way. Of course, I never had much interest in birth control or pinpoint bombing. I always left that to other people. How about you, Willie?'

The black man shrugged.

'I stay away from that hard stuff,' he reported. 'Why, I don't think I could bomb a pinpoint if I tried. I was only a sergeant, you know.'

Lovely.

It was just lovely.

Schonbacher was right on the hairy edge of hysteria, Falco was more than willing to kill him, the ex-Marine was fighting some private war against officers and/or whites and a small army was forging a ring of men and metal on the surface. So far as Dell could see, the only one not causing problems at the moment was the homicidal holy man – and there was no way of predicting what that mental basket case might do next.

Just lovely.

Almost as lovely as his wife had been – at the beginning.

She hadn't been at all lovely during the last three years – not since the drinking began – and by the time she died that fine model's face had been hateful and haunted. Suddenly he saw her again, on the bedroom floor with the purple marks on her throat and death in those extraordinary hazel eyes.

He turned his attention back to the small screen.

Some three quarters of a mile away, a brigadier general with airborne insignia sat in one of those STRIKE communications vans speaking into a radio. The entire force was in position, deployed and ready to carry out the plan.

'Stand by,' advised General Stonesifer. 'We're expecting the final go-ahead any minute now.'

The Paratroop general promised to stand by.

As he spoke, more than six thousand miles to the east a traffic controller at Tempelhof Airport in West Berlin noticed some unusual spots on his radar screen. No transports were expected now in the small hours before dawn. He watched them for some twenty seconds, checked his equipment for malfunction and then called his supervisor from an adjacent office.

The number of dots was growing, and they were all converging on the air corridors that led into Berlin from Communist territory.

Six . . . nine . . . thirteen.

No, fourteen – and all moving at speeds above those of any commercial airliner.

'What do you think?' the controller politely asked his supervisor.

'I think we'd better notify the appropriate authorities,' replied the senior controller.

Even in the new Germany, people 'notify the appropriate authorities.'

About nineteen minutes after the dots first bloomed on the Tempelhof tower screen, a telephone sounded in US Air Force headquarters in Wiesbaden.

'Yes, I know. They're on our radar too,' the duty officer said. 'Right . . . right, we're checking it out now.'

In accord with the decision of the Central Committee of the Communist Party of the Union of Soviet Socialist Republics, Yamshchik had begun.

CHAPTER TWENTY-ONE

'From a professional point of view, Mr President, Dell is probably the most interesting,' the woman from Akron said.

It was 10:05 P.M. in the District of Columbia, and they had just finished the detailed psychoanalytical evaluations of Hoxey and Schonbacher.

That left only Lawrence Dell.

'And he's the most difficult, of course,' her husband added.

Then the telephone that served the SAC hot line to Offutt rang, and Stevens left the black leather armchair to take the call at his desk.

'Yes ... yes, General. ... That's pretty quick work. I suppose I ought to commend you and the STRIKE people. ... I see. ... No, not yet. ... I'll let you know. I don't want anybody going off half cocked on this. ... You tell them to wait. ... Yes, I know the plan and frankly I'm not at all enthusiastic about it. ... I'll let you know,' he announced, 'and probably within the next hour or two. Until then, tell them to wait – with their fingers off those triggers. ... Good.'

He sighed as he put down the instrument.

'The task force has arrived and they're ready to attack,' Stevens told his former wingman, 'but I'm not ready – not yet.'

'I'd say you made that pretty clear. How about getting back to Major Dell now?'

'Nothing on Powell's wife yet, Vince?'

Bonomi shook his head, and the Chief Executive returned to the armchair to listen to what the CIA analysts had to say about the former Deputy Intelligence Officer of the 168th.

'Since you're familiar with the basic facts of his origins and family relationships,' Pinney began, 'let me merely note in passing that one could say he was the middle child – with an older brother and a younger sister – and middle children are sometimes thought to get lost in the shuffle. Let me also mention that interviews with his parents, other relatives, former neighbors and childhood friends provide no evidence that Major Dell was, in fact, lost in the shuffle. So far as anyone can recall, he had a better than average childhood in a better than average home with superior parents who gave him plenty of affection and attention. So far as we know, the boy continued to receive plenty of affection and attention after his younger sister appeared. There was, of course, the normal sibling rivalry with the older brother.'

'That's Richard, the one who became a stock broker,' noted the woman.

'What about today? How does Major Dell feel about them now?'

The doctors exchanged glances as they paused to phrase their estimate.

'I'd say that he gets along with them fairly well, although he isn't exactly the sentimental type,' the Georgian judged. 'He sees his parents at least once a year – his father's still practicing in New Haven, you know – and he usually remembers to phone his brother and his sister on their birthdays and Christmas. It isn't what you'd call a very close family relationship, but certainly no worse than most. Better than most, and probably warmer than you might expect from a man of such ambition.'

'It's very interesting,' confirmed his leggy colleague. 'That ambition and the question of children – quite interesting.'

'Just how ambitious is or was Major Dell?' probed the President.

'Well, it seems clear ... fairly clear ... that he always wanted to be the best. Had to be. He wasn't satisfied to be just a good pitcher on his prep-school baseball team; he had to be the best in the state. He wasn't content to go out with pretty girls, only beautiful ones. It wasn't enough to be a first-class math student; he had to win a national merit scholarship in math for college. He was admitted to five universities, and I still don't understand why he chose the Air Force Academy. No offense, General, but he could have gone to MIT or Yale or some others.'

'No offense,' assured Bonomi.

173

'Maybe he chose the Air Force Academy because he calculated that he had a better chance to star there,' Stevens speculated.

The lady from Akron beamed.

'That's very perceptive of you, Mr President,' she congratulated.

'You ought to see him do his card tricks,' Bonomi advised in a tone that communicated his impatience with their polite patronizing.

'Easy, Vince. Go ahead, Doctor.'

'The word "star" is well chosen,' Pinney said, 'for that's what this man has sought to be all his life. Oh, he had good manners and the casual style that people call "cool" all right, but it was quite deliberate. He wanted to be a star, to be admired. He even looks like some sort of film or stage star; he's theatrical – in a polished way. Not cheap or vulgar like those stand-up comics, but motivated by what you might call the WASP version of those same drives. He's never asked for a free ride, of course. He's both intelligent and a hard worker, and he's tried to avoid making any enemies.'

'The Air Force Chief of Staff can't have enemies,' recited the woman.

'Yes, Dell has told a few people that he intended to become Air Force Chief of Staff – that's the highest rank in the entire Air Force,' Pinney confirmed – 'and the girl he married was not only an extraordinarily lovely model but also the sister of a British earl.'

Nothing but the best for Lawrence Dell.

'You said something about children?'

'Yes, Mr President,' the Atlantan responded, 'he doesn't seem to relate too well to children. He apparently shows only nominal interest in his nephews and nieces, and his own nine years of marriage didn't produce a single offspring. Since he had a reputation as an energetic and successful lover with the girls in Colorado Springs – when he was at the Air Academy there – one might guess that he has continued to favor contraception during intercourse.'

Stevens closed his tired eyes for a moment, reopened them.

'Exactly what does this children thing mean?' he asked.

Dr Osgood arched her eyebrows meaningfully.

Actually it wasn't that bad.

She might have pursed her lips and shrugged in addition.

'We can't say with any degree of certainty,' she answered. 'It could hint that there was *something* – something in his own childhood – that nobody knows or remembers or wants to remember. Considering that this man is so ambitious and so conscious of his image, you'd think that he'd want children of his own because they'd be helpful socially. But he didn't father any.'

'And why would a surgeon's son become a career Air Force officer?' wondered Bonomi. 'It doesn't fit the pattern. I don't think one surgeon's son in one thousand would pick such a way to spend his life. The money's not much and the status isn't any better. I don't get it.'

'On the basis of the limited data available, General,' she answered, 'we don't *get* Major Lawrence Dell. There are key pieces missing. It's very interesting.'

'What would he do? What could he do? Why would he do it?' the President challenged.

'Now? After the way he was treated by the Air Force, abused in the press, he might do anything. He was a brilliant officer, the escape from the Death House was very cleverly done and as for the capture of a presumably impregnable missile base,' she said, 'well, you can characterize that yourself.'

'I don't see him as any big genius,' Bonomi disagreed. 'Killing his wife wasn't too smart for a man with such great ambitions.'

The two doctors exchanged family looks again.

'What is it?' asked the President.

Pinney cleared his throat before he answered.

'To put it bluntly, sir, who said he killed his wife?'

'He was convicted,' Bonomi replied, 'by a jury of his peers. No racial prejudice there, Doctor.'

'He was convicted on circumstantial evidence, and it took the jury three days to reach a verdict. Of course, as the President said, the question of justice may be of academic interest at the moment. However, if you're interested, I could tell you what the psychiatrists who saw him before the trial said.'

'I'm interested.'

'Well, Mr President, they made two findings – only one of which was relevant to the legal processes of the State of Montana. First, they found that he was legally sane and knew what he was doing and what the results of his acts would be. That was reported to the court. Second, the doctors out there – after many hours of interviews and many more hours of evaluating those sessions – concluded that it was unlikely that this man would kill his wife.'

Stevens sat up, stared.

'And what do the two distinguished CIA doctors here have to say?' he demanded.

The woman answered.

'We'd say that – for whatever it might be worth – there's a distinct possibility that Major Dell didn't kill anybody.'

'But you're not sure?'

'No, Mr President,' she replied frankly, 'we're not sure at all.'

The hot-line telephone jangled again.

CHAPTER TWENTY-TWO

'I've got that phone number you requested,' the CINCSAC said.

As he spoke into the phone, he looked down from the Battle Staff area on the upper level. Everything seemed to be normal and routine below, but McKenzie knew that they knew. The men and women on duty at the CP knew, even if they didn't show it. They knew that something unusual was going on, and while they probably didn't guess what it was there were undoubtedly more than a few who realized that it was serious. The CINCSAC down in the bunker all of Sunday, the flow of grim looks and urgent calls, the cluster of key officers in the Battle Staff area – these things had to be noticed and judged.

'The area code for Helena is 406, and the number is 111-2012,' McKenzie told the President. 'That's an apartment in a two-family house on Jane Street, 317 Jane Street. Mrs Powell is there now, General Stonesifer reports.'

'Good.'

'Mr President, I'd like to suggest that we give her some warning or preparation for the call. Otherwise, there's a chance she might not recognize your voice or might not believe that it's really you phoning.'

'That's a good idea. How do you mean to do it?'

'Colonel Clantar – he's the senior Intelligence Officer of the 168th – is in a car watching the house right now. We can radio him, and you can phone in about ten minutes. He'll show her his credentials and talk to her in the meanwhile.'

David Stevens agreed, then returned to the disturbing discussion of Major Dell. He questioned and tested as the two CIA analysts explained how they had come to the conclusion that Dell's 'personality profile' was such that it was rather unlikely he'd murder his wife. He wasn't the sort of man who lost his temper, who exploded under strain, bitterness or frustration. He'd always handled those things in a realistic and effective way – abnormally so. While it was true that Diana Dell had been drinking heavily and probably unfaithful, it was equally true that this man wouldn't – you might almost say couldn't – risk his career by such an act.

'I'm not saying that Lawrence Dell is incapable of violence,' the Georgian pointed out carefully, 'but a single act of this sort – personal violence against an individual civilian – isn't his thing. Isn't his bag, as our son would say.'

'The major's perfectly capable of killing a foreign power's air base or capital city,' Dr Osgood explained, 'and his choice of a military career confirms this attitude toward impersonal mass violence – that is, violence against a large remote group or place.'

'Somebody once quoted the late Bugsy Siegel as saying that the American public had little to fear from organized criminals because gangsters basically only killed each other,' Stevens recalled. 'Are you saying that a man such as Dell only kills strangers, faceless foreigners far away?'

'That's about it, Mr President,' she agreed, 'or at least that's what his pattern would strongly indicate.'

'So if that's the case, Doctor,' the Chief Executive reasoned, 'then it's unlikely that he killed his wife but he's perfectly capable of firing those ICBMs.'

'Exactly. Mind you, we're not saying that we're *sure* he was convicted improperly for a crime he didn't commit – but there's definitely that possibility.'

'What the hell are we going to do with possibilities, dammit?' Bonomi erupted.

Dr Pinney looked puzzled.

Dr Osgood looked delicately disappointed.

'Why, you'll consider them in reaching your decisions, General,' she explained in tones that a teacher might use on a dull fourteen-year-old.

'You have to consider all the factors to reach an intelligent and logical conclusion,' agreed her husband.

'What conclusion?'

'Why, that's up to you ... and the President, of course,'

Pinney replied. 'Our job is to collect, sift and interpret the data. Then the people who make the decisions about action are better equipped to decide and act. In the case of these five men, we don't even have anything like all the data. Why, we don't even have the actual Rorschachs – just evaluations of them by doctors we never heard of before. We're not magicians, you know.'

'Edward,' his wife said soothingly.

'Well, we're not,' he insisted in a voice edged with defensiveness. 'We're well-trained, thoroughly experienced, serious specialists who have demonstrated our capabilities in this complex field of personality profiles – but we're not machines or computers. We can't give you absolute answers or simple formulas. We're not like those acne lotions advertised on television that guarantee teenagers a perfect complexion within nine days, or your money back.'

The President nodded.

'I understand, of course, but there's no chance of anybody getting his money back if we're wrong on this one, Doctor,' he judged. 'Well, I guess I ought to thank you both – and I do. Now I have a phone call to make and a decision.'

He thanked them again as they left, and then he returned to the handsome swivel chair at the historic desk.

'They're right about at least one thing, Vince,' he brooded. 'Dell is the most interesting – the smartest and the most interesting.'

'Maybe so, but I don't see that we've got time for this sort of philosophizing. You ought to save it for your memoirs, Mr President, if you live long enough to write them.'

Bonomi was an honest and able and loyal man, but he didn't have much philosophy. That was an unfortunate weakness, even though his line of work didn't require a great deal of philosophy. He had principles and integrity all right, but very little philosophy.

'How far will Dell go in his fear and anger?' Stevens continued. 'Millions of people will cheat on their income taxes or their wives, but how many of them would kill? How many of them would kill thousands or millions, tens of millions?'

'That's a problem they don't have to worry about, Dave.

They've turned that over to professionals – to you and me and a few thousand others – to decide, and they can make virtuous wisecracks about what brutal bastards we are. It's easy for them to look down on the hired help, but we didn't create the jobs or do the hiring.'

After all these years, Vince Bonomi was having – and articulating – second thoughts, Stevens realized. He wasn't rejecting his choice of a career, but – whether he knew it or not – he was having second thoughts. Yes, he was suffering the pangs of philosophy – perhaps as the result of age.

Or maybe it was the threat of Viper Three.

'But you were a volunteer, Vince – just like Dell. If you'd been kicked out of the Air Force after years of conscientious service, if you'd been sentenced to die for a single desperate act – one that perhaps you didn't even commit – would you fire those missiles?'

'I'm not him,' Bonomi parried.

'No, but you're a professional and you've had much of the same training and sort of life. Would you launch?'

The general puffed on his cigar, considered.

'To get even or to save your own life – even for a while – would you launch, Vince?'

Bonomi ground out the Corona irritably.

'No, but I'm stupid. He's smarter than I am, and meaner. He's more screwed up too. I may be one of the brutal bastards, but I couldn't do it. We're not the same, even if we wore the same blue uniform. I've got four sons, and he doesn't have any. Shit, there could be a hundred differences.'

'I suppose so.'

'Why don't you make your phone call, dammit?'

The President reached for the telephone.

'Maybe I would launch,' his former wingman muttered. 'Maybe I would if I were in his shoes.'

'No, you wouldn't. Maybe there are nineteen other generals – on both sides of the Iron Curtain – who'd launch, Vince, but *you* wouldn't.'

Before Bonomi could answer, Stevens gave the Helena number to his secretary and some thirty seconds later he was talking to the wife of Willieboy Justice Powell. He spoke gently to the woman, explaining the problem carefully and pointing out that she could help save the life of her husband and many, many other people. His tones were sober but respectful; he didn't threaten or browbeat or order and he did his best not to frighten her. As he spoke, he found himself wondering what this woman looked like – and he decided that she was tall and attractive and dignified. Was she white or black or perhaps Indian? It was impossible to tell from her voice.

'If he ... if they come out now, the death sentences will be commuted and he'll only have to spend a few years in prison, is that what you're saying, Mr President?' she asked gravely.

'That's what I'm saying. I'm giving you my word.'

She hesitated for several seconds.

'You're not saying what will happen if he doesn't come up now, if they all refuse to surrender,' she observed.

Now the President hesitated.

'I'd rather not, Mrs Powell,' he finally replied. 'It would obviously be much less pleasant – for all of us.'

'You'll kill them, won't you?'

'Mrs Powell,' he began to reply.

'Never mind. I know you'll kill them. I suppose that, from your point of view, you'd have to.'

'I didn't say that, Mrs Powell,' Stevens protested.

'No, and that was thoughtful of you. But you'll kill them all. I don't mean you personally, but someone in the Government will do it for you – and that will leave me a widow with a fatherless child. I probably wouldn't even collect his Social Security pension, would I?'

'I didn't call to threaten anyone,' Stevens said truthfully. 'I'm trying to save lives, your husband's and millions of others. I know that your husband's worth saving, that he's no professional criminal.'

'You don't know anything about my husband,' she contradicted sharply, 'and there's really no reason you should. ... It doesn't matter. I'll call him in a few minutes, if Colonel Clantar here can arrange it. I'm afraid I don't know the number.'

'I'm sure he can arrange it. Thank you, Mrs Powell. I hope he'll listen to you.'

She chuckled softly, sadly.

'That proves you don't know my husband, Mr President,' she said a moment before she ended the conversation.

'Smart woman,' Bonomi judged when Stevens turned to face him.

'What the hell are you talking about?'

'She's right, that's what I'm talking about. Even if they pull this off without launching and get away with their bags of money,' Bonomi reasoned, 'they'd never get to enjoy it. This Government – no Government – would stand for that sort of humiliation. Wherever they went – unless they made it to Red China – Michaelson's people would hunt them down. Sooner or later, in five months or five years, his people – the ones you call *my* people – would kill them. You might not even know about it.'

'You're crazy, Vince.'

The general shook his head.

'No, not a bit, Dave. They'd hunt them down sooner or later.'

'Not if I told them not to.'

Bonomi sighed.

'But you wouldn't. They'd talk you into it, Dave, or if they couldn't they'd just go ahead anyway. Do you really have any idea as to how many people our intelligence agencies have killed – for reasons and on orders – in the last year? I don't, and I don't ask either. Did you ever ask?'

'No, I never thought about it.'

'You're not supposed to, Mr President. You're not supposed to ask and you're not supposed to know. It's not your business. The big stuff – the budget, the new civil-rights law, nominating judges and ambassadors, the arms-limitation negotiations – that's your business. By the way, if it's any consolation to you the Russians and the Chinese probably killed nine times as many – maybe sixteen times as many.'

'It's no goddam consolation at all, you son of a bitch. I don't know why you brought this up.'

'Sorry, Mr President, but you've always told me that you liked me to say whatever—'

There was a double rap at the door.

One of the junior military aides entered, reported that Colonel Clantar was about to put the call through the Malmstrom switchboard to Viper Three and General Stonesifer had arranged for a patch so that the President could listen.

'We're ready to plug it into the conference speaker,' the captain announced.

'All right,' Stevens agreed.

It didn't take long – less than a minute – before the voices issued from the small walnut speaker box on the desk.

The conversation was brief and – somehow – simultaneously tender and formal, as if they knew that strangers were listening. She told him that she and the boy were well, and she put the child on the phone for a minute. Powell assured them both that he was 'all right,' and said that they shouldn't worry because things would 'work out soon.' She explained that she was worried, and suddenly the ex-Marine understood that the military had her under surveillance or in custody. When he asked, she answered that there were Air Force officers with her but no one had threatened her or the child.

'The President was very specific about that,' she reported.

'The President?'

'Yes, he phoned a few minutes ago to ask me to talk to you, Honey,' Martha Powell announced, 'and he gave me his word that you men would get your sentences commuted to a few years – if you come up now.'

Powell told her what he thought of the President's word, and she asked him again to think of her and the child – and all the other children.

'Let the President think about them; he gets two hundred thousand dollars a year for thinking big,' Willieboy Powell answered scornfully. 'He's only trying to scare us, Baby. He's bluffing. We know he's bluffing, and he knows that he's got to pay up. We'll be on our way out of this damned country in less than twenty-four hours, and you'll both be coming with us. You'd better pack your bags now.'

There was an odd sound; it might have been a controlled choked-down sob.

'I think they mean to kill you, all of you,' she whispered.

'I *know* they do, but they won't.'

'Willie?'

'Yes?'

'*Please,* Willie.'

'See you tomorrow night,' he replied firmly.

That was it.

'Well, she tried,' Stevens said in tones of acceptance.

'She wasn't even close, Dave. She tried all right, but she didn't lay a glove on him. Of course, I never thought she would.'

The President sighed, closed his eyes for a moment.

'To tell the truth, Vince, I didn't either. Why should he trust anybody anymore? I'd hoped that the word of the President might still mean something, but I guess that's gone too.'

'Your predecessors took care of that, Dave, with all that fancy lying in the UN and those TV speeches. Of course, nobody believes the Prime Minister of Britain or the head of the Russian Government or the president of Harvard either. I don't suppose . . . well, it's the nature of our times.'

'You're getting more philosophical by the minute, General.'

'Terror is maturing me,' Bonomi acknowledged.

Then he looked at his wrist watch.

'You ought to be hearing from McKenzie and Stu Woodside in about eighty-four seconds,' he estimated.

'What are you talking about, Vince?'

'Mr President, I may be terrified but I'm not hysterical. I'm still aware of what's happening. McKenzie will want the go-ahead for the attack, and Woodside will ask for the shift to DEFCON Four. He's the JCS chairman, and that's what he *ought* to do now that Mrs Powell failed and you're about to okay the attack. . . . Don't look so innocent, Dave. For God's sake, you certainly must realize that both of them were listening to her conversation with her husband. There must have been twenty generals plugged into that line, here in Washington, the SAC brass at Offutt and Malmstrom and probably K.O. Warsaw's crew down at STRIKE.'

'DEFCON Four?' Stevens considered soberly.

'If I were the JCS chairman, I'd ask for Three. Dave, for all the moral and humanistic questions involved in this mess it's still – so far as the military are concerned – a military crisis.'

'That's all they see, I suppose, and I can't blame them.'

'The brutal bastards are only doing their job,' Bonomi confirmed.

'Which side are you on, Vince – mine or theirs?'

'I didn't know there were two sides on this one.'

Then the CINCSAC called, and after a brief discussion Stevens reluctantly authorized the attack. Less than two minutes later, General Stuart C. Woodside was on the line renewing his request for DEFCON Four. Being as canny a bargainer as the JCS chairman should be, he actually asked for DEFCON Three and 'settled' for Four.

At 10:49 P.M. (Washington time), US armed forces around the world received a coded radio signal raising the defense readiness condition to Four.

This message was also heard and recorded, of course, by several well-equipped listening posts manned by Soviet and Chinese intelligence units. Seven different 'electronic eavesdropping detachments' in Europe and Asia, plus two of those Russian trawlers that cruise off New England and Alaska with so many antennas, noted and relayed the message back to their headquarters. Within a few hours, the cleverest cryptographers in Moscow and Peking would be at work with their minds and machines to pry out the hidden meaning.

CHAPTER TWENTY-THREE

'Go,' said General Stonesifer to the wholesome-looking major who'd been waiting impatiently for what had seemed much more than two hours. 'The word is *go*.'

Major J. C. Lebeau, who had excellent reflexes in addition to paratrooper's insignia and very clear memories of the eastern border of Cambodia, went. He saluted first, of course, and then he went from Stonesifer's office to the jeep that carried him to the helicopter pad three quarters of a mile away.

'Time to haul ass, Norm,' he announced in that delightful New Orleans accent.

Captain Norman Tippett, who was not only several years younger but also enjoyed an even deeper Dixie drawl, beamed happily and he was still beaming when he ordered a sergeant to 'Get those mothers moving.' The men of the airborne platoon poured out of the nearby 'ready hut' on the trot and quickly filed into the two waiting helicopters with their weapons and ropes and bags of assault gear.

'See you on the roof, Norm,' Lebeau announced as Tippett watched the last of his squad enter the aircraft. 'Wait a minute, here come the Special Weapons boys – right on schedule.'

Six men stepped out of the station wagon, three carrying sub-machine guns and two holding square metal containers bound with straps. The sixth had a clipboard and a look of great sobriety. On the face of it, Lebeau reckoned that the three were protecting the two who carried the atomic charges and the one with the clipboard was in command. After some years in the US Army, he'd learned that the one with the clipboard – anyone with any clipboard – was in command. He was right, for this man was a full colonel.

'Major Lebeau?'

'Yessir.'

'May I see your ID, please?' asked the one with the clipboard.

The paratroop officer produced the plastic card, and the colonel from the Special Weapons Detachment studied it carefully before he thrust forward the clipboard.

'Would you please sign for delivery? Top line, next to where it says "Type 133A Demolition Charges dash Two."'

The 133A was a compact atomic warhead equivalent to fifty tons of high explosive, and two of them would deliver the blast of two hundred thousand pounds of TNT or dynamite. The 133A was the third smallest weapon in the US nuclear arsenal, a toy compared to the warheads on those Minutemen.

Major Jean Charles Lebeau signed.

'Is there any deposit on the boxes?' he asked.

'No, not a penny,' bristled the colonel. 'You've been checked out on these gadgets and their timing devices, I assume.'

'Sure have. Took the course down in New Mexico only three months ago. Captain Tippett took the same course last December. We can handle them, sir.'

The man with the clipboard nodded, and his men put the two boxes at Lebeau's feet.

'Tippett! Tippett, get your ass over here!' the paratroop major bellowed.

He had no sense of history. This would be the first time that the 133A would be used in combat, the first time that any nuclear weapon would be detonated in anger in the Western Heisphere. To use such language at such a moment was ... well, it was deplorable.

'This one's for you, Norm,' Lebeau announced, 'and you take good care of it because I just signed for it. You take good care of it, you hear?'

'Yessir. It's the 133A, right?'

'You bet your ass it's the 133A.'

Simply deplorable.

'We've got two in case one of the choppers craps out on us, Norm,' Lebeau reminded, 'so if my bird doesn't make it you take your charge down and put it right up against that big mother of a steel door.'

'Set the timer for ten minutes, and bug out – right?'

Lebeau patted him on the shoulder.

'Good boy. Told you he knew what to do. Well, Colonel, you've got your nice little signed receipt — all correct and official — and I've got your two fine boxes. I'd be obliged, sir, if you'd step back a bit because we're going to take off in about one and half minutes and these goddam choppers kick up an awful amount of wind and dust.'

For a moment, the colonel considered wishing him good luck.

Somebody ought to say something suitable at an historic moment such as this, and if this crude paratrooper wouldn't, then it was up to the 26th Special Weapons Detachment.

'Major Lebeau,' the colonel began.

'See you later,' the big major shouted and then the roar of the rotors drowned out everything.

The unhappy man with the clipboard retreated some thirty yards, watched as the helicopters lurched into the air and swooped off into the dark night. There was almost no moonlight, for patchy clusters of clouds still stained the sky — and that would be good for the attack.

The helicopters climbed higher and higher, their riding lights twinkling like some man-made stars. The Special Weapons colonel stared as the pinpoints receded into the blackness, and when they vanished he glanced at his watch.

It was 11:50, local time, just ten minutes before word reached the JCS 'war room' in the Pentagon that all the landline telephone circuits into West Berlin had gone dead.

CHAPTER TWENTY-FOUR

'Choppers airborne,' Stonesifer reported on the direct line to SAC headquarters in Nebraska.

McKenzie and the assembled Battle Staff heard him, President Stevens and Bonomi heard him, General Kermit O. Warsaw heard him – and so did all but one member of the Joint Chiefs of Staff. The commanding officer of the Marine Corps, General H. D. 'Hounddog' Pitcher, was still in Bethesda Naval Hospital recovering from a gall-bladder operation. His deputy was sitting in for him, however, and vigilantly defending the Corps' legitimate interest against those bastards from the other armed services. There was also three other men in the JCS 'war room,' Secretary of Defense Darby and the head of the Defense Intelligence Agency and Evan Michaelson. Michaelson would have preferred to listen in his own office at CIA headquarters, but the military had refused to arrange this on the grounds of security. This was probably a pretext, Michaelson suspected, an excuse to score a point in the endless interdepartmental guerrilla warfare.

He was right.

There were no members of the Women's Liberation Front, the Students for a Democratic Society, the Black Panthers, the Daughters of Bilitis, the Polish UN Mission or the Jefferson Airplane present. It was strictly an Establishment group in that Pentagon chamber, with every one of them over forty-five and not a beard or an Indian headband in the crowd.

Square and uptight.

Definitely uptight.

You could see it in the faces, the hard, tense faces.

'No calls,' ordered the JCS chairman. 'This is Number One Priority, Colonel,' he told his aide, 'and I don't want any interruptions or distractions unless it's NORAD reporting a Russian missile attack . . . or something of equal urgency. You got that?'

'Yes, sir.'

'Okay, now put me through to the Jericho Task Force commander.'

Jericho was the code name STRIKE had given to the composite unit ringing Viper Three.

'Satellite TV circuit ready, sir,' reported a Signal Corps major. 'She's coming in on Screen Two now. There, nice and clear.'

Woodside and the others looked up, and there was a clear picture of the Viper Three guardhouse.

'They've got a scrambler on that camera, I hope,' the Chief of Naval Operations worried.

'Oh yes, sir. We've double-checked that,' assured the communications officer.

'You've got a great image, Pete,' the Army Chief of Staff complimented Crane, 'better than the one I pick up on my set at home.'

'The set-up cost enough, goddamit,' Crane acknowledged.

'Jericho Task Force commander, sir.'

Woodside picked up the gray telephone.

'Woodside here. Yes, your picture's coming in fine, but that's not what I'm calling about. You all set? . . . One minute, huh?'

As he spoke, the Chief of Air Staff was summoned to another telephone to talk to the North American Air Defense Command.

The three-star general at the NORAD bunker inside that Colorado mountain wanted to know about the shift to DEFCON Four.

'What about it?' Crane demanded.

'Is something up, Pete?'

'Yes, you could say that – but I can't say much more, Harry. We're trying to straighten it out right now.'

'How bad is it?'

'It's *not good*, and if we can't fix it within the next couple of hours I'm betting we'll go to Three by morning. Don't repeat this to anybody,' Crane advised, and even as he spoke he realized that half a dozen NORAD generals would know about it within ninety seconds.

'Any suggestions, Pete?'

'I'd stay close to the store tonight. As a matter of fact, I'd plan on eating in for the next eighteen hours or so – just as a precaution.'

'Okay. . . . Say, Pete, I think you ought to know that there's not a damn thing on any of our screens. I've double checked with Greenland and Alaska and England, and the Navy picket ships and planes too. We don't have anything, not anything. I thought you ought to know that.'

'I knew it. Listen, there's nothing up yet – nothing for radar to spot. Don't get steamy, Harry – not right now anyways. The Army thinks they can fix the whole thing.'

Suddenly the grinding noises of tanks issued from a speaker beneath the TV screen – the one designated Screen Two – as the audio channel to the task force transmitter was opened.

'Here we go,' announced Crane. 'I'll call you back in an hour or so.'

It was, in the simple sincere prose of the TV news announcers who describe Thanksgiving Day parades, Presidential inaugurations, half-time entertainment at football games, Hollywood weddings and Midwestern tornados, quite a sight. The searchlights crisscrossed the area with the dazzling glamour usually associated with the opening of a major new film or laundromat, and the tanks moving back and forth looked like lost rhinos that had wandered onto the wrong film set. There was a great deal of noise and activity as men and vehicles moved across the screen, as trucks and half-tracks disembarked fresh troops and equipment.

The men in the capsule watched, unaware that other men were studying the same scene on other TV screens.

'What are they doing?' Schonbacher worried.

'I don't know,' reported the ex-major. 'There's a helluva lot of activity, but it may just be the normal confusion of any growing military operation. It looks like reinforcements moving in and some sort of regrouping.'

'I don't like it,' said Powell.

'I don't like it either, even though they're all staying outside the fence. As a matter of fact,' Dell noticed, 'some of them seem to have pulled back a little. It's hard to judge distance on this little screen, but I think some of them are back a bit.'

'Maybe they're going to bomb the guardhouse?' Falco suggested.

Dell and Powell both shook their heads simultaneously.

It wouldn't make any sense.

It wouldn't do any good.

'This is Jericho CP,' said the task force commander to that other audience. 'We've picked up the choppers at a range of about three miles on infra-red, and they're moving in high according to plan.'

The helicopters would approach with their lights extinguished at 3,500 feet – up above the scanning angle of the capsule's protective camera – and when they'd reached a blind spot directly above the guardhouse the two machines would rotor down slowly and quietly, as quietly as possible, to fifty feet above the roof. The roar of the tanks was to cover the helicopter sounds.

'Here they come.'

The two shapes on the Pentagon TV screen grew larger, and in less than a minute they were identifiable as Bell troop-carrying helicopters. Closer and closer, they cut through the night until they were directly above the guardhouse – about one thousand yards above – and then began to rotor down. They descended steadily to five hundred yards, at which altitude one waited and continued to hover while the other fluttered down to some twenty yards above the roof. A white nylon climbing line spilled out, and a few moments later the first of the airborne troopers began his descent – hand over hand.

He reached the roof, looked around and signaled with his sub-machine gun. Seconds later, a flexible ladder dropped from the craft and the rest of the squad started down with their assault gear.

'So far so good,' McKenzie judged hopefully.

His aide looked much less contented.

'I know, I know what's bothering you, Doug,' calculated the CINCSAC. 'A flaw in the system. A security gap, right? If these choppers can come in through the dead spot right overhead, why couldn't enemy choppers – right?'

'That's right, sir. We'll have to plug that gap, sir.'

The same point was being made – a bit less pleasantly – in the Pentagon, where the Army Chief of Staff was noting with pride how his jumpers had found a hole in the SAC launch-site defenses.

'Don't mean to hurt your feelings, Pete,' he concluded.

'We always welcome constructive criticism,' Crane answered coldly.

Now the first helicopter was empty and it began to climb up, rising to five hundred feet and then moving a dozen yards off to permit the other machine to go down the same invisible shaft.

'There they go,' Woodside said as Lebeau and his unit put their climbing ropes over the side of the building and started to climb down warily.

It was at that moment that Dell began to rotate the camera on the roof.

'Move it, move it,' ordered the paratroop officer.

Three . . . four . . . five men were over the side, and the electronic eye was still turning slowly.

'Hurry up, hurry up.'

The sixth and seventh men were having some problems with their climbing ropes.

'Get your ass over that roof, Farley,' Lebeau told his sergeant, 'or I'll boot it over.'

The camera was moving again.

Now the sergeant was out of sight, leaving only Lebeau and one twenty-year-old from Kansas.

'If you can't climb, Bryman, jump,' the major ordered.

The lens was almost upon them.

Taking the officer at his word, the corporal – who knew a good deal about how to fall – jumped. As he did so, Lebeau slid over the edge himself with one of the boxes – all of five seconds before the camera reached that area.

'Shit, shit, shit – that was close,' McKenzie whispered to himself as the crisis slid by.

In the JCS 'war room,' some very important people expressed some very similar thoughts – although the language used wasn't quite as blunt.

The second helicopter was descending.

The first squad was halfway down to the ground now, safely

below the scanning area of the rooftop camera. One by one the troopers reached the surface, flattened against the wall and slipped through the open door into the guardroom. They made little noise, for they wore sneakers. They stood there in the darkness panting as Lebeau ran a quick count.

Five, six, seven.

Bryman.

The man who'd jumped.

Where the hell was Bryman?

Lebeau heard an odd sound, spun with his M-16 at the ready and saw someone or something crawling in over the threshold.

'That you, Bryman?' he asked softly.

'Yes, sir.'

'You okay, boy?'

'I'm okay, sir. I think I broke my foot, sir, but I'm okay.'

'Hurt bad?'

'Hurts like hell, sir.'

Lebeau considered this, reached a decision.

He gave the injured soldier his walkie-talkie.

'You stay up here, Bryman. Cover the door, just in case there's some other way besides the elevator for these mothers to come up. Cover the door, and take care of the radio. If I need anything, you'll tell 'em – right?'

'Right, sir.'

Lebeau turned, hesitated.

'Hey, Bryman. How's your ankle?'

'I think my ankle's busted too, sir. I'm not used to jumping in sneakers.'

'You're okay. Yes, you're okay,' Lebeau repeated as if this litany could heal bones and ligaments.

They heard Tippett's squad stepping onto the roof above them.

'Bryman, get on the radio and warn them to watch out for that goddam camera,' the major ordered a moment later. 'And, Farley, come here and carry this special nuclear device.'

He spoke the last three words with irony, mocking the jargon. The sergeant picked up the warhead container and followed the tiny beam of Lebeau's masked flashlight down the corridor. The others trailed behind silently, and in a minute they all faced the closed metal accordion door of the freight elevator.

The cab itself was at the bottom of the shaft.

'Goddam,' said Major Jean Charles Lebeau.

'There's a control over here,' whispered Sergeant Farley. 'I think it might bring up the elevator.'

'And it might set off some goddam alarm. This whole goddam place is rigged with goddam alarms, and there are more alarms on the goddam alarms. ... No, get out your cutters and whittle on the door slats. Chop us a hole big enough to stick a hand in and open it from the inside.'

As Farley set to work, the men heard the sounds of their comrades slipping off the roof and descending via the climbing ropes.

'Bryman,' Lebeau called out softly, 'you better radio that we're hacking away at this elevator accordeen door with our cutters and Tippett's on his way down.'

'I don't see anything, Larry,' Falco said cheerfully ninety-eight feet away. 'Just the same old crap they've been going through for half an hour.'

'That's what bothers me. There has to be a reason for it.'

'They're up to something,' predicted the puffy rapist.

'Crap.'

'No, Stud,' disagreed Willieboy Powell, 'it looks *wrong*. There's too much action for this hour of the night. Something's not *right* up there. I've got to agree with Harvey.'

'Screw Harvey and his sweaty hands and his big mouth.'

Dell continued to rotate the camera.

'Leave Harve alone, will you, Stud?' he asked. 'He's not feeling too well, you know.'

'He might feel a lot worse. ... Okay, you guys watch. I'm going to sleep. Let me know how the picture comes out, will you?'

'Sweet dreams,' Dell proposed.

'No, dirty ones,' predicted the assassin.

His estimate proved to be realistic, for within five minutes after he'd shoved Lieutenant Canellis into the upper bunk with Towne and appropriated the lower one for himself 'Stud' Falco was reliving – in excellent color – a weekend he'd spent with three high-spirited young women in a suite at the El San Juan Hotel in Puerto Rico. One had been a redhead, a natural redhead, he'd discovered by meticulous study. It was a wonderful dream, and, while it might not compare too well with those tapes made by the video-recorder in the bedroom of a certain roguish publisher in Chicago, it was both a heart-warming recollection of what had been and a delightful promise of what lay ahead.

'They're all inside now,' reported the Jericho commander, 'and so far everything's looking *real* good.'

'What do we do now?' grumbled the Army's Chief of Staff.

'Have you ever considered prayer?' Woodside answered.

The senior Army general eyed the JCS chairman thoughtfully, trying to estimate whether he was being serious or sardonic.

'What do you think, Vince?' the President asked less than five miles away.

'I'm not thinking, just perspiring profusely.'

'I'm wondering how the hell we ever got into this.'

'You mean Viper Three or the whole fang-and-claw global missile mess?'

It was nearly 2:30 A.M. in Washington, and Stevens was red-eyed with fatigue. He yawned, sighed and yawned again.

'The whole mess, Vince.'

'I don't know, Dave,' Bonomi replied with his own yawn. 'I can't even figure out what a nice boy like me is doing in a place like this.'

'You were never cut out for the White House,' Stevens agreed, 'but that still doesn't answer the question. What the hell are we doing – all of us – with H-bombs and intercontinental missiles and squadrons of atomic submarines that can burn out whole cities with their rockets? What kind of a world have we created in which an auto mechanic talks to his wife – and twenty generals listen in?'

'Part of it's his fault, you know, Dave. If he'd stayed in his garage and kept out of that bar nobody would give a damn about his family life.'

Bonomi heard the sigh from the armchair.

'Yes, part of it is his fault – but what about the part that's ours?' wondered the Ohioan.

Suddenly Corporal Bryman's voice crackled from the TV set.

'Second squad entering the guardhouse.'

Tippet led his unit through the room and back to where Lebeau was watching the crouching sergeant work the cutters.

'J.C.?' asked the captain.

'Glad you could make it, Norm. Hang on a second, will you? I think Farley's just about got it whacked.'

Tippett put down the box with audible relief, glad to be free of the forty-two-pound burden.

Farley twisted the edged tool back and forth, squeezed again and cut through. He reached inside, groped for a few moments before he finally tripped the catch.

'She's open,' he said softly.

Lebeau nudged him aside, pulled back the accordian gate and pointed his lamp down the shaft. The top of the elevator car was dimly visible some dozen yards below. Much nearer and of more immediate interest were the steel cables, for they were the way to the bottom. Lebeau focussed his beam on them, saw that they glistened with a thin layer of oil.

'Looks a little slick, Norm,' he told his second-in-command. 'A man might make it with just his weapon, but I'm not sure what the hell would happen to a man carrying one of these charges. He might go down like a rock.'

'Suppose I give it a try?'

'Without the charge,' Lebeau stipulated.

Tippett pulled on a pair of gloves, reached through the opening and saw the cable was just out of reach.

'You're a qualified certified jumper, Norm,' Lebeau whispered slyly, 'so you'd better jump for it.'

The captain backed off a few yards, took a running start and leaped into the shaft with arms outstretched. His left hand caught one of the cables and he half spun as he struggled to secure a firm grip, and after some dozen efforts he managed to grasp the wires with both hands. He hung there gasping for a while before he began heading down, a fitful, jerky journey of starts and stops and swaying crises.

He reached the roof of the car, caught his breath and waved a thumbs-up 'come ahead' to the men watching.

'No sirree, that's just too goddam exciting. Too goddam chicken-picking exciting,' Lebeau judged, 'and goddam dangerous. Get your extra climbing ropes, boys.'

Four men – Lebeau and three others – would descend on the white nylon lines.

Four men, two to carry the charges and the other two to cover them with rapid-fire guns.

'I didn't go airborne to climb down no elevator shafts,' grumbled one of the men Lebeau picked, but he slung his weapon and attached his rope carefully.

'You're going to be a big famous hero, Kopecki,' promised the major. 'They're going to name interstate highways and public urinals after you, boy.'

Kopecki didn't try to match wits with his commander; he simply started down. The others followed within seconds, and it was an easy descent – for those not burdened by the 133As. For those carrying the atomic charges, it was a terrible muscle-stretching horror that seemed much longer than two and a half minutes.

Tippett gestured to the opening he'd made by removing one of the elevator car's ceiling panels, and the gunners went through first.

'You okay?' he asked Lebeau.

'Just dandy, considering my age and laziness and lousy disposition. Move your fat butt, Norm, the Yankees are counting on you!'

They were lucky.

The elevator door was open, so there was nothing to touch or move or cut, and that meant less risk of kicking off some sophisticated alarm. Jean Charles Lebeau put one index finger to his lips, led the way to the big steel door, yes, it was a massive mother all right, but one, certainly two, 133As would punch it in and simultaneously stun everyone inside with the blast.

Stun?

That was a terribly cautious and dishonest estimate.

The blast of one hundred tons of high explosives in this

confined area would almost surely kill them, pulp them into pink jelly.

All of them, the convicts and the two men of the 168th.

That pair – they'd surely name federal office buildings and USAF bases in their memories. No mere Walter Reed urinals or public incinerators for those martyrs. Hell, they might even retitle a couple of dormitories at the Air Force Academy – and all Lebeau would get, if anything, was a Silver Star. The prospect was not exhilarating, since he already had a Silver Star and a $275 golden retriever and a girl named Patty who was bronzed all over and loved fruit and nuts and Judy Collins records. She was really something to look at, as Lebeau often remarked.

'I can hardly see anything,' Dell said less than nineteen yards away. 'It's the lights. They keep flashing their lights on our camera, and it's hard to see in that glare.'

'Think they're doing it deliberately?'

'I don't know, Willieboy. Hard to tell.'

Outside the four-foot-thick door, Lebeau began to untie the straps that sealed one of the boxes.

In twelve, maybe thirteen minutes, it would be all over.

Two or three to open the containers and set the charges, and ten to get back up to the helicopters. No nine. It wouldn't pay to cut things too fine.

'Bet there's nearly a thousand men out there,' Powell judged as Dell moved the rooftop camera again, 'just itching to kill us.'

'They're not all itching to kill us, are they?'

'No, Major. Some of them are itching to wash their feet and some are itching to get laid and some aren't itching at all, but plenty are itching to kill us.'

'But I haven't done anything. Why would they want to kill me?' protested the former SAC officer.

'You've done something. You killed a woman, didn't you?'

Before Lawrence Dell could answer, Sergeant Francis Farley reached down to start untying the second box and almost brushed against the huge door. He didn't touch it, but that wasn't necessary.

His body heat was enough to trigger the thermostat alarm.

A blue light began to flash on the commander's console, and

a klaxon groaned louder and louder with unpleasant metallic urgency.

Falco awoke immediately, and as he leaped from the bed he saw Powell picking up one of the machine guns.

'Stud, you and Willie cover the door,' Dell commanded. 'The bastards are at the door.'

Falco turned and bent down for his weapon on the floor, and just at that moment Captain Sanford Towne and Lieutenant Philip Canellis hurled themselves down on him from the upper bunk.

CHAPTER TWENTY-FIVE

The missilemen were going for the second machine gun, and how they'd untied their bonds didn't matter now. All that counted was who got his hands on the rapid-fire weapon, Falco or one of the SAC officers. The three fought desperately in a tangle of arms and legs for several seconds. Suddenly Canellis broke free with one fist closed around the stock of the gun, shouting in hoarse triumph as he turned toward the control console.

The homicidal holy man fired the stolen .38 police revolver from the doorway to the other compartment, breaking his right arm and shoulder and gouging a half-inch-deep furrow through the flesh of his hip. Canellis dropped the weapon, fell bleeding from the three wounds with a shrill scream. Falco seized the gun. In one motion, he swiveled to ram the muzzle into Towne's stomach and the captain doubled up instantly.

'Okay?' Dell asked.

'Okay,' confirmed the assassin, 'thanks to Deacon. Nice shooting, Deacon.'

Hoxey answered something, but Lawrence Dell wasn't listening.

He was speaking into the telephone.

'We're about to launch. We've broken the safety seals on the firing switches, and we'll launch in two minutes if you don't pull out your assault team. Two minutes,' he threatened, 'starting from now.'

'Now, Dell,' the CINCSAC began.

'The keys are in my hand right now. Get those bastards out and up – out and up – fast.'

It would be inaccurate to say that there was pandemonium in the JCS 'war room.' Senior commanders and intelligence directors are not given to pandemonium, but there was some con-

201

sternation, a certain amount of shouting and a great deal of distress, perspiration and abrupt gastric upset. There was, in fact, considerable consternation.

'The countdown is on,' they heard Dell announce. 'One-twenty ... one-nineteen ... one-eighteen ... one-seventeen ... one-sixteen.'

'Get 'em out!' decided the President.

Bonomi picked up the hot-line phone, repeated the Chief Executive's edict.

'One hundred five ... one hundred four ... one hundred three ... one hundred two.'

They could hear the klaxon still going in the background.

'General Woodside says they can set their charges in only another minute,' McKenzie reported.

Stevens jumped up, seized the phone.

'I said get 'em out. This is the President. Do it!'

'Major Dell, we're pulling those men out immediately,' McKenzie conceded. 'It may take more than two minutes for them to climb up, however.'

'They can use the elevator. Out! Now! Ninety-five ... ninety-four ... ninety-three.'

Both the boxes were open when Bryman shouted the order down the shaft.

'The President says get out! Just leave everything and come up in the elevator – fast!'

No Silver Star for Jean Charles Lebeau after all.

'Hurry up! Hurry up! Those crazy cons are going to launch!'

The five paratroopers ran to the elevator, took it to the surface and led the others out the front door. The major helped Bryman hobble across the twenty yards to the gate.

'We had it made, had it made,' lamented Tippett a few steps behind them.

'Thirty-eight ... thirty-seven ... thirty-six ... thirty-five.'

'Move it! Move it out!' boomed the voice of the task-force commander over an electronic bull horn.

Half a dozen powerful searchlights illuminated the scene as if it were a sound stage, and hundreds of tense men watched as the assault party reached the gate.

'It's locked, dammit!' shouted Lebeau.

'Switch in the left gatepost,' answered the bull horn.

'Seventeen . . . sixteen . . . fifteen . . . fourteen.'

They rushed out, slammed the gate shut behind them.

'Nine . . . eight.'

'They're all out, Dell,' McKenzie reported. 'All out, every one of them.'

The former launch-site security officer didn't reply immediately.

He eyed the instrument panel, studied the gauges and then reset the thermo-alarm on the door.

The klaxon stopped, and for a moment the silence seemed even more menacing than the rhythmic alarm itself had been.

'All out? No tricks?' Dell asked.

'That's right.'

More silence.

The Jericho camera swept the scene in slow panorama, then panned up to catch the two helicopters climbing up to head back to Malmstrom.

'We'll see,' Dell acknowledged cautiously. 'The countdown stopped at eight, General, and that's exactly where it'll start again if you try anything else. You tell that to the President. It'll start at eight.'

'I'll tell him.'

There really wasn't any more for either of them to say.

In the Pentagon, the men in the JCS chamber were speaking intently about what had happened and what might have gone wrong and what to do next – until the message from Germany arrived. All the telephone lines into West Berlin had been cut, Soviet MIGs were crisscrossing the air corridors into the city and East German troops were piling up traffic from West Germany into the former capital by blocking the autobahns. The situation was getting worse all the time, with each report bringing word of further 'deterioration.' As for the three 'checkpoints' through which people moved from East Berlin to West Berlin and vice versa, they'd been sealed by tanks and the interzone subway halted.

The crisis was mounting, building by the hour, and no one knew just how far the Communists meant to go – or why.

Perhaps it would be necessary to go to DEFCON Three.

In the morning, when the President was rested and feeling a little better, General Woodside would ask him.

_____

CHAPTER TWENTY-SIX

It was going to be some time before David Stevens would feel
at all better, even for a moment. At this moment, he felt grim
and troubled and taut.

'They wouldn't have launched, I guess,' he reasoned aloud.

'Right,' Bonomi confirmed.

'They wouldn't have launched because they'd be shooting
everything, and they wouldn't have anything else. No cards left,
nothing.'

'Right, but now they're mad . . . and scared.'

'Yes, Vince, now they're mad and scared and they might do
anything now. Now they're really desperate, really on the knife
edge.'

'Check.'

'And they don't feel quite so safe any more. Assuming they can't
know exactly what those paratroopers were doing and what
hardware they carried, those men in Viper Three still know that
soldiers got through all the alarms to reach the capsule door.'

Bonomi felt it all now in a sudden wave of fatigue, sweat,
worry and – most tangibly – the scratchy awareness that he
needed a shave. That, which should have been the least, was
inexplicably the most bothering.

'Maybe they would launch now. Is that what you're saying,
Dave?'

The cigar tasted terrible. It was a good Canary Island petit
corona that had cost fifty cents, but it tasted terrible and the
whole room – the whole big office – smelled bad after the day of
steady smoking.

'That's exactly what I'm saying. I think I made a mistake in
risking this attack. I'm not blaming the military, you understand, but it was a big mistake – my big mistake. I'm not
supposed to make big mistakes, Vince.'

'You don't make many, Mr President. As a matter of fact, I can honestly tell you – not just as a friend – that you've made damned few. Of course you might destroy the whole world if you goof this time,' the general admitted wryly, 'but I wouldn't worry about that.'

'I'm not you. I'm worrying.'

For those who keep score cards on Christmas Eve highway fatalities, the illegitimacy rate among California high-school girls, suicides in Sweden and international crises, there were a number of other people worrying in a number of other places at the same time.

In Bonn, the Chancellor of the Federal Republic was acutely worried about the news from Berlin.

In Moscow, five full marshals of the Red Army – including Chief of Staff Barzinko and Chief Marshal of Armored Troops Aleksei Soyuzov – were just as troubled. The cryptographic section of the GRU had broken the American message escalating the worldwide US defense readiness to DEFCON Four, and this seemed to be an obvious reaction to Yamshchik.

Stupid, stupid, stupid.

The whole operation was stupid, staging another Berlin crisis to impress the other Communist states with Soviet toughness a few weeks before the Bucharest Conference.

Stupid, stupid, stupid.

These were the thoughts that Soyuzov would have articulated if he'd been certain that the room wasn't bugged, but it probably was.

Nevertheless, it was all stupid.

Yamshchik was stupid and the *Amerikanski* reaction was stupid and the Central Committee's answer to that reaction would, beyond any doubt, be stupid. And the newspaper evaluations in London and Peking and Mexico City would be just as stupid, although basically unimportant. What was important was that the Central Committee should be cautious, analytical, practical, not ideological or egotistical.

'The operation itself has gone well,' Barzinko reiterated hopefully, 'and we have executed every phase of the plan exactly on schedule.'

'Yes, it was well done,' agreed the head of the Red Air Force loyally.

'We have done what the plan called for,' Barzinko continued, 'and now it is up to the diplomats and the propaganda people to extract the maximum benefits from our achievement.'

'Of course,' chorused two marshals.

Soyuzov said nothing.

'Don't you agree, Aleksei?' one of them asked.

'My leg hurts,' he replied noncommittally.

'It always hurts in this weather,' Barzinko reminded the others soothingly with the smooth conference skill that had contributed so much to his rise. He was a master at glossing over, at compromising, at adjusting. 'As I was saying, the operation is a success and I have so informed the Minister of Defense and he has notified the Central Committee.'

'Has anyone notified them about the change to DEFCON Four?' challenged the tank veteran.

It was an unnecessary question spoken with unnecessary bluntness, but that was typical of Soyuzov. It should have been clear to everyone in the room that Marshal Barzinko had passed the news to the minister, and the Minister had relayed it to the Central Committee. That was, after all, standard procedure. There was no reason to be disturbed about this, and no reason to think that the Central Committee would do anything more than take note of the information. Even with all the pressure from the Chinese to sink or take over the Bucharest meeting, the Central Committee certainly wasn't going to do anything precipitate.

'The Minister has been notified,' Barzinko announced calmly, 'and we can assume that word has reached the Central Committee. I don't think, however—'

The arrival of the Ministry of Defense courier interrupted the marshal's remarks. The brief message stated that the Central Committee was determined that the USSR would not be intimidated by the American reaction, which was only a bluff anyway.

Four of Soyuzov's armored divisions in Poland would move – immediately – to within thirty miles of the West German frontier.

CHAPTER TWENTY-SEVEN

By two A.M. almost everyone at Malmstrom was asleep. Of course, the Air Police guarding the base perimeter and the others who sealed the hospital's isolation ward were awake – and so were Brigadier General Stonesifer and five of his top colonels and the Duty Controller. But almost everyone else – including Captain Dr Stanley Bigelman and the battered missilemen and the Air Intelligence officers who'd brought in Dr Langer and Nurse Kelleran – was asleep. Bigelman was tossing gloomily in a dream that featured Dr Langer and Nurse Kelleran miming the last seven chapters of *Fanny Hill* with a skill that would have impressed Marcel Marceau. It was all quite vivid, with plenty of background music in excellent stereophonic sound. If he were awake, Bigelman would have had the sense to realize that Langer and the nurse would never dare to sleep together in a room in an Air Force hospital.

Eleven yards from where Bigelman snored, Dr. Langer and Nurse Kelleran slept sweetly in each other's arms. The shapely blonde wore an especially beatific smile, one rooted in her deep female intuition that she'd be Mrs Langer before summer. Only time would tell, but she believed.

While she believed and smiled, Dell paced the confined space of the Launch Control Center with the bitter look of distrust. He knew that he'd never had the slightest reason to trust any of them – the brass and the Government people – since he'd been sentenced to die, and he hadn't. No, it wasn't simply distrust now. It was anger, no longer suppressed.

He'd been angry for a very long time – for a variety of reasons. The strain of endless intelligence, charm, diligence and success as the brightest and the handsomest was only one of the reasons. There were others, and there was the shock of the surprise attacks – external and internal.

'We're doing one helluva business in tourniquets,' Powell announced as he finished with Canellis.

'How is he?'

'He's okay, Major. He's not at his best, but who is?'

Falco laughed.

'That punk's lucky he's alive,' judged the assassin.

'And we're all lucky that Deacon was on the ball.'

'Right, Larry. Of course if I'd had the piece I'd have killed him,' acknowledged the underworld executioner, 'but then I was never paid just to wound somebody. I never got a contract like that.'

'You should have killed him, killed them both!'

The black man shook his head.

You could always count on good old Harvey to say something vicious, to press for some gratuitous and excessive violence.

Good old Harve must have been hell on frogs and pussy cats with his Scout knife as a child.

'They're both idiots,' Dell scorned. 'Dumb bastard apprentice heroes. God, I've always hated that type. Harvey may be right – this time.'

For no reason – none that made any sense – he saw her face for a split second. Diana, as she'd been at the beginning. Beautiful.

'Major, if you'd been one of those two tied up there,' Powell probed, 'what would you have done?'

'I wouldn't have—'

'Major, wouldn't you have done the same thing?'

Now the anger in Dell was visible, almost tangible.

Not just his eyes and his face.

His whole body was rigid with rage.

'Hey, Larry,' chuckled Falco, 'Willieboy thinks you've got the makings of a hero too. That's nothing to be sore about.'

'We must all be heroes for the Savior,' intoned Hoxey solemnly, 'for Judgement Day is drawing near. I hear the bugle calls to Armageddon.'

'Man, I don't hear a thing,' Falco confessed. 'Maybe I'm tuned to a different wave length. I'm getting Tony Bennett, loud and clear.'

'I'm getting fed up with all this, especially the two-bit psychiatry by garage mechanics. Is that clear?'

'Yes, Major.'

'And I'm tired of that "major" shit too. Is that clear, Willieboy?'

'Don't blow your cool, Larry,' urged Falco. 'After all, Deac may be right and it wouldn't be nice to be all hateful and nasty on Judgement Day. Hang loose.'

'The bugles sing!' Hoxey rejoiced.

'Right,' said the assassin, 'and they'll be playing "The Girl from Ipanema" by Tuesday night.'

'That's Brazil,' the ex-Marine pointed out, 'and we're going to Peru.'

'There are girls in Peru too, and I think I'll go back to sleep to dream about them. Why don't we continue the bitching in the morning?'

Without waiting for an answer, Falco turned, took a last look at the TV screen, saw nothing different and adjourned to the upper bunk. A moment later, he climbed out to re-examine the new bonds of the two prisoners.

'You know it's kind of dumb to waste a sack – certainly the lower one – on these two clowns, even if they are a bit bloody.' He yawned.

'Those beds should be for *us*,' complained the rapist.

Falco tossed down the two pillows.

'You guys can rest your heads on those. Hope the floor's not too hard.'

Powell watched him settle down into the upper bunk again.

'What gives *you* the exclusive right to the bed?' he asked.

'Brains. I had the brains to take it while you deep thinkers were busy talking and worrying. It's what they call native intelligence. . . . Good night.'

Schonbacher quickly appropriated one of the pillows, took it to the tunnel doorway and settled down uncomfortably on the linoleum floor. Just to make it clear that he was uncomfortable, he issued a number of unmistakably 'uncomfortable' sounds that officially registered his discontent. Hoxey simply sat in one corner, closed his eyes and retreated into his pious paranoia. It was impossible to tell whether he was awake or asleep, Powell realized, but then it probably didn't matter much anyway.

Dell was still turning the knob that rotated the camera, still checking and rechecking the enemy on the surface.

'Anything?' asked Powell.

'I don't know. We didn't see anything last time. I wonder how those bastards got in. We've got to know, got to know.'

Or they might try it again.

The former SAC officer didn't say the words, but he didn't have to.

If there was any such thing as a good officer. Willieboy Powell reflected, Dell was a good officer. He thought ahead, he organized, he planned realistically and he tried to anticipate what the enemy might do. He was a cold man, but a competent one. The enemy? The enemy was David Stevens and Martin McKenzie and the entire armed forces of the United States – including the Marine Corps in which Powell had spent eight years. Everyone in the country – white and black and brown, young and old, male and female – they were all the enemy.

'I wish that I knew more about the set-up of these bases,' the former sergeant volunteered, 'but this is all strange country to me.'

'I know all about the set-up ... every bit of it ... and I can't figure it out ... I know it all ... the whole security system ... top to bottom.'

Then Lawrence Dell smiled.

'That's it,' he celebrated. 'That's it all right. They came in through the top, above the field of the camera.'

'Choppers?'

Dell nodded emphatically.

'Had to be. Had to be. Those slick bastards couldn't get through on the ground, so they threw a forward pass. Onto the roof, then into the guardhouse and down.'

'Elevator?'

'No, Willie, the elevator didn't move. It would have registered on our console here. They came down the shaft on ropes or ladders, pried open the top of the elevator car and started to work on the door. That must have been the way, but they can't do it again.'

'Why not?'

'Because they left the goddam elevator up at the surface level when we made them run! Now they can't come down the shaft except by running the elevator, and we'll know it!'

'So we're okay?'

'We're okay.'

Dell was beaming.

He knew. He was in control again, and he was triumphant.

'Take the other pillow and go to sleep,' he offered. 'I can sleep in the commander's chair, so you take the pillow.'

Yes, Dell would like the commander's red chair.

'I'll wake you in two hours and you can take the next shift,' he told the ex-sergeant.

Still taking care of the enlisted men, *his* men.

Powell lay down and drifted off into blackness. Still radiating that immense smile – much larger even than the one suffusing the face of the satisfied nurse in the Malmstrom isolation ward – Lawrence Dell sat back in the chair and watched the little figures and lights on the screen. He hadn't slept for more than twenty-four hours, but he felt good as he observed the pigmies. Now that he knew, his enemies were pigmies again and he didn't need to be angry anymore.

The bitterness drained away in the silence, with only the low soothing hum of the air conditioning barely audible.

The fear – the fear and the histamines that had flooded with it – started to ebb, and his eyes began to hurt.

Benzedrine.

They should have looted a drugstore on the way to seize some Benzedrine. He'd overlooked that somehow, he realized wearily. He walked to the sink, splashed cold water on his face and felt better. He washed his hands and face carefully, and he was much more awake when he returned to the chair.

Twenty minutes later he was asleep.

Schonbacher listened to the rhythmic breathing for several minutes, flickering his eyes open for brief moments to look. Yes, the weariness had won. They were all asleep, and it was time for Harvey Schonbacher to save himself.

The firing keys would be his passport.

The rapist rose to one knee wearily, glanced around again

before he stood erect. It would be so simple. He'd taken off his shoes before lying down, and now he could move quietly. That was essential. He moved close to the commander's chair, scanned the room once more and drew his pistol. He struck Dell on the skull twice, saw the handsome head slump forward.

Good.

Schonbacher reached into the unconscious man's pocket, groped and struggled and finally succeeded. He sighed, glanced at the sleepers. Then he walked carefully out of the capsule and up the tunnel that led to the huge door. It was such a simple plan. He would deliver the keys to the Army and the Government would replay him by setting him free. The others who slept would no longer be a threat, and the military could exterminate those fools at its leisure.

He reached the door, slipped the keys into his coverall pocket and reached for the handle that controlled the massive bolts. He took a firm grip, twisted.

Click.

It was quite a loud click, and the former jungle fighter awoke instantly. Powell grabbed his machine gun, looked up and saw the rapist up the tunnel tugging at the door. The combat veteran reacted instantly, and his first burst killed Harvey Schonbacher.

As the fat man fell, Powell was already sprinting up the shaft to the door. The door was all that counted now. The former sergeant stepped around the butchered thing on the floor, re-locked the bolts. Only then did he bother to glance down at the corpse, and as he did so he spotted the familiar shape of a firing key silhouetted in the blood-splattered coverall.

'Bastard,' he said to Falco, who now stood beside him. 'The bastard took the keys, and he was on his way out with them.'

The assassin responded with a stream of obscenities.

Powell looked at the porky body, realized that he'd never shot anyone except in war. It seemed strange, and he said so.

'You're just out of practice, Willie.' Falco laughed.

Powell recovered the keys and they returned to the Launch Control Center, went to work to help the unconscious man in the Commander's chair.

'Schonbacher hit him with something . . . you can see where,' the syndicate executioner noted. 'Must have done it when he got the fucking keys.'

'Harvey was always too violent and too stupid,' the black man answered as he raised Dell's eyelids – a test he'd learned from a medic in battle. 'That idiot wasn't going anywhere even if he got out the door.'

'He wasn't?'

'No. Say, get a wet cloth, would you, Stud?'

Falco returned with it twenty seconds later, and Powell applied it to the cut on Dell's temple.

'Why wasn't he going any place, Willie?'

'Because he wasn't a balloon. He had no way to reach the surface even if he got out the door,' Powell explained, 'because the elevator was upstairs anyway. He was just an idiot.'

Dell's eyelids moved. He'd be all right.

'No loss. With Harve gone, the split for each of us will be bigger,' Falco calculated. 'Say, you still feel funny about gunning that fat slob?'

Willieboy Justice Powell considered the question soberly.

'Yes, I still feel funny,' he replied.

CHAPTER TWENTY-EIGHT

On a normal day or what passed for one in the District of Columbia, Brigadier General Vincent Bonomi awoke at 7:30 A.M. and was showered, shaved, dressed and breakfasted by eight when the CIA couriers arrived in the car. On this schedule which prevailed on weekdays when David Stevens was in Washington, Bonomi reached the White House at 8:35 and at 8:45 was briefing the Chief Executive.

This Monday morning was different.

For one thing, Bonomi awoke in a guest room at the White House instead of his own home. For another thing, it was only 6:10 when he was awakened and he was not at his rosy best after less than four hours of sleep. But there was a third thing, and that counted the most.

'Sorry to get you up at this hour, General,' apologized the brisk young military aide, 'but the President wants to see you *immediately*.'

He probably wasn't sorry at all.

He probably welcomed this opportunity to harass a general.

He was a twenty-six-year-old captain, wasn't he?

'Coffee, sir?' he offered cheerily. 'I brought along a pitcher and a cup, General.'

He was one of the eager-beaver 'gung ho' types; he'd be wearing a major's leaves by thirty and he'd be married to a congressman's daughter. Hartung. That's what the nameplate on his jacket said. Major Hartung? Colonel Hartung? Maybe, for he was very keen – especially for this hour. Of course the bushy-tailed bastard hadn't been sweating Viper Three all Sunday and hadn't sat up half the night either.

'Sugar?' offered the efficient captain as Bonomi sat up and poured his first cup.

He probably didn't take any sugar, the general brooded.

He was lean and dietwise and didn't smoke and was terribly fit.

Screw him.

'Two sugars,' Bonomi said defiantly.

Screw them all.

After his second cup of coffee, Bonomi felt better.

'Where is he?'

'The President, General?'

'No, Marlene Dietrich,' Bonomi replied irritably as he took off the top of the pajamas the White House had provided.

Captain Hartung smiled pleasantly.

He thought that all generals, senior Department of the Army officials and members of the Senate Military Affairs Committee were witty.

'The President's in his bedroom – just upstairs. He's been up for more than half an hour, since the telex came in and the Secretary of State called.'

Bonomi wondered, then looked at his rumpled underclothes, shirt and uniform.

'I've taken the liberty of telephoning your home, sir, and we've sent a car to collect fresh clothing. I hope you don't mind, General.'

'Very thoughtful. I'm going to take a one-minute shower now.'

The car hadn't returned by the time Bonomi finished showering and shaving, so he put on the soiled garments and hurried to talk to David Stevens. Stevens was still in his pajamas and bathrobe, concluding a telephone conversation.

'Nine o'clock – that's it,' he finished.

He turned to Bonomi.

'Well, General, you look perfectly terrible this glorious Monday morning. Did you sleep in your clothes?'

'I feel perfectly terrible, and I didn't sleep in my clothes – and at this very moment fresh, crisp garments are en route here in a White House car. You didn't wake me up to discuss my personal appearance though, did you?'

'No. Berlin.'

Bonomi blinked several times.

'The Russians have completely sealed off Berlin, blocked the autobahns and closed the checkpoints and flooded the commercial air corridors with MIGs.'

'Dandy, just dandy.'

'Caldwell is going on the "Today" show at 7:15, I'm told, and the word is that he's going to blame this Red affront to the West on US military weakness. How do you like that?'

'I *love* it. Dave, let's forget about Caldwell. Remember that version of the Twenty-third Psalm that Bill Frost quotes? The Lord is my shepherd, so let his mother worry. Let's play it that way. This Berlin thing – why?'

'We're not sure. Grosvenor believes that they're putting on pressure to get recognition for East Germany again, and Michaelson suspects darker and more devious motives . . . Of course, he always suspects darker and more devious motives.'

'What do you think, Mr President?'

'Good morning, you son of a bitch?'

Bonomi shook his head.

'I mean it. How do you figure it, Dave?'

'I'm not sure . . . but I've got a hunch that they're looking for a free ride, a propaganda victory, just before our elections. They figure that they can get something for nothing now, that we'll be tame and hesitant. They'll look strong and tough, and we'll be the old paper tiger again.'

'Well?'

The President stood up, walked to the window and looked down at the lawn.

'No, they've made a mistake. No tiger, paper or saber-toothed. Election or no election, Viper Three or no Viper Three, we're not going to panic.'

'You're a pretty smart fella, Dave.'

Stevens nodded in appreciation.

'I know you're just saying that to get one of those fat Government jobs,' he teased, 'but I don't mind. In any case, while this Berlin thing is serious I can't see it as crucial. From a military point of view, if they meant to hit us they'd never tip their hand like this, would they?'

'Probably not. Everybody on both sides seems to be thinking in terms of a big surprise, a massive preemptive strike.'

Then the President saw his own reflection in the window.

'Come on in and talk to me while I shave. I want to chew on this and organize my thoughts before the NSC meeting. I've called it for nine. Your clothes ought to be here by then.'

'I hope so,' Bonomi replied, 'because I wouldn't want to embarrass you, or the CIA, or the Air Force.'

David Stevens shaved and washed and dressed and spoke with his old friend, and then at 7:15 they watched Senator Caldwell denounce the 'musty, moribund Stevens administration' on NBC–TV's 'Today' show. At 7:35, Ray Gumbiner was on the phone to discuss the political implications of the newest Berlin crisis and Caldwell's use of it.

'It's neck and neck right now, Dave,' he warned, 'and you can't let him take the initiative on this sort of thing. You've got to issue a statement of your own – fast. Fast enough to make the afternoon editions and the evening news shows.'

'Ray, I'll make a statement when I've figured it all out very carefully,' Stevens answered patiently. 'I'm not just some horny Senator with hot pants for the White House, not anymore. I'm the President of the United States, and when I speak I speak for the United States – so I can't sound off with ringing patriotic platitudes and marching songs the way Caldwell can.'

'Dave, I know you're tired,' the canny chairman of the national committee cajoled, 'but a good strong statement – right away – would certainly be in the country's interest. Don't you agree?'

'How strong and how fast – that's the question.'

'Pretty strong and pretty fast – if you want to stay President. You've got to show the country that you're not tired, not scared, that you know exactly what to do.'

The President of the United States couldn't help laughing.

'What's so goddam funny about that, Dave?' Gumbiner demanded. 'Nobody else knows exactly what to do about anything – not even dandruff or bad manners – and everybody wants the President to be smart and clean and confident. You can prove you're all those things – even if you aren't – with the right statement.'

'Ray, I don't want to escalate this confrontation. I want to keep it small and unemotional, not to give in but not to insult or defy the other side.'

As Gumbiner argued that the Soviets probably wouldn't take any official US statements too seriously anyway, Stevens realized that he couldn't discuss Viper Three with the party professional. No matter how it was solved, word about the disaster there would surely get out before Election Day and it would undoubtedly be wise – from a political point of view – to notify Gumbiner in advance so that he could cope better *later*. But if Gumbiner were notified, he'd probably make it a lot more difficult for the President to cope *now*. It was entirely logical and respectable for a political party's chairman to see almost everything in terms of politics, of winning elections, but David Stevens had to live with other considerations as well.

'I'll talk to Grosvenor about a statement when he gets here at nine, Ray,' promised Stevens. 'You can count on that.'

'A strong statement?'

'Ray, I want to win that election as much as you do – more, if you can believe it.'

'Then sock it to 'em, Mr President, and sock it to 'em hard.'

Several other phone calls and messages on the Berlin crisis reached the President during the next hour, and Bonomi's clothes arrived in time for him to change just before the National Security Council convened in the Cabinet Room. Secretary of State Grosvenor came prepared with a draft of a statement that was sincere, noncommittal and full of references to treaties and previous US statements. Peter Ustinov could have delivered it very well, but it wasn't quite right for David Stevens. Secretary of Defense Darby brought in an entire attaché case filled with contingency plans. The Defense Department and the Joint Chiefs maintain a complete library of contingency plans, as well as all the back issues of the *National Geographic*. Assuming that the President had already read the *National Geographic*, Darby offered three different contingency plans named Beer Barrel, Harper Valley and Sandspit – all geared to coping with Berlin crises. The CIA's contribution included a digest of a tapped telephone conversation between a Soviet marshal named Korbynin, who was in East Germany, and Red Army headquarters in Moscow – plus a political analysis of probable Soviet intentions compiled by the Agency's Russian Affairs Unit. It was, in fact, quite a perceptive analysis that offered a number of possibilities relating to Southeast Asia and the Near East and also a secret set of talks that the Soviets were to be having with the Chinese in January. Michaelson's presentation was impressive, but it didn't nearly answer the questions that troubled David Stevens.

'By the way,' Michaelson concluded with premeditated casualness, 'the name of the game appears to be "Coachman". That's "Yamshchik" in Russian. Korbynin spoke of Yamshchik several times, and we know that he's the field commander of the operation. NSA has reported a number of references to Yamshchik in the past month or so, and now with Korbynin's transcript we can be pretty certain that this is the operation they've been preparing.'

Knowing the name of the game was fine, but knowing the score would be even better. Coachman – it didn't communicate anything. The Russians hadn't said anything yet either. If they played their usual game, they'd wait for a US statement and then rip it to pieces with a barrage of invective, innuendo and gutsy clichés. They could afford to wait, for they had Berlin isolated and they had the initiative.

'Gentlemen, even though the Soviets' objectives are not clear,' reckoned the President, 'and I'm not minimizing the contributions and estimates we've just heard, we've got to prepare to move. Until we do move – in a day or two – we'll have to say something reassuring for the sake of our friends in Bonn and Berlin.'

'The German ambassador's been on the phone three times this morning, pushing and pleading,' Grosvenor reported, 'and the British and French ambassadors have been asking what we're going to do.'

'That figures,' snapped the Secretary of Defense. 'They're not going to do a goddam thing themselves, nothing that'll cost a dime anyway. They'll expect us to do it all, and then their newspapers will blame the whole thing on us anyway and their film directors will sign petitions denouncing American meddling.'

'You're starting to sound like Senator Caldwell, Bob,' Michaelson needled.

'As I was saying,' Stevens continued, 'we'll issue a statement this afternoon – at State. It isn't necessary for me to jump into this yet, so you put out the statement, Arthur. Call a press conference for two o'clock, Arthur, and you'll make the late-afternoon editions and the six-and seven-o'clock news shows. Keep it calm but firm, and that ought to buy us some time to decide on physical action. . . . Bob,' he said to the Secretary of Defense, 'Sandspit – that's just the airlift, I think – how long would it take you to get the transports and the fighter escorts mobilized?'

'We can mount a token operation like that in twenty-four hours, and thirty-six hours after that we can be in full swing with a cargo plane touching down in Berlin every fifteen minutes.'

'I lean toward that – that's the minimum and the least likely to provoke escalation, I'd think. We could start it without the fighter escorts, add those only if necessary.'

There was a knock at the door. Captain Hartung entered with a message for Darby that had just come in by JCS courier.

'Mr President, it looks as if the Russians are already moving to escalate,' announced the Secretary of Defense after he'd scanned the eight lines of typing. 'Pictures taken by our reconnaissance satellites indicate that at least three Soviet armored divisions have left their bases in Poland. They appear to be heading west. Two are already in East Germany.'

Stevens saw Bonomi shrug, and he agreed.

You couldn't tell what this meant, not for certain.

'As a precaution, purely as a precaution,' Darby began, 'I'd suggest—'

'Thanks, but no thanks,' Stevens interrupted. 'No, we'll watch and evaluate for a while. Alert all our intelligence units to keep an eye on these divisions, to track them, but that's all for the moment. Now I want to talk about Viper Three. At this minute, it looks a helluva lot more menacing than Berlin.'

Arthur Renfrew Grosvenor looked unhappy.

'Arthur,' expostulated the President, 'we have a Berlin crisis almost every year or two. It's getting to be a tradition – like Mother's Day. Now let's face up to Viper Three.'

'Mr President, the Defense Department and the Joint Chiefs have given this problem a great deal of further thought and very careful study,' Darby announced earnestly, 'and we have a new plan.'

'Yes?'

'This would not involve an assault on the capsule, which has such an elaborate and sophisticated alarm system,' Darby continued, 'but rather a way to prevent the rockets from leaving the silos. We can do it with tanks, M-60s, fifty-one tonners.'

'I'm listening,' acknowledged the President.

Marshal Feodor Barzinko was also interested in the recent developments, unusual developments, in SAC's Montana missile force. A signal had just come in from the Soviet fishing trawler *Orlov* on patrol near Vancouver. The vessel had relayed a message from an agent in southwestern Canada, who'd received a phone call from a woman in Great Falls. The woman – a switchboard operator – reported that something unusual was going on at Malmstrom Air Force Base. No one was being allowed to leave, and outgoing calls had been cut to almost zero. That wasn't all. A two-mile section of highway out near the Minuteman installations had been closed off to civilian traffic by Army troops, and the reason given to motorists was some vague talk about a security exercise.

It didn't ring true.

A SAC security exercise wouldn't require Army troops, for the American Air Force handled its own security.

Marshal Barzinko decided that those tricky *Amerikanski* were up to something, a conclusion that immediately turned his thoughts to Berlin and DEFCON Four. Yes, the Central Committee had been right to shift those tank divisions.

It might even be necessary to move additional forces west, and it probably wouldn't hurt to raise the defense readiness of the Red Army one notch either.

Maybe two.

CHAPTER TWENTY-NINE

'I'll let you know by one o'clock or so,' Stevens promised the Secretary of Defense as the National Security Council meeting ended.

'It's certainly worth considering, isn't it?' Darby nudged. 'We roll a fifty-one-ton tank onto the lid of each of the silos – simultaneously – and the compressed-air equipment won't have enough push to open for firing. The tanks are on the way right now. They'll be there by one all right.'

'I'll let you know, Bob,' the President repeated.

After the NSC members departed, the White House press secretary entered with word that scores of journalists were asking when the Chief Executive would issue a statement on the Berlin situation. A number of senior Congressmen and Senators had called with the same question. Stevens instructed him to announce that the Secretary of State would talk about Berlin at a 2:00 P.M. press conference, and to state that the President was giving the matter very serious study to prepare for his own comments 'as soon as the situation was clarified fully'.

'That sounds better than "no comment", but not a great deal better,' observed Tim Grasser. Timothy Grasser had handled Stevens' press relations for the past eleven years, and his ability was matched by his frankness.

'Don't make waves, Tim,' Stevens advised.

'Just between us, when is this situation likely to be *clarified fully*? Tuesday? Wednesday? You're debating Caldwell again on Wednesday night, you know.'

'I know. Goodbye, Tim.'

'You're sounding very executive and Presidential these days,' Grasser commented.

'That's because I'm the President. Anything else, Tim?'

'Bill Frost is outside with some memo you asked for.'

'Send him in. It never pays to get on the wrong side of the Attorney General; he can have you investigated.'

Grasser was unimpressed.

'Not me. I haven't committed a federal crime since I shot a migratory bird with a twenty-two when I was fourteen years old, and the statute of limitation's run out on that.'

'Send him in, Tim.'

Frost handed over the memorandum a minute later.

'Proves beyond a doubt that you've got the right to pay out that money,' he assured. 'Thirty-nine pages of brilliant legal reasoning, full of Constitutional references and citations of Supreme Court decisions. *Winston v. Jacobson, Barr v. Dalton* and *Markell v. the United States*. Great cases you may recall from your law school days. I was up half the night with my number-one legal genius, Jerry Morris, to write this magnificent document. He used to be a professor at Northwestern Law, you know, which gives him an advantage. I find academics exceptionally talented at sneaky reasoning and dirty deeds.'

'Will it stand up, Bill?'

The Attorney General had this wonderful gift for arching his eyebrows, which he demonstrated again.

'Probably. It's long and it's boring and difficult to understand. Three quarters of the country and two thirds of the Congress ought to accept it on those grounds alone. I wanted to make it so long that even the New York *Times* wouldn't reprint the full text, but Morris pointed out that's impossible. There is no official document that long. I can guarantee one thing though. There isn't a newsman at any of the three networks who'll be able to decode it.'

'Excellent.'

'They'll have to bring in professors from Harvard and Columbia just to understand the punctuation,' Frost boasted. 'By the way, I don't mean to pry but where *do* we stand with Viper Three, Mr President?'

'We don't. We sit. The Army tried an attack last night and nearly made it. Now Darby's got another plan that the CJS says can't miss, and we – that's an editorial we – are sitting and considering the proposition.'

'I don't believe in sure things, Mr President. What do you think about the new plan, General?'

Bonomi felt for a cigar in his pocket, found none.

'I don't think it's a sure thing, but it could work. On paper it ought to work fine.'

'If it does you'll be a big hero, Dave,' Frost predicted. 'It might win you the election. Good old resolute Dave Stevens stood cool and clever, and he defeated the forces of evil and saved the world. Touchdown run in the last four minutes of play, a ninety-three-yard gallop through the whole enemy team!'

'And if it doesn't work,' calculated the President, 'the convicts will launch and the Soviets and Chinese will hit back and there won't be anybody left to vote anyway. You got any advice, Bill?'

'Do you believe in prayer?'

'Not that much,' Stevens admitted. 'I know that a chief of state is supposed to turn to God in moments like this, but I'm not sure that He'd hear me. And if He did, I'm not sure He'd care. Maybe I'm a freak. I've heard that all the Presidents before me believed in prayer. I'm not an atheist, you understand, but I suspect that David Stevens had better try to solve this one without counting on divine assistance.

'*You* believe in prayer?' Bonomi challenged the Attorney General.

'I even believe in the Easter bunny, and I'm not Christian.'

'That doesn't answer his question, Bill.'

'Mr President, I don't know how to answer his question – and that's why I'm avoiding it so wittily. Politicians who run for elective office are supposed to believe in prayer and the Almighty, or at least to make frequent references to both. I never ran for elective office, so I never had to face the problem myself.'

'Were you serious when you suggested that I pray?' Stevens pressed.

'Half serious. It couldn't hurt, I'll tell you that. I don't imagine that you'll get a flash of lightning and the voice of God with an angel choir in the background, but it might help. Some people whom I respect a good deal believe it can help – at least with moral questions. I doubt that the Almighty would simply haul those convicts out of Viper Three – He doesn't run an Emergency Road Service – but prayer might help you to sort out your thoughts and convictions. There isn't much time left, you know.'

Less than nine hours.

'I'm going to talk to Dell again,' Stevens announced. 'Maybe I can offer him something more.'

'The only thing he wants – really wants and needs – is a complete pardon,' Frost replied. 'I don't think that the money is that important to him. If he has any brains, he'll realize that it could be more trouble than it's worth.'

'A complete pardon? I can't do that. That's up to the Governor of Montana, and he's Caldwell's friend.'

Frost waved his finger reprovingly.

'Mr President, there are one hundred and thirty-nine things that the Governor of Montana – or any other state – wants from the President, and one hundred forty-one ways that the President can screw any Governor. For example, you could turn the FBI and Internal Revenue loose on him – they'd find *something* – or you could push for that dam he wants or make him an ambassador. You could make him our man at the UN, or even put him on the Supreme Court.'

'Wilcox on the Supreme Court? You've got to be kidding!' Bonomi scoffed.

'If I were the President,' the Attorney General said soberly, 'I'd promise him anything – and I'd deliver if he did.'

Stevens considered for several moments.

'I don't think they'd buy it, Bill – not without the money,' he finally replied, 'but I'd better find out.'

Using the SAC hot line, Stevens put through the call to Viper Three and made his new offer. He explained it simply, persuasively. A full pardon and, if they wished, safe-conduct out of the United States.

'I see. . . . I see. . . . I understand. . . . Six o'clock, your time. . . . Goodbye, Major.'

Stevens put the red phone away in the drawer.

'Well?'

'He won't budge. He doesn't trust me *or* Wilcox, and he won't budge an inch.'

'He said no?' Frost wondered hopelessly.

'He said no. No deal except on his original terms.'

The desk telephone rang.

It was the chairman of the Joint Chiefs of Staff.

The M-60 tanks had arrived and could attack the silos whenever the President gave the word.

CHAPTER THIRTY

'Stand by. That's all I can say now,' Stevens replied and then hung up the phone before the Secretary of Defense could argue with him.

'They're ready to move in with the tanks, Vince.'

'Well, what's your pleasure, Mr President?'

'No pleasure at all, dammit. I don't like it – not any part of it. My instincts tell me not to roll those goddam tanks, Vince, and the people who're supposed to be my top military advisers tell me just the opposite.'

'I'm kind of partial to your instincts, Dave. It may sound weird for an Air Force general to say that, but in a gut situation like this I'd favor your gut over Darby's or Woodside's any time. And that isn't just loyalty talking – that's *my* gut judgement.'

'That routine with the tanks isn't a bad idea, you know.' Stevens mused aloud.

'No, it isn't. It's certainly better than the TAC fighter-bomber scheme.'

'A lot less chance of missing the silos,' reasoned the President, 'but still *something* could go wrong.'

'Right.'

'One of the tanks could stall or break down, couldn't it?'

'Right.'

Stevens looked up at his friend.

'You're starting to sound like a yes-man, Vince.'

'Not a chance in hell, Mr President. I barely made one lousy star, and I never expect to wear two.'

'I bet you wouldn't turn it down. I could fix it easy enough, you know. Two stars – *Major* General Vincent Bonomi? I could make you my military aide.'

His former wingman grunted.

'Not me, you bastard. I couldn't take all the crap that goes with the White House game. I can barely put up with the CIA. Let's stop playing games and get back to those goddam tanks.'

'All right, we'll talk about it some other time. Now, as for the tanks—'

The intercom buzzed.

Timmy Grasser's voice sounded from the box.

'Can I come in – right away? It's important, real important.'

'Come on in,' Stevens yielded.

A minute later the White House press secretary closed the office door behind him. His face wore a look of tension and uncertainty.

'I just had a phone call from Don Wellington. He's the NBC man at the Pentagon, and a buddy of mine for years. We used to drink together a lot,' Grasser announced.

'Yes?'

'He's no clown, you know. At the risk of sounding sanctimonious, he's a serious journalist.'

The President nodded.

'He seems to know about something that I don't know – something *here*. He called to ask me to check it out.'

'Timmy, why don't you just speak your piece?'

'Okay, Mr President. He's had a fantastic tip that one of our missile bases has been captured by a gang of escaped convicts.'

'Is that it?'

'There's more. The Army wants to blast them out, and you're too worried about the election to give them the okay.'

'That's quite a yarn,' Stevens fenced. 'What do you think of it, General?'

'Holy shit!'

Stevens shook his head.

'That isn't very constructive, General,' he reproved.

'Is it true?' demanded Grasser.

'Can you stall him, Tim?'

'I don't know. Aren't you going to answer my question? Is it true?'

The Chief Executive nodded.

'Mother of God!' the press secretary groaned.

That didn't help, but it was a lot less vulgar than 'Holy shit!'

'Sorry we didn't tell you, Timmy. There are only twenty or

thirty people in Washington who know, and I didn't think that it was essential that you be one of them. No disrespect, you understand, just tight security.'

'Where did Wellington get the tip?' Bonomi asked.

'He wouldn't say.'

'Some son of a bitch at the Pentagon leaked it to put the heat on you to buy that goddam tank deal, Dave,' Bonomi said angrily. 'Some smart ass with three or four stars, I'd bet.'

The President of the United States leaned back in his swivel chair, sighed.

'We'll get him later, Vince. Right now we've got to buy time. What did you tell Wellington, Tim?'

'I told him it sounded crazy – maybe some crap planted by Caldwell's buddies over there.'

'Did he buy it?'

Grasser shook his head.

'Not really. He asked me to check it out, said it came from a very good source. I'm supposed to phone him back – within an hour.'

'Bring him over here,' ordered the President. 'Tell him that you can give him the whole story if he gets over here immediately. I'd better talk to him myself.'

After Grasser left, David Stevens discussed his plan with Bonomi and explained what he had in mind. It might work, and then again it might not, so Vince Bonomi decided that it wouldn't hurt to prepare a back-up plan of his own.

'I want to grab a sandwich and check on the Berlin thing, Dave,' he lied to the President. 'Be back in twenty minutes.'

But he didn't eat or telephone when he left the office. He found Captain Hartung in the corridor outside the Presidential Suite.

'I may need a handgun, Captain. Have you got one?'

Hartung was completely unfazed.

'We don't wear them on White House duty, General, but I've got a pistol I keep locked in my desk drawer.'

'Loaded?'

'No, but I've got a clip and could load it. Of course, sir, the Secret Service men are all armed. If you'd prefer, I'm sure you could borrow a .38 from them.'

'Not without a lot of questions. I'd rather do business with you. You don't waste time with questions.'

'You seem to be in a hurry, General,' evaded the junior officer deftly, 'so I'd better get the gun.'

'And get another one of the military aides – somebody like yourself.'

'Someone who doesn't ask a lot of questions, sir?'

Bonomi nodded.

'I want you both to stand by in the outer office of the Presidential Suite. There *may* be a little trouble, and I *may* need you. Any questions?'

'No, sir. If you'll excuse me, I'll try to locate Lieutenant McInerney. He was middleweight boxing champ at the Academy last year.'

Bonomi smiled.

'I gather you got the message, Captain.'

'I hope so, sir. I think you made it pretty clear, General. Shall he bring a sidearm, sir?'

'No. There probably won't be any trouble at all, you understand, but I'm compulsively cautious.'

Now it was Hartung who smiled.

'That's not what I've heard, General.'

'Get the gun.'

Five minutes after noon, Don Wellington was ushered into the office of the President of the United States. The tall NBC reporter with the crewcut and attractively open face was visibly surprised, but still composed.

'Mr President, this is my friend, Don Wellington,' introduced Grasser.

'Glad to meet you, Mr Wellington.'

'I'm pleased . . . and surprised to meet you, Mr President.'

'Sit down, please. Sit down and we can talk frankly. . . . Huh, frankly? When a politician says that he's usually about to lie his head off – but I suppose you know that.'

'I've been in Washington for eight years, Mr President,' Wellington acknowledged as he settled into a black leather chair.

'Good, then we can skip all the formalities and polite

evasions. There *is* a crisis that's being kept from the public, and General Bonomi and I,' the President explained with a nod of introduction toward his ex-wingman seated on the couch, 'were up half the night trying to handle it. So were a couple of dozen top military and civilian executives.'

'The missile base? It has been seized by escaped cons?'

'Yes. You want the story? Here it is. A subterranean Minuteman capsule of the 168th Strategic Missile Wing out in Montana has been captured by five men who broke out of the Death House at the state penitentiary in Helena. One of the five was a SAC major in for killing his wife. He showed them how to do it, I imagine. His name is Dell, and the code name of the capsule is Viper Three. It's about eighteen or twenty miles from Malmstrom Air Force Base near Great Falls.'

Wellington eyed him warily, skeptically.

'Is this off the record, Mr President?'

'No, it's all on the record – and you're getting the story as an exclusive.'

'I don't understand, Mr President.'

'Just listen. Don,' Grasser urged.

'I'm listening.'

'There's more. They've threatened to launch the ICBMs – ten of them – if we don't pay them $5,000,000 and fly them out of the country in Air Force One.'

'You aren't putting me on?'

'I've never been more serious in my life – or more scared. I'm giving you the story you came to get. This is news, and the American people are entitled to know about it. I understand that. The public has a right to the truth, especially about something as important as this.'

Wellington shook his head.

'I'm sorry, Mr President, but I think you're putting me on. You're reading all my lines, arguing my arguments.'

'No, there's no argument. No one in this room disputes the public's right to be fully informed or your duty to inform the public. . . . The only question is when.'

'I knew there was a catch. You want me to kill the story.'

'No, I'm asking you to hold it – for a day or two.'

Wellington stood up abruptly.

'You're a very clever man, Mr President. First you soften me up by volunteering all the facts I'd have to break my back to get, and then you ask me to hold back the story until its suits your political plans.'

'No, there's nothing political in this. The issue is simply national security, perhaps – at the risk of sounding melodramatic – national survival.'

'I'm not buying. There's been an awful blunder, and you're afraid it might cost you the election. That's the word I got.'

'Bullshit!'

'Take it easy, Vince,' counseled the President.

'Why should I? NBC doesn't scare me. You're talking a lot of crap, chum. The missile base security system that failed was developed years before this Administration took office, and it was a pretty good system too. I don't know how those hoods found the gap, but I do know that somebody lied to you about why we're being cautious about attacking Viper Three. Tell him.'

'All right, it's simple enough. If the attack is less than completely successful, they could fire their missiles and start World War III. What I'm asking you to do, Mr Wellington—'

'It's the Bay of Pigs again, and I'm not going to be conned,' interrupted the reporter. 'One of your well meaning predecessors managed to con the well meaning *New York Times* into holding back the story on that little caper, and it was a disgrace and a disaster for everyone. Don't give me any of that sweet-talk about responsible journalism and duty to my country, Mr President. I'm not buying.'

'We're in the middle of another Berlin crisis, another confrontation with the Soviets,' Stevens pointed out soberly, 'and how do you think they'd react if they heard that some US missiles might be flying their way – unofficially, of course?'

'That's your problem, Mr President. I'd imagine that it might be smarter to level with them and everyone else – unless re-election is all you care about these days.'

'All I'm asking for is twenty-four hours. That short delay won't affect the election, but we could get them out of Viper Three – one way or another.'

'I'm sorry.'

Stevens looked over at Bonomi, was surprised to see his former wingman composed and impassive.

'Mr Wellington,' said the Chief Executive, 'you might as well have it all. Here's a folder with biographies of the five convicts. You may find it useful in preparing your story.'

The television correspondent accepted the packet, frowned.

'Now why in hell did you do that, Mr President?'

'For truth and accuracy. That's what we both believe in, isn't it?'

Wellington shrugged, started for the door.

'Don,' Grasser pleaded.

The NBC correspondent shook his head, put his hand on the doorknob.

'Don, you've got to be crazy to do this,' warned the press secretary.

'I'd be crazier to believe a politician in a tight election. I'd be out of my skull.'

'I'm afraid you're being used, Mr Wellington.'

The correspondent paused, turned.

'Mr President, I've been used, conned, lied to, taken on junkets, half-informed, misinformed and variously abused by some of the best and most patriotic pros in the business. Over the past few years, I've had my phone tapped, my house bugged, my car tailed – the works. I don't even know which government outfit – or outfits – did it. I don't care. . . . Thanks for the biographies, and the other information, though.'

'Where do you live?' challenged Bonomi.

'Arlington. What's that got to do with anything?'

'Just figuring. If the Russians drop one of their SS–11s on Washington, the hydrogen warhead would take out your wife and kids in Arlington too.'

'You're a real bastard, aren't you, General?'

'You ought to know.'

Wellington spun, opened the door and stepped across the threshhold.

He stopped, re-entered the room and closed the portal behind him.

'You're a real bastard,' he repeated bitterly.

Then he turned to Stevens.

'I don't really believe you, not really.'

He sounded as if he were about to cry.

'Thank you, Mr Wellington.'

'I don't believe you for one minute, dammit.'

'I appreciate what you're doing. I know it can't be easy.'

Wellington stood shaking his head.

'I must be crazy, absolutely crazy.'

'You're a hero, Don,' judged Grasser. 'Don Wellington, the hard-boiled hero. You're a genuine patriot, Don.'

'I'm an idiot, a stupid, gullible, sentimental idiot!'

'Sit down, Mr Wellington,' urged Stevens. 'We'll get some pictures of these men for you. You can use them tomorrow. You can still have your exclusive and your Pulitzer Prize – just a day late.'

'I'm not doing it for you. It's just that I despise the phoney Caldwell, and I hate to be used.'

He wasn't going to mention his wife and children – pride.

'Vince, get Mr Wellington everything else he needs.'

Bonomi rose, walked quickly to the door.

'Were you really going to let me just walk out of here?' the journalist asked.

'*I* wasn't,' replied Bonomi.

He swung open the door, pointed to the pair of military aides.

'I had them ready to take you.'

'Suppose they couldn't?'

Bonomi opened his tunic, disclosed the gun in his belt.

'Mother of God!' Grasser gasped.

'You said that before. Yes, I would have shot him – to wound, not to kill.'

'I was right,' Wellington said. 'You're a real bastard.'

'No, just a sentimental patriot like you.'

'Don't be too hard on General Bonomi,' advised the President.

'Why not?'

Stevens drummed on the desk for a moment before he replied.

'Well, I guess that I ought to confess something. I had four Secret Service agents waiting for you down the corridor.'

Wellington pointed at the man behind the desk.

'You're a real bastard too, Mr President.'

'But I thought you knew that before you walked in that door, didn't you?'

Wellington nodded.

'Yes, I knew it – but I didn't believe it,' he confessed in reluctant surrender.

Then he started asking more questions about the situation at Viper Three.

CHAPTER THIRTY-ONE

At two o'clock, the Secretary of State announced the official position of the United States on Berlin in those fine New England tones for which Arthur Renfrew Grosvenor was renowned.

'Wonderful,' Ray Gumbiner said at half past two.

'Encouraging and statesmanlike,' declared the West German ambassador at 2:40.

'Lies and nonsense,' scorned Radio Moscow an hour after that.

The German diplomat and the Russian broadcaster were both judging Grosvenor's statement, but Gumbiner was reacting to the announcement that President Stevens had just taken off from Andrews Air Force Base for a visit to Strategic Air Command Headquarters near Omaha. It was perfect. It was smart. Stevens didn't have to issue a tough statement, for his inspection tour of SAC – the main US nuclear force – at this time said it all. The United States wasn't threatening or blustering, but Stevens was making it clear that this country wasn't going to be pushed around either.

'He's a genius,' Gumbiner told the deputy campaign chairman.

'He's an idiot,' Dell said to Falco.

'The President of the USA is an idiot? That's a terrible thing to say – even if he is an idiot.'

'Well,' the ex-major sighed as he ever so gently fingered the bandage on his temple, 'I feel terrible. And he is an idiot – to think we'd trust him after last night.'

'Your head okay?' the assassin asked.

'I'll survive. . . . That was a neat job of bandaging, Willie, and I guess I ought to thank you. I don't think I did, did I?'

'No, but don't bother.'

'And we all owe you something for your alertness, the way

you stopped Harvey from opening the door,' Dell continued.

'Reflex action. I heard a noise, saw him, pointed my weapon and squeezed. Nothing very creative about that.'

'Perhaps not creative, but useful.'

Powell shrugged off Dell's compliment.

'I guess that's me,' the former sergeant answered noncommittally. 'Not very creative but useful.'

There wasn't any point in pressing it further, for Willieboy Powell was still – clearly and stubbornly – fighting that old private war.

'Where's Hoxey?' Dell asked.

Falco gestured toward the tunnel.

There he was, seated on the floor near the huge door, praying for the corpse beside him.

'He's trying to save Schonbacher's soul,' suggested Powell.

The assassin laughed softly.

'Doesn't he know that fat Harvey didn't have a soul?' Falco jeered. 'He was just a selfish stupid slob, no guts and no soul.'

'Do you think he had a soul?' Dell asked the black man.

'I don't know. I never heard him sing.'

It wasn't a very good joke, but it was something – a small sign that Willieboy Powell hadn't written off humor and warmth completely.

'*I* think Harvey had a soul,' announced the renegade major. 'Maybe a miserable and tarnished soul, but he had a soul – that is, if there is such a thing as a soul.'

'I didn't know you cared about souls,' said Powell.

'I'm not sure that I do. I didn't say that I did, anyway. I just remarked that if there was such a thing *even* old Harve had one.'

'If that's the case, then maybe *even* Lawrence Dell has a soul?'

'Unlikely ... but possible. Say, you're quite a philosopher, Willie. I didn't realize that you were a philosopher, or are you just trying to bug me?'

Powell smiled.

'Now why would I want to do that?' he evaded gracefully. 'No, I've just been trying to understand you a little better.'

'And how are you making out?'

'Not too well, but I'm getting a few glimmers.'

'I wouldn't waste much effort on it,' Dell counseled, 'since we ought to be in Peru by this time tomorrow and I imagine we'll all split up about ten minutes after that.'

'You really think they're going to pay up?' Falco asked.

'I'm sure of it. I know it.'

'In your soul?' wondered Powell.

'In my soul – *if* I have one.'

There was a groan from one of the wounded captives, and Dell brought two cups of water to the men in the bunk.

'You know, you're not as cold-blooded a son of a bitch as I thought you were,' Powell told the former SAC officer.

'You know, I was just thinking the same thing about you.'

'That doesn't mean I like you,' Powell warned.

Dell gave each prisoner a few sips.

'Don't worry, Willie,' he answered, 'I never thought you did.'

Then Falco began talking about Peru, the anti-American feelings of its revolutionary government that would bar extradition and the good life that the fugitives would enjoy there.

'Custom-made clothes, beautiful women, champagne,' he anticipated.

'The local drink is something called Pisco,' Dell pointed out. 'It's a country cousin of Tequila. I don't know how much champagne you'll find in Lima.'

Falco was utterly undiscouraged.

'A man with one million two hundred and fifty thousand dollars in US currency can get champagne anywhere,' he predicted. 'No, I'm not worrying about the drinks. It's the President and the troops up above us here that still have me itchy.'

'Stevens will pay,' Dell predicted, 'unless the Army can talk him into another attack of some sort.'

'What about tricks? They could gun us once we're on the surface.'

'Stud, that's what some sly general might try. That's what Senator Caldwell would do, but he doesn't get to be President till January. I think this President is just old-fashioned enough to keep his word if he gives it. To put it another way, I'm betting that Stevens has soul.'

'There's that dirty word again,' Powell joked.

239

Now Hoxey was singing a psalm, chanting in a loud nasal voice to ease the journey on which Harvey Schonbacher had so violently embarked.

'Does he have to wail that way?' Falco complained.

Dell and Powell nodded in unison.

Beyond any doubt, Hoxey had to and it might well be dangerous to disturb him in this religious experience. The assassin accepted this estimate with a shrug, turned to watching the troops on the surface again. It was a bright clear afternoon, and the ring of men and weapons could be seen quite distinctly. The camera did not pick up the M-60 tanks, for they had been positioned beyond its 300-yard range. There was less activity and movement than there had been the night before. Everyone was waiting, waiting for the word from the President.

One of those was General Martin McKenzie, who was standing on the edge of the concrete apron at Offutt as Air Force One taxied to a halt. The other big jet – the 707 chartered by the press covering Stevens' campaign – was pulling to a stop about one hundred yards behind, and as soon as it ceased moving the stairs were lowered and a crowd of reporters and photographers surged out to cover the President's arrival at the base. The CINCSAC wasn't paying much attention to them, however – not as much as he usually would – for he was focussed on Stevens' decision about Viper Three.

There he was, descending from Air Force One in a cluster of Secret Service men and White House aides. McKenzie was puzzled to see a USAF brigadier general in the Presidential party. The SAC commander stared at the unfamiliar face for a long moment.

'That's General Bonomi,' Winters volunteered discreetly. 'He flew eighty-sixes with the President in Korea. Hot pilot, they say.'

'How hot?' McKenzie asked out of the side of his mouth.

'A real pistol. Eight kills, sir – and five more probables.'

The band broke into 'Hail to the Chief' and McKenzie strode forward briskly to greet the President, trying to smile and to conceal the questions that were troubling him.

Why had the President decided to visit SAC headquarters now?

Why was he traveling with this 'real pistol' who had eight kills – and five more probables?

Most important, what would he say about the attack plan proposed by the Joint Chiefs?

'Welcome to SAC, Mr President,' McKenzie said.

Pictures. More pictures. A handshake, repeated four times for still more pictures. Then they entered the limousine and drove to the headquarters building, where McKenzie led the way down to the bunker. After the inevitable ten-minute briefing, the two men adjourned with Bonomi to the Battle Staff seats on the upper level.

'I'm glad to see SAC's battle ready,' Stevens said, 'but that isn't why I'm here. I assume that you're *always* battle-ready. You're the first team, and I count on you.'

'Thank you, Mr President.'

'You've heard about the JCS plan to plug the silos with tanks?'

McKenzie nodded.

'That's why I'm here. The Berlin situation's getting warmer steadily, and the latest reports indicate that those damn fool Russians are moving mechanized divisions and preparing to disperse their bomber squadrons. I've got to settle the Viper Three mess before something very serious happens – something unthinkable. I've got to settle it today.'

The CINCSAC nodded again.

'I've made up my mind on the JCS plan,' Stevens announced, and then he explained what he'd decided should be done.

'What do you think?' he asked.

'I think you're right, Mr President, and, if you don't mind my saying so, I think you've got a lot of guts. Do you want me to come with you?'

'No, you'd better stay here. If something goes wrong, you'd better be here. You know what I want you to do?'

'Yessir. I'll take care of it right away.'

When they reached the door that led from the lobby to the portico outside where dozens of journalists waited impatiently, Stevens paused to brace himself again.

'Good luck, Mr President,' McKenzie said.

'I'll need all I can get. Thanks.'

'Mr President, the authority to launch the nuclear strike force is entirely yours,' Martin McKenzie acknowledged, 'but it is within the prerogatives of the CINCSAC to take the precaution of having all our long-range bombers manned and moved down to the end of the runway – ready for take-off. I'm thinking of doing that when I get word that you've reached Malmstrom, unless you object.'

'I see.'

'We haven't done it since the Cuban missile crisis, sir. I think you ought to know that.'

Stevens looked over to his former wingman.

'It won't show up on Russian radar,' Bonomi calculated, 'and it shouldn't get them too excited. I'd say they wouldn't even know about it for a day, and by then it won't matter.'

'All right,' the President assented cautiously, 'but wait until I'm *leaving* Malmstrom to join the task force. Wait as long as you safely can.'

They shook hands again and went out to speak briefly to the press about the power of SAC as a force for world peace and America's commitment to peace. Twenty minutes later, Air Force One rolled down the runway and took off for the return to Washington. The press plane followed. Nine minutes after it was airborne, however, the pilot announced to the reporters that he was going to have to make an emergency landing because of electrical malfunction in two motors.

The journalists were furious as they watched the President's plane disappear into the clouds.

They would have been even more angry if they'd known that their pilot was lying.

CHAPTER THIRTY-TWO

Everyone seemed to be angry.

A spokesman for the Chinese People's Republic told Radio Peking that 'the entire Berlin affair' was simply 'a cheap and obscene farce cooked up by the scummy American imperialists and the cynical whores of Moscow' that was designed to 'trick the Socialist world.' To show his Marxist impartiality, he excoriated both the USA and the USSR as 'moral dung heaps infested by worms such as Gangster Stevens and the hoodlums of the so-called Central Committee of the so-called Communist Party of the so-called Soviet Union.' Radio Peking broadcast this searing statement every hour on the hour, with a recorded version of three thousand voices singing 'The East Is Red' as background music.

In Moscow, Marshal Aleksei Soyuzov was even more angry but his prose was somewhat less lyrical. It was, however, quite explicit and the Minister of Defense had to admit that it had a certain logic. He wouldn't agree that Barzinko was 'an imbecile weakling,' but he did promise to discuss Soyuzov's arguments for slowing Yamshchik with the Deputy Chairman of the Central Committee. This did little to mollify the tanker, and Soyuzov left the minister's office with the thought that the minister wasn't much more effective than Barzinko. The Minister of Defense was also angry, furious that Soyuzov should put him in such a difficult position between the Red Army Chief of Staff and the Central Committee.

And there was considerable rage in Washington. Senator Caldwell's running mate for the Vice Presidency, Governor Bankhead, had told some eight hundred members of the Daughters of the American Revolution that the 'weak sweet-talk of the knee-jerk liberals in the Stevens administration' was no answer to the 'brutal Soviet aggression in Berlin,' and he'd said a lot of other strong phrases that would make colorful copy for the press. The angry remarks made that afternoon by Private Herman Obstler at the Pentagon were even more colorful, but would be less widely reported since a number of them were obscene. Obstler had been on guard duty outside the famous five-sided building when a previously peaceful demonstration by the Women's Liberation Front erupted into violence. Somebody had hit him in the groin with a sign demanding why there were no females on the Joint Chiefs of Staff, and somebody else bit the corporal – twice.

In Great Falls, the city editor of the *Tribune* was rather irritated by the run-around he was getting from the public information officer at Malmstrom. He might have felt a little less bitter if he'd known that the managing editor of the *Leader*, the local evening paper, had received the same vague answers to his identical questions about that closed-off stretch of highway. Then again, he might not, since the *Tribune* had more circulation and a Sunday edition, which the *Leader* lacked.

At the air base itself, Captain Bigelman was getting 'pissed off' at being confined to the isolation ward. He rather enjoyed using the quaint phrase, which he'd acquired shortly after reaching Malmstrom, for it proved that he was as earthy as the next man, but he didn't like being locked up this way.

'I ought to call my brother,' he ruminated. 'He's a lawyer. He'd get me a writ of habeas corpus. I may send a registered letter to the American Civil Liberties Union too. They can't just lock us up like this, you know. It's in the Bill of Rights. Magna Carta, all that stuff.'

Neither Langer nor the nurse replied.

'Aren't either of you going to do anything about this?' Bigelman challenged indignantly.

'I could sing the first two verses of the *"Marseillaise,"* ' Langer offered.

'And very well too,' added his beaming blonde companion.

Bigelman glared, realized that he could expect no help from this pair and walked to the barred window. Glancing out into the late afternoon, he saw a large plane – no, it wasn't one of the B-52s – glide down to a perfect landing nearly a mile away.

Not being a member of the American Society for Psychic Research, he could not guess that the big transport was Air Force One.

General Stonesifer didn't have to guess.

He'd known for an hour – since the CINCSAC's call – and he'd been waiting with the two helicopters for nearly twenty minutes. Stonesifer glanced at his wristwatch as the Presidential jet touched down, saw that it was 5:35. At 5:37, the swept-wing transport stopped less than one hundred feet from the helicopters and the Chief Executive was on the ground himself ninety seconds later. Right behind him was a one-star general carrying two large canvas pouches, each of which contained something that was obviously heavy.

The President was in no mood to chat.

After the briefest of handshakes and introductions, he brushed off the Malmstrom commander's effort to discuss the tank assault and walked directly to one of the helicopters. The general with the grim face and the canvas sacks followed him into the machine, which was airborne almost immediately.

At 5:54, Falco was in the toilet and Powell was making instant coffee and Hoxey was reciting some of his favorite Old Testament quotes to the two prisoners – intensely. Dell was still in the red commander's chair, feeling vaguely hungry and specifically tense. It was almost time.

'Look in the freezer, would you?' he called out over his shoulder as he watched the TV screen. 'I think we ought to eat pretty soon,' he suggested a moment later.

Then he saw the two helicopters move into view, settle down about one hundred yards outside the Viper Three perimeter. A small crowd bunched up around the two machines. About three minutes after that, the crowd opened and a pair of figures walked forward toward the gate in the fence. Dell stared at the men – one carrying two bags – until the phone on the console sounded.

'Yes. ... Yes. ... Okay. ... he can come down with the sacks, but tell the other man to wait outside the guardhouse – out in the open, where we can see him,' Dell told the caller.

He was radiating that big Warner Brothers smile as he put down the telephone.

'Gentlemen, guess who's coming to dinner?' he asked.

Powell, Hoxey and Falco, who was zipping his trousers as he left the toilet, all waited for him to answer his own question.

Dell pointed at the screen.

'The President of the United States!'

They had won.

In Moscow, Aleksei Soyuzov had lost. The Minister of Defense and the Chief of Staff had lost their patience with his 'lack of cooperation and respect,' and the order had already been drafted relieving him of the post of Chief Marshal of Armored Troops. One stubborn old tanker could not be permitted to interfere with Yamshchik simply because he didn't understand the political realities of Cold War diplomacy. He was getting off rather lightly, everyone agreed. In the Stalin era he would have faced a firing squad.

CHAPTER THIRTY-THREE

'We made it! We made it!' chanted the assassin exuberantly.

'We beat 'em!' Powell shouted in tones of mixed joy and surprise.

Dell's grin grew larger and larger.

'You didn't really believe we'd do it, did you?' he tested the former Marine.

'Man, I didn't. I most certainly didn't,' Powell confessed. 'It sounded good back in the Death House, but I never thought it would work. Not all the way. Nobody ever beats the system – nobody like us, anyway.'

'We beat them – right down to their knees,' Dell said with unconcealed pride. 'We beat them all, the generals, the engineers, the politicians.'

'We beat the shit out of them!' bellowed Falco. 'Five million bucks! Five million bucks – for two lousy keys! Fantastic!'

The ex-major nodded.

It was fantastic. There was no need to be modest now.

'Five million for two keys,' he reflected as he took out the pair of them from his pocket. 'Willie, I know that you didn't want to return these – but you did. That was sensible, since we'd had enough trouble over them. Now, in appreciation for your courageous and exemplary service above and beyond the call of duty, I hereby decorate you with the Order of the Key.'

He gave one of the keys to Powell.

'You earned it,' Dell said in parody of an officer presenting a medal to a battlefield hero.

On the screen, they could see the President approaching the guardhouse door slowly with the two pouches. Standing a dozen yards away, Vincent Bonomi also watched Stevens. It was the end of David Stevens' political career, the former wingman realized, for once word of this surrender and payment got out Caldwell and Bankhead would rip him to pieces. They'd call him a coward. The defense professionals would never admit that what had happened at Viper Three was in any way their fault, so they'd pass the buck to Stevens and insist that they'd been overruled. Of the whole group, McKenzie was the only one with the courage not to fight in this situation and the intelligence to realize that hardware couldn't solve everything. But the CINCSAC was an unusually independent and outspoken man, a maverick who probably wouldn't remain CINCSAC once Caldwell was in the White House.

'Peru! Peru! Women by the yard – that's what those keys are going to buy us!' exulted 'Stud' Falco. 'Too bad you can't keep your souvenir, Willieboy, but we're selling them for a very good price.'

'No, we're not,' Hoxey declared.

The three men at the console turned, saw the madman had a revolver in each hand.

'Evil, evil, evil. The world is seething with sin and evil,' Hoxey announced.

'What the hell is he talking about?' wondered the assassin.

'Sin and corruption! Sodom and Gomorrah! Filth and horror stalk the streets! The anti-Christ feasts in our churches and homes!'

'What's all this crap?'

'Easy, Stud,' warned Dell.

'For chrissakes, I'm goddamed tired of this hillbilly weirdo,' Falco bulled ahead irritably. 'I've put up with all his moaning and wailing and mumbling half-assed prayers long enough. He gives me the creeps.'

'Fire! Fire! The time for the great cleansing fire has come!' Hoxey said shrilly.

'Deacon,' Dell began softly. 'It's going to be all right, Deacon. We'll be out soon, and you'll have your own place to pray. People will listen to you now, Deacon.'

'Give me the keys.'

'Don't give him anything, Larry. He's out of his fucking skull, a forty-four carat loony. You're psycho, Deacon,' Falco announced, 'but I'm not. And I'm not going to let any maniac screw this deal up.'

Hoxey fired each gun once.

'Goddam maniac,' Falco cursed as he clutched the two burning holes in his stomach.

Hoxey pulled the triggers again, and the assassin lay dead.

'Give me the keys, Larry,' Marvin Hoxey repeated mechanically.

Dell held them out toward him.

'Put them on the console and get back against the wall there.'

The former SAC officer obeyed, retreated to the other side of the small chamber.

'You too, over with him, Willie.'

He was speaking in a strange, gentle voice, almost like a patient, benign father.

'Armageddon, it is time to purge the earth with fire so that our Lord may begin again,' Hoxey declared. He put down one gun, reached out and tore the safety tapes that protected the firing switches.

'I heard what you said, Larry,' he explained. 'If the missiles are launched, then there'll be a great atomic war and everybody will die. I'm going to launch those missiles. It's God's will.'

Dell tried to reason with him, and then Powell tried and then they both appealed for mercy for the women and children, for all the innocents.

'There are no innocents. All are polluted by lust and hate and scorn for the greatness of God,' he answered smugly.

He flicked the switches, one by one.

Dell watched him, showing none of the fear that gripped Powell.

'He can't do it,' the SAC veteran said flatly.

'I have the strength of great armies! It is the Lord's mighty strength!'

'Nobody can,' Dell announced. 'No *one man* can launch. The locks for the firing keys were deliberately positioned more than eight feet apart, beyond any one man's reach. The firing system was engineered so that it would take two men to launch.'

'I'll turn one key and then the other,' said the sly fanatic.

His eyes.

They were awful.

'Both keys have to be turned simultaneously, Deacon.'

249

Hoxey stared at them wildly.

'You can't launch alone, Deacon, so why don't you give me back the keys? Or give them to Willie, if you prefer.'

Hoxey shook his head.

'I'll turn one key, Larry, and you'll turn the other. If you don't, I'll have to shoot you.'

Dell sighed.

'I guess you'll have to shoot me, Deacon,' he replied.

The madman turned to Powell.

'You'll help me, Willie,' he pleaded. 'You know what an evil world this is. You know how cruelly it's treated your people. You know that this is the world of the anti-Christ. Help me to end the sin, *please*.'

'It may not be much,' the black man admitted, 'but it's the only game in town. It's the only world we've got, Deacon.'

'*Please*, Willie.'

'No, you'll have to shoot me too – and then you'll have nobody left to turn the other key.'

A light flashed on the console, signaling that the President was on his way down in the elevator.

'It won't work,' Dell told the psychotic. 'You can't launch these ten birds.'

'Then I'll blow up one of them – the one in the silo that's connected to the capsule by the tunnel. I'll kill all those evil soldiers on the surface, those men of violence who defy God's call for peace.'

Lawrence Dell tried again.

'Kill for peace? That's not a very original idea, or a sound one. You'll go straight to hell. Thou shalt not kill, The Bible says.'

'I shall smite the infidels for God!'

Then he turned, picked up one of the machine guns and backed out of the capsule into the shaft that led some ninety yards to the No. 8 rocket of the flight named Viper Three.

The two men waited, looked at each other.

'What do you say, Larry?' Powell asked.

He'd never called Dell by his first name before.

'I guess we've got to take him,' the former major answered.

They each put on one of the bulletproof vests, and Dell picked up a sack of tear-gas grenades.

'Respirators,' he said.

When they had donned the gas masks, they took up weapons and set out for the silo. As they started up the shaft they could hear hammering and shooting, the sounds of the madman's frantic efforts to explode the missile's fuel tank or warhead. He seemed to be focussed on the rocket. That might be helpful.

Then a burst of bullets made them both drop to the floor, and they knew that it wasn't going to be that easy. Dell hurled one grenade, then another. Within seconds thickening eddies of tear gas dimmed the tunnel. Hoxey fired again blindly. The gas would reach him soon, Dell calculated. He reached out, found Powell and nudged him against one wall.

Wet.

Dell's hand was wet, and he suddenly realized that the ex-Marine had been hit. Powell was gone into the gas cloud now, crawling and crouching just the way he'd moved through those jungles. Dell moved up along the other wall. More bullets flew past, and Powell's rapid-fire gun blasted back. Dell raced forward, saw Powell and fired over his shoulder.

There was a scream, and both masked men shot at the sound.

Now there was quiet.

Slowly and warily, they inched forward until they saw the Minuteman's tail. The body of Marvin Hoxey rested beside it. Dell reached down, took the madman's guns and rolled the figure over. Dead or dying – it hardly mattered which. It was as unimportant as which of the two men had dropped him. It could have been either or both. Now Powell loomed out of the vapors, lurched and would have fallen if Dell hadn't caught him. It was a bad wound in the right thigh, bad but not likely to be fatal. Dell helped him back to the capsule, where they both removed their masks.

'Now it's my turn to do the bandaging,' Dell said, and with Powell's advice he was able to apply it well enough to stop the flow of blood.

There was a buzzer sounding.

The President was at the door.

'He's out there with five million dollars and our plane to Peru. It's going to be two and a half million apiece now,' Dell announced.

They started slowly toward the huge door, Powell with his arm around the SAC veteran for support.

'What do you think we ought to do, Larry?'

'You mean the money?'

The black man nodded.

'They'll kill us – sooner or later – if we take the money,' he reasoned. 'They'll hunt us down and kill us.'

Dell looked at the bandage, saw that it was already soaked. Powell was bleeding badly, needed a doctor. He'd never live to reach Peru.

'That's exactly what I was thinking, Willie.'

They were halfway up the shaft.

'Willie, what would you say if I suggested that we surrender to the President?'

Powell stopped, considered, sighed.

'I'd say yes. We beat them once, but we couldn't do it forever. Nobody's that smart or that lucky, not even you, Larry.'

It was ridiculous. Why should he *fail*, fail for this stranger to whom he owed nothing?

'Not even me,' he confessed with surprising good cheer.

There was Schonbacher's rigid corpse, directly ahead.

'I want to ask you something, Larry. Just one thing.'

'Sure.'

'If they'd attacked us again or if the President hadn't come with the money, would you have launched?'

Dell laughed softly.

'You'll never know, Willieboy. That's one thing you'll never know. I'm not sure myself.'

They reached the door.

'We did win, you know,' Powell said.

'We won it all,' Dell agreed wearily as he reached for the bolt.

'I wonder what comes next, Larry.'

The man with the film star's face shrugged again.

'What do you mean?'

'Stevens' offer of a full pardon and safe-conduct out of the country? Does that still hold, Larry?'

'Here's where we find out,' Lawrence Dell replied as he drew back the bolt and swung open the massive door to face the President of the United States.

THE OMEN

David Seltzer

The bloodchiller of a book that became one of the most sensational and terrifying films ever made. The powerful, spell-binding story of a child who is not a child and a man who must become less than a father and more than a man.

Robert Thorn is a wealthy American diplomat, a close friend of the President, with a beautiful wife and a highly successful career. One night in Rome, he exchanges his still-born son for a new-born orphan. Only Thorn and the priest who arranged the swap could tell the difference. Kathy and Robert Thorn called the child Damien. Five years later, in England, the strange occurrences begin. Damien's nanny commits suicide. A mysterious new nanny, with a ferocious black dog, suddenly appears to guard the child. A wide-eyed priest tells Thorn that Damien is the spawn of the devil, then dies in a gruesome and inexplicable accident. Kathy Thorn is critically hurt in a fall. An agonised and frenzied search takes Robert Thorn from Rome to Jerusalem, and then back to London aware of the terrible truth, aware of what he must try to do. For Damien is indeed the anti-Christ ... the Beast of Revelations ... the precursor of Armageddon.

The sensational film of THE OMEN stars Gregory Peck, Lee Remick, David Warner and Billie Whitelaw. Produced by Harvey Bernhard and Mace Neufield. Directed by Richard Donner. Distributed by Twentieth Century Fox.

70 SUTTON PLACE

Joseph DiMona

A searing novel about the private lives of the beautiful people – by the author of LAST MAN AT ARLINGTON.

70 Sutton Place is the most exclusive apartment block in New York – a palace for the very rich and the very famous. People like Pamela Morrow, the film star every man wanted; John MacArthur, the glamorous senator with a roving eye; Madame White, the legendary black blues singer; Harley Widener, the theatre producer; Jay Kohner, the magazine publisher; Bob Taylor, the advertising executive.

But New York is a jungle, and even the very rich can't stay isolated for ever. When both the Mafia and a Black Power group decide to infiltrate the block, the sensuous calm and glitter of 70 Sutton Place is shattered, and its residents find themselves trapped in a web of terror and violence that threatens not only their guilty secrets, but also their lives.

NICOAT
SALES DEPT.,
. BOX 11
ALMOUTH
CORNWALL TR10 9EN

Please send me the following titles

Quantity	SBN	Title	Amount
————			————
————			————
————			————
————			————
————			————
			————
		TOTAL	

Please enclose a cheque or postal order made out to
FUTURA PUBLICATIONS LIMITED for the amount
due, including 10p per book to allow for postage and
packing. Orders will take about three weeks to reach
you and we cannot accept responsibility for orders
containing cash.

PLEASE PRINT CLEARLY

NAME ....

ADDRESS ....

....